Also by Matteo Strukul

Medici ~ Ascendancy
Medici ~ Supremacy

MEDICI
Legacy

MATTEO STRUKUL

Translated from the Italian
by Richard McKenna

An Aries Book

First published in Italian as *Una Regina al potere*
in 2018 by Newton Compton

First published in the UK in 2021 by Head of Zeus Ltd
This paperback edition first published in 2022 by Head of Zeus Ltd,
part of Bloomsbury Publishing Plc

9 7 5 3 1 2 4 6 8

A catalogue record for this book is available from
the British Library.

ISBN (PB): 9781786692191
ISBN (E): 9781786692160

Typeset by Silicon Chips Services Ltd UK

Printed and bound in Great Britain by
CPI Group (UK) Ltd, Croydon CR0 4YY

MIX
Paper from
responsible sources
FSC® C171272

Head of Zeus Ltd
5–8 Hardwick Street
London EC1R 4RG
WWW.HEADOFZEUS.COM

To Silvia

JUNE 1525

Prologue

Seeming almost to challenge the heavens, the cathedral of Santa Maria del Fiore loomed over the city.

Catherine trotted towards it. Her aunt had been worried she might be frightened by the building's imposing grandeur, but she wasn't. She raised her large eyes towards the red dome, as though wishing to measure its height.

'How tall is it, Aunt?' she asked, her eyes entranced by its splendour.

Clarice looked at the little girl. 'It's almost four hundred feet from the base to the lantern above the dome,' she replied.

Catherine's eyes widened in astonishment. 'So high?'

Her aunt nodded. The sun shone in the sky, and the cathedral seemed to capture its rays and amplify their magnificence, enveloping itself in a golden cloud.

Catherine hadn't finished. She loved asking questions. Questions cost no effort. Answers were quite another story, she thought, but she was a child and knew no answers – or at least that was what the adults believed, so she took the opportunity to ask whatever she wanted.

'And who built it?'

'A great artist.'

'What was his name?'

'Filippo Brunelleschi. He was the most skilful and extraordinary architect in history. Though the truth is that he wasn't actually an architect at all. He was a goldsmith. It was he who solved the problem of the dome.'

'What do you mean?' asked Catherine, with a chuckle. Another question. She loved this game.

'That for more than a hundred years the cathedral was without a dome. It was open to the elements – uncovered...'

'And then what happened?' the little girl asked. The story was starting to capture her interest.

'The *Opera del Duomo* that supervised the choice of projects for building a possible covering had to choose between two magnificent proposals: one by Lorenzo Ghiberti and the other by Filippo Brunelleschi. The first was championed by the Strozzi family and the second by the Medici, the family to which I belong.'

'I belong to it too, don't I?' asked Catherine. She knew that she did, but found it reassuring to be reminded of the fact.

Her aunt nodded. 'That's right.'

'What happened at the end of the story?'

'Ghiberti and Brunelleschi both won, and so the *Opera del Duomo* decided to entrust them with the direction of the works for the construction of the dome. But it was Filippo who had the most effective and revolutionary ideas.'

'And then what happened?' asked Catherine.

'For a few years, Lorenzo and Filippo worked side by side, with the latter devising almost all the solutions for erecting a dome with a span of nearly two hundred feet. But then the great mad goldsmith fell ill, and decided to stay at home.'

'And was it true?'

'What?'

'That he was ill?'

Clarice laughed. 'How clever you are!'

'Am I?' asked Catherine, raising an eyebrow with a hint of innocent mischief that made her aunt laugh even more.

'Yes.'

'So was it true?' the little girl insisted.

'Of course not. As you have already worked out for yourself, Filippo simply wanted to ensure that all Lorenzo's inadequacies would be put on display. He stayed away from the building site until the representatives of the *Opera del Duomo* went to visit him at home because the work was no longer proceeding as planned. When the most important families in the city asked him to return, he demanded that he be given complete control of the work.'

'And did he succeed?'

'What do you think?'

'Of course he did,' said Catherine confidently, 'because the Medici had chosen him.'

Clarice looked at her niece in surprise. 'You have learned the lesson well,' she said.

'It's all thanks to you, Aunt.'

'Do you really think so?'

'Of course I do.'

'Very well, then. Now that you know how the dome was built, what do you say about going home? Am I mistaken, or do you have Latin to study?'

'Ugh.'

'Come along. How do you think you will become a real Medici without study?'

'Oh, all right then,' the little girl said, throwing up her hands and mimicking the expression that her uncle often assumed when, while speaking to Clarice, he realized he had no chance of prevailing. 'But can we stay and look at the dome for a little while longer?'

'Very well,' replied her aunt, stroking Catherine's head.

Then she too raised her eyes, and was bewitched by the sight of the great dome of Santa Maria del Fiore.

It was truly beautiful.

AUGUST 1536

1

The Dauphin

He had screamed until his throat was raw.

An excruciating pain like liquid fire scorching his very soul had torn at him, and he had grasped at his chest, dropping the crystal goblet of water, which had shattered on the floor.

And now Francis' eyes were glassy and his head lay on his shoulder. His white hands dangled over the arms of the chair, the fingers white and cold. The face was a mask, its features still beautiful yet carved with a rigor that knew only one name.

He could not answer the voices that called to him. He was dead.

There was banging on the door of his room. Soldiers, trying to break their way in. At the umpteenth charge, the door finally gave way.

Monsieur Raymond de Polignac, captain of the second company of the French pikemen, rushed into the dauphin's room, followed by the rest of his men and a couple of maidservants. When he saw Francis slumped lifelessly in the armchair, he dropped his wide-brimmed hat with its large white feather to the floor.

'Your Highness,' he murmured in a broken voice. One of the maids screamed and Raymond gestured to a spearman, who immediately led the two women out of the dauphin's room.

Raymond looked at the simple chair with its blue velvet upholstery and thought of his king, who had just lost his favourite son. He shook his head, went over to Francis and gently closed his eyes, then retrieved his plumed hat from the floor and raised it to his chest.

With a sigh, he looked at the golden rays of sunlight which filtered into the room through the gap between the brocade curtains. The smell of death was already starting to fill the air.

The war had arrived there. Charles V of Habsburg had invaded Provence and even reached Tournon-sur-Rhône, but now that humid summer, all mosquitoes and sweat, had begun to weaken his troops, making them enervated and sickly, he was thinking of returning to Savoy. And that wasn't all. Francis I, the King of France, had made scorched earth of his own kingdom: the fields had been burned, the wells poisoned and the countryside emptied, and nothing now grew there.

The land had been murdered by its own sovereign for the sole purpose of preventing it from offering anything to the army of the emperor of Austria and Spain.

'Give me a few moments and I shall write to the king. You will deliver my missive directly into the hands of His Majesty, who is currently in Lyon,' he ordered the guards who were with him. 'I will explain what has happened. Meanwhile, call doctors and surgeons. I will handle questioning them in order to ascertain the causes of death. No one must know what has happened until I give orders. Dark days await France.'

While he was speaking, Monsieur de Polignac wasted no time. He sat down at the dauphin's desk and in a fine hand wrote a few lines, then placed the sheets inside an envelope. With the flame of a candle, he melted the wax and applied his own seal to it.

His pikemen departed, and while one of them went to the stables to dispatch a courier to Lyon, Monsieur de Polignac looked at the dead youth.

He had closed the dauphin's eyes out of pity for the poor boy, but apart from that they mustn't move a hair on his head until the doctors arrived. The room must remain intact, exactly as he had found it.

He had no idea of the reason for the tragedy, but it would not be he who prevented its causes from being ascertained with certainty.

Motionless, his mind sinking into an ocean of unanswered questions, he stood in the centre of the room: had Francis died of natural causes? If not, who could have wanted to assassinate the dauphin? And to what end? Though if you thought about it, there was an embarrassment of possibilities.

The light of the rising sun glinting off the sword at his belt, Polignac sighed and adjusted his velvet doublet. As he walked around the room, the heels of the boots seemed to mark out the passage of time, and he slipped off his left glove and began beating it upon the palm of his right hand. This went on until Monsieur Guillaume Maubert, the dauphin's personal surgeon, entered the room.

Polignac looked at Maubert with sincere consternation, his bitterness at events clearly visible in his beautiful pale-blue eyes. Smoothing his thin moustaches with the forefinger of his right hand, he observed with interest the short little man with his mischievous face, and saw his expression change as soon as he realized what had happened. Those ruddy cheeks, the dishevelled hair and the small, lively eyes would have fooled even the most attentive observer into doubting that Maubert might be up to the task at hand, but Polignac was capable of looking far beyond appearances, and he knew that behind that undistinguished appearance lurked a brilliant mind.

'Monsieur Maubert,' he said, 'I will waste no time with words. I thank you for coming. The circumstances that bring us together are the saddest possible. What I ask of you is to take all the time you need to establish with certainty the causes of the dauphin's death.'

'Has the king been told?' asked the surgeon in a quiet voice.

'I have already sent dispatches to Lyon.'

'Excellent. Very well, then. Let's begin.'

'Needless to say, absolute secrecy must be maintained on the matter, at least until we know beyond any reasonable doubt the reasons for Francis' death.'

'Of course.'

Catherine felt the cool breeze on her face. In that hot and humid August, an early morning ride was a pleasure she had no desire to forgo.

David, her beloved roan gelding, galloped across the bright green fields. She had chosen the name in homage to the statue by Donatello as a way of underlining that she was a Medici and a Florentine: origins of which she was proud, despite many at court insisting on considering her nothing more than an Italian merchant for that very reason.

They did so in perfect disregard of her being the wife of Henry of Valois, and therefore Duchess of Orléans and Princess of France. But Catherine didn't care: she knew she was hated and at the same time feared at court. Even the way she rode her horse like an Amazon was looked upon with suspicion by the damsels of the king, prime among them his mistress, Madame d'Étampes. The beautiful duchess made no attempt to hide her contempt for Catherine, which was mitigated only by the fact that the sovereign had welcomed her with enthusiasm and a hint of admiration from the first moment he had seen her, precisely because of that resourcefulness of hers.

She smiled. There was so much that was graceful in that clear dawn. The sparkling breeze made the countless scents which filled the air with sweet and invigorating fragrances, prime among them eucalyptus and wild lavender, even more intense. Catherine breathed in deeply, grateful for those moments of solitude in which she could abandon herself to the seductive beauty of nature.

Ahead, she saw the vineyards, which looked almost as if they were parading stiffly across the gentle hills, and the waters of the Rhône, sparkling like a ribbon of liquid silver in the diaphanous light of a vibrant yet pale-blue sky.

How beautiful the countryside was, dotted with farms with red-tiled roofs and majestic olive trees that emphasized the Mediterranean charm of the *Midi*.

Soon the sun would reach its zenith, and it would be necessary to withdraw into the great halls of the castle or seek relief in the coolness of the shadows.

She thought with pleasure about the glass of ice water that she would soon drink.

2

The Count of Montecuccoli

After concluding all necessary investigations, Monsieur Guillaume Maubert had hypothesized that the cause of the dauphin's death might have been totally natural, but that he could not in any case exclude other possibilities. Even that of poisoning.

When he had heard that word, Captain Raymond de Polignac had asked Maubert to maintain the most total reserve and had wasted no time in making his own rapid and discreet enquiries. Perhaps it would all turn out to be nothing, but he preferred to run no risks.

The news had not been allowed to emerge because the dauphin's personal physician needed time to see if his suspicions would be confirmed.

By then, the king should have received Polignac's letter and be on his way to Tournon-sur-Rhône.

In the meantime, the captain had learned that the previous afternoon Francis had been gulping down quantities of ice-cold water in a wholly cavalier way: the heat had gone to his head, and he had attempted in this way to guarantee himself at least a little coolness.

This, anyway, was what a certain Gasquet, one of Francis' pages, had told him. He had also added that one person who did not look fondly upon the dauphin was one of his squires: Sebastiano di Montecuccoli, Count of Modena.

Gasquet had explained that while he was at the camp in Tournon-sur-Rhône awaiting the arrival of his father, who was due in a few days with more troops to set off against the imperial armies of Charles V, the dauphin had spent his time playing Royal Tennis.

And he had played against Sebastiano di Montecuccoli. After which, hot from the fiery sun, while everyone had been seeking refreshment in the shade of the tents, he had remained there drinking cold water with the count. Gasquet remembered that it had been the squire who sent him to fill two large amphoras with cold water. And that wasn't all: Montecuccoli had accompanied Gasquet to the well.

So now, Captain Raymond de Polignac was speaking to the nobleman to try to understand what had happened.

He didn't know the individual in question, but had formed a decidedly negative impression of the man as soon as they had met: Montecuccoli had seemed treacherous, his manner so elusive that Polignac instinctively found it unpleasant. He had narrow features and cold eyes, and it was hard to ascertain precisely what tasks he carried out on behalf of the dauphin.

'So if I understand correctly, you came to court with Catherine de' Medici, the wife of the Duke of Orléans?'

'That's right,' answered Montecuccoli. There was an irritating smirk on his face, as if he knew exactly what Polignac's intentions were. He played with a lock of his brown hair, twisting it around the forefinger of his right hand. He looked extremely well-cared-for: his skin was soft and pale, his expression relaxed, and he wore an elegant velvet doublet. His appearance was above reproach, that was certain.

'And yet you became a squire of the dauphin,' said Polignac, barely able to believe the words as he said them.

'Yes, one might put it that way.'

Polignac raised an eyebrow. The man's manner, so indolent and vague, left him increasingly perplexed.

'And was it also you who advised the dauphin to drink a large quantity of cold water the other day?'

'Captain, Francis was bored and so he asked me to play a ball game with him. I advised him against it, given that the sun was hot enough to set the grass ablaze, but he refused to listen to reason. After the game we were so hot that the dauphin decided to send a page to bring us fresh water to drink.'

'And you accompanied this page... what was he called... Gasquet, to the well?'

'Precisely.'

Polignac sighed.

'Very well,' he said, 'I have taken note of what you have told me. I would ask you not to leave the Tournon-sur-Rhône camp for any reason over the coming days.'

'Has something happened to the dauphin?'

'Nothing to worry about. A slight illness. I am simply checking up on a few things.'

'Very good,' said Montecuccoli, but it was clear that he didn't believe a word of what the captain of the pikemen had told him.

Raymond de Polignac stood up and shook the count's hand then, without another word, headed for the door.

When he saw the pallor of death upon his firstborn, Francis I wept.

He could not hold back his tears: not simply because this was his favourite son, but also because of the awful episode to which he himself had consigned the youth ten years earlier.

The sovereign had never recovered from that shame and torment – he had harboured a sense of guilt towards his children, and towards Francis in particular, from which, after that harsh and unjust death, he would never now be released.

He remembered vividly how, after signing that ignominious treaty in Madrid, he had consented to its unworthy terms of surrender which allowed him to return to France only upon condition that he left his children as hostages. Thus it was that Francis and Henry had been handed over to the emperor of Habsburg, who for over three years had left them to rot in the dungeons of the castle of Madrid.

That imprisonment had scarred Francis' soul. Forever. And all his father's efforts to heal the wound had been of no use. With the new war against Charles V turning in his favour, Francis I had hoped to be able to fight alongside his son and to regain his esteem, but fate had tricked him for the second time.

As soon as he had read Polignac's missive, the king had leapt into the saddle of his horse and set off at a gallop for Tournon-sur-Rhône.

The sight of his son, consumed by death, his skin now greenish, had brought to mind the time of anguish and failure that had led him to betray his own children.

And that memory was now the most awful of punishments.

His only consolation was the manner in which Captain Raymond de Polignac was conducting the investigation into the dauphin's death: de Polignac was a soldier of great valour and loyalty, and he had no doubt that he would get to the bottom of the mystery.

'Do all you can,' said Francis I. 'I grant you all the necessary authority and ask that you put Montecuccoli under arrest. His conduct is at the very least suspect, and a few days in the cell pending the results of further investigations certainly won't kill him. And as for the news of my son's death, there is no reason to remain silent about it any longer.'

'Do you really believe so, Your Majesty?'

'I know what you think, Captain, and in principle I agree with you. Why stoke the fires of panic and hatred? What good would that do now, when the army of Charles V is in deadlock thanks to the intolerable heat of this fiery summer? But on the other hand, imagine the energy that national mourning might unleash. Francis was much loved, and since nothing will bring him back to me, it might as well be known. I need only a few days, just long enough for his mother to see him and for his mortal remains to be brought to Lyon. I will make certain that he is taken there today.'

'Very well,' replied the captain.

'Another thing.'

'Of course, Your Majesty.'

'Let the name of Montecuccoli be leaked as that of a possible suspect. I have the impression that the people will spread the news on his account.'

'Very good, Your Majesty. If I may say, he strikes me

as a man without scruples, and he is certainly hiding something. Though not particularly shrewd, he may have nothing to fear.'

'Because he is innocent or because he has total confidence in his abilities?'

'That is what we must ascertain. One more thing, Your Majesty...'

'Yes, de Polignac?'

'Montecuccoli confessed that he had come to the French court in the retinue of Catherine de' Medici.'

Francis I gave his captain an incredulous look, and for a moment he was silent, unable to utter a single word.

'I see,' he said gravely. 'Fear not. I shall investigate every possibility. As soon as I return to Lyon tomorrow, I will speak with Catherine and try to get to the bottom of this.'

'Very well. And... Your Majesty, far be it from me to insinuate anything, but with the death of Francis...' Polignac hesitated.

'Henry becomes dauphin of France, and therefore she with him? Is this what you are trying to say?'

'Precisely.'

The king sighed.

'Very well, then,' he said. 'Let us hope that Catherine has a good explanation.'

3

The Confusions of a King

The king was visibly distressed.

The news of the dauphin's death, and his probable murder, had not failed to upset France: Francis had been much loved, and Catherine herself had adored him. The queen mother had been shut up inside her apartments for days now, while the king tried to exorcize his pain with long rides on horseback.

The war continued, but the hot summer was the most treacherous and cruel enemy of the imperial troops led by Antonio de Leyva and Ferrante Gonzaga: the invaders' men perished in large numbers, and they suffered so deeply from their lack of victories that the French were expecting them to retreat at any time.

It was therefore with concern and bitterness that Catherine found herself summoned by the king himself.

That morning, still distraught at the death of Francis, she had worn a white dress as a sign of mourning, as was the French custom. Her skin, naturally pale, and her light-brown hair made her the portrait of melancholy and grief.

She entered the room with all the humility and modesty of which she was capable, for she knew that while in one way what had happened to Francis strengthened her position, in another it weakened it, because it cast suspicion upon her. She, after all, was the principal beneficiary of a death which made her a French dauphine.

When she saw Francis I, dressed in black, his magnificent velvet jacket adorned with gold buttons and his dark beard endlessly curled and teased, the sight produced in her a reverence so profound that for a few moments she could barely breathe.

'Come, come, *ma fille*, what are these formalities?' said the king affectionately. 'Embrace me, rather, for I know how dear Francis was to you.' And so saying he walked towards her and squeezed Catherine to his chest.

She could not hold back her tears, for it was true – she had adored Francis. She had married Henry, of course, but her husband had revealed his inadequacies all too soon: he was diffident and suspicious, and above all he was completely under the thumb of the harlot who had always held his leash. Diane of Poitiers – the most beautiful woman in France, and perhaps in the world – was his mistress and lover, and Catherine had rapidly and with immense sorrow discovered how difficult her life at court would be. This, of course, had not stopped her from loving Henry, who was handsome, young and strong, but Francis was cut from a completely different kind of cloth. He was a man of honour and of principles.

And now he was dead.

Her tears, therefore, were genuine, because they were the fruit of a suffering which bordered upon despair. The king was now the only ally she had left.

'Your Majesty, you cannot imagine how much I will miss him,' she said.

Francis I sighed. Then, not without a touch of embarrassment, he broke away from the embrace and looked Catherine in the eye. On his face was an expression of profound sadness. He had absolutely no desire to speak to her about Montecuccoli, and yet knew that he could not escape the task.

Catherine realized at once that something was amiss, so without waiting any longer she decided to take the bull by the horns.

'Something distresses you, my lord. Something that goes far beyond the death of your son. I can see it in your eyes, so tell me what it is you wish to ask me and I will answer you frankly.'

Francis I shook his head.

'How clever you are, Catherine, my child – for you

I am an open book. Yes, I admit, it is so. I will tell you everything, but in the meantime, let us at least sit down.' And as he spoke those words, the king pointed to two comfortable armchairs upholstered with blue velvet and adorned with the royal coat of arms, the golden lilies of France.

As Catherine sat down, the king began his story.

'You see, my daughter, when I learned of the death of my beloved Francis a few days ago, my heart was pricked by other voices.'

'Are you referring to the rumours that he was murdered?'

'I am, Catherine. The problem is that it is not merely a question of rumours. Let me speak more clearly: it was the dauphin's personal surgeon, Monsieur Guillaume Maubert, who maintained that, though appearing natural, his death might actually be a cunningly disguised murder.'

As she heard those words, Catherine raised her hand to her mouth and her eyes widened. She was beginning to see where the conversation was leading.

And she was afraid.

The king nodded indulgently, as if he knew what she was thinking. 'That's right,' he said. 'And mind you, Guillaume Maubert is not a man to make such statements lightly. But there is more. Fortunately for me, an excellent soldier – Raymond de Polignac, captain of the fourth company of pikemen – had already begun to investigate Francis' death, and when I arrived in Tournon-sur-Rhône to embrace my son for the last time, he informed me of his suspicions.'

'And whom does he suspect?' asked Catherine, with tears in her eyes.

The king sighed.

'It seems that a certain Sebastiano di Montecuccoli, Count of Modena, somehow persuaded Francis to drink an immoderate quantity of ice water after an extempore game of Royal Tennis. I can scarcely hold back my anger if I think of it...' The king's voice trembled with emotion and resentment. 'In any case, nobody knows whether Montecuccoli took advantage of the occasion to pour some poison into Francis' glass. But what I want to tell you, Catherine, is that when Captain Polignac asked Montecuccoli to explain his role at court, he did not hesitate for a moment to say that he had come as part of your retinue, and that his statement would be supported by his obviously Italian origins.'

Catherine was stunned. The man's statement was so false that for a moment she was unable to answer, and her face went white. But then anger and indignation took over.

'I have never had this gentleman in my service. I didn't know his name or identity until you told me it. I have no idea who this Montecuccoli is. Indeed, in my eyes he is only one thing: the man who has deprived me of my beloved Francis. And you know very well how much I cared for him, how close a friend he was to me, as much as and even more than my husband, who has practically ignored me since our wedding day. And I will say no more.'

Francis I weighed Catherine's words then decided to press her further. For the sake of certainty, he wished to be absolutely sure of what she was saying.

'Are you sure you are hiding nothing from me? I apologize for asking you again, *ma fille*, but I must.'

'Your Majesty, I will say only one thing: if you no longer trust me, if your suspicion is such as to obscure the loyalty and sincerity I have always shown towards you, then do not be afraid, you can order my head cut off this very instant.'

Her eyes blazing brightly, Catherine held the king's gaze with such confidence that the truth she spoke was tangible in all its power.

The king breathed a sigh of relief. He had seen the fierce light in Catherine's eyes, and unless she was a masterful actress, he was sure she was telling the truth. On the other hand, he could not be silent about the perplexities that gnawed away at the bottom of his soul: he loved her too much, and he knew that revealing his own doubts to her would be the best way to strengthen the position of this shrewd and courageous young woman.

'Catherine, your words are a balm to me. I know that my son Henry is... inconsistent. But I cannot find it in me to criticize him. I know my own weaknesses, and I confess that I am the person least suited to reminding him of his obligations. Apart from anything else, Henry hates me…'

'He does not, Your Majesty.'

'Yes, he does, ever since I abandoned him as a hostage to his jailers in Madrid. And I cannot blame him for it. And yet, what matters now is lineage. I do not wish to seem cynical to you, Catherine, but I already know what people in court will soon start saying – that Henry and you were the first to benefit from Francis' tragic death. You are the dauphins of France now. I do not wish to know how often Henry visits your bed, but for your own safety and security I suggest that you give him a child soon. I will always protect you, Catherine, because I see in your eyes the intelligence and sensitivity which are among the qualities I most admire in a woman, but you are so close to the throne that you can no longer afford to be without an heir…'

'Your Majesty…' said Catherine, attempting to interrupt.

'Let me finish, *ma fille*. What I am telling you is this: give birth to a son, and do it as soon as possible. It is the only way to protect yourself from the arrows of Diane of Poitiers. Pay close attention, Catherine: Clement VII has been dead for two years now, and Francis, who was so very fond of you, has also gone. I am the last friend you have left, and you will agree that I am speaking to you with extreme frankness. But if I do so it is precisely because I love you so much – precisely because in you I see the daughter I never had. Your knowledge of philosophy and astrology astounds me, as does the skill and resourcefulness you demonstrate on horseback and even during the hunt that make you seem some modern-day Artemis. And I have the same opinion of your taste and of the sober elegance that has always characterized you. There, I have said it! But if you believe that will be enough to save you then you are naive. And since I believe that you are not, find a way to bring Henry back to your bed and make him understand that a child will strengthen his position as heir. I expect to remain on the throne a few more years, but it is pointless to bury our heads in the sand. Have I made myself clear?'

Catherine nodded. There were many things she wanted to say, but she knew very well that it made no sense to say any of them. Indeed, in its harsh frankness, the king's little speech was far more useful than it might seem, not least in the way it suggested to her exactly the bearing she must maintain.

'I will do as you say, Your Majesty...' replied Catherine obediently.

'And you are wise to do so, believe me. I also recommend this line of conduct to my unfortunate son,' he added bluntly, 'for without heirs you will not have a long life at court.'

'Your Majesty... what about the other matter?'

'Are you referring to Montecuccoli?'

Catherine nodded.

'*Ma fille...* do you really think that I would have spoken to you with such frankness if I did not already believe you? In any case, put the matter from your mind: I will tell Polignac what I saw in your eyes and I heard in your voice, and you will have nothing to fear. I am convinced that justice will soon be done. Now leave me, so that I may arrange dispatches to indicate to my good captain in which direction to take the investigation.'

Without another word, the king stood up and offered his hand to Catherine.

'Now you are the wife of the dauphin of France, though I confess I would have preferred to see you become it in very different circumstances...' For a moment his voice broke with emotion. 'Promise me that you will honour this title with your actions.'

'I promise it,' she said.

'And now go,' concluded the king. 'Time is a tyrant.'

4

Revelatory Letters

Upon his return from his nocturnal mission, Raymond de Polignac found not one but two letters awaiting him upon his desk. He was drenched in sweat and had gathered his long brown hair into a ponytail, but the damp heat was so intense, even at night, that it was still causing him problems. He would have done better to cut the lot off, but as well as being fashionable, his long hair was the only hint of vanity he had retained over the years and he had no desire to give it up. Luckily, though, Sergeant Bouillon had been zealous enough to provide him with a jug of cold water and some raspberry jelly.

He took off his jacket and opened the collar of his lace shirt, hoping this would allow him to breathe at least a little more easily, then he poured some water into a glass and drained it, wiping his lips with the back of his hand. Taking a small silver spoon from the tray upon which the cup of jelly stood, he sampled it. It was cool and delicious, and the raspberries were exquisite. He took another sip of water, then picked up the envelope bearing the royal seals and broke them.

The letter was addressed to 'Monsieur Raymond de Polignac, captain of the fourth company of pikemen of the King of France'.

He read quickly.

My dear Polignac,

I have done as you suggested and have recently spoken with Catherine de' Medici, the Duchess of Urbino and wife of my son Henry II, the duke of Orléans and new dauphin of France. I told her what Sebastiano di Montecuccoli the Count of Modena had claimed, and she answered me firmly and most sincerely that she never met such a man nor had he ever been part of her retinue.

I can assure you that the way she expressed her position and the disdain in her words were those of an innocent woman. I do not believe that Catherine is involved in any way in a possible conspiracy against me or against France. This is all you need to know. You may therefore proceed to interrogate the prisoner, since I imagine he has been put in irons as per my order – and I would add, do not skimp on the whip.

I look forward to hearing from you,

His Majesty the King of France, Francis I, formerly Francis of Orléans

As soon as he had finished reading, Polignac broke the seals of the second missive, which bore the symbol of the royal army.

Like the first, it was addressed to 'Monsieur Raymond de Polignac, captain of the fourth company of pikemen of the King of France'.

My Dearest Captain,

My name is Bernard Sorel, lieutenant of the second pike company of His Majesty the King. I thought it useful to write to you to share with you what happened this morning, as I believe it might help explain the dramatic events of recent days. I refer to the rumours which have reached my ears regarding the possible murder of the dauphin at the hands of a certain Sebastiano di Montecuccoli.

Without further ado, allow me to tell you what happened to me. Some time ago I suffered a leg injury caused by an arquebus ball, and after undergoing the attentions of surgeons, I was told to take a period of rest and thus took up residence in Lyon, at the inn of the Falconer, run by Madame de Lille, a jovial, vivacious lady who spoiled her guests as best she could. As you can well imagine, the dramatic events of the murder of the dauphin of France are upon everyone's lips, and so also the name of the possible culprit: Sebastiano di Montecuccoli.

You can imagine my amazement therefore when, just the other day, Madame de Lille approached me to confess that a man with precisely that name had stayed with her some time before, and then gone on to the front and the camp at Tournon-sur-Rhône. When he did so, he had decided to leave a valise with her while he was seeking new lodgings, and to send a servant to retrieve it in the following days.

Even more incredible was the coincidence that this servant was now at the door of the inn asking for the valise and that, before handing it over to him, Madame de Lille had come to me to ask me a favour.

Since she did not want her honesty to be questioned in the future, it was her intention to open the suitcase, in the presence of two witnesses, to show that nothing had been removed from it during M. Montecuccoli's absence.

Naturally, with what was being said about this latter person in mind, together with the thought of being able to make myself useful to Madame de Lille who has always been so good to me, I decided to do her this little favour, and I went downstairs with her, and in the presence of another gentleman, Monsieur Henry de Rocheforte, opened the valise.

The servant confirmed that nothing had been stolen, and while Madame inventoried its contents, Monsieur de Rocheforte, who is by profession an apothecary, identified inside the valise two curious transparent bottles containing rather suspicious-looking powders.

Examining them more carefully, Monsieur de Rocheforte concluded that they were poison and, after asking the servant to open the first of the two, he smelled its aroma and announced that it must be arsenic.

At that point, the situation had become embarrassing – so embarrassing that I thought it appropriate to point out that, as an officer of the second company of pikemen of His Majesty the King of France, I was obliged to seize the valise and to ensure that it was delivered to my superior. As my company is at the moment detached in Provence, it seemed safer and quicker for me to have it sent to you, who are so much closer to where I am stationed, than to Colonel François de Chatillon, and so I proceeded to ship the valise. It seemed all the more important in light of the fact that Sebastiano di Montecuccoli is himself in Tournon-sur-Rhône.

I hope that I have done the right thing and have been of some use to you.

In the meantime, please accept my greetings and my best wishes for a quick victory against those imperial dogs of Charles V.

With all my respect, yours,

Bernard Sorel,

Lieutenant Second Company Pikemen of His Majesty the King of France, Francis I

What a stroke of luck, thought Raymond de Polignac. Along with the letter signed by Lieutenant Sorel he found the leather valise belonging to Sebastiano di Montecuccoli, and immediately went to open it to check its contents. Apart from some personal effects, two pairs of gloves, three shirts of cambric linen and a pair of bright-red velvet trousers, what he immediately noticed were the two glass bottles of which the lieutenant had spoken in his missive.

He picked them up to examine their contents, and saw colourless crystalline dust. He summoned a soldier and ordered him to go and tell Monsieur Guillaume Maubert to join him in his quarters as soon as possible.

There was a question of the utmost urgency which needed to be brought to the surgeon's attention.

5

The Golden Bell

The king was right, and she had been a fool not to have thought of it before. She had been worrying about that slut Diane of Poitiers and her influence over Henry, but the problem was a far simpler and far more practical one.

If her husband continued to frequent her rival's bed, it would be extremely difficult for her to conceive a child.

And above and beyond the benevolence of the sovereign, who once more had shown her all his esteem and affection, she would soon have to start worrying more about her safety than her honour. Children would serve to consolidate a position which, already delicate because of her foreign origins, was now dangerous, if not actually desperate, because of the double suspicion that on the one hand linked her to Sebastiano di Montecuccoli's absurd declarations and on the other, to these spurious aspirations to the throne.

In truth, Catherine cared little about this second aspect, but the courtiers, nobles and paper-pushers would certainly think differently, that was clear! Who if not her and Henry stood to gain the greatest advantage from Francis' death? Who was it that the crime had made the dauphin of France and, one day, king?

Catherine turned these matters over and over in her mind as she attempted to identify a solution to her problems, but she certainly wouldn't be able to conceive a son by terrorizing her husband.

No! There was a subtler, more artful way of obtaining the result she needed to survive in this court so full of envy and corruption.

While she looked at herself in the mirror, appreciating her full lips and beautiful brown hair, and acknowledging the eyes, somewhat dull in colour, and the imperfect nose that nature had chosen to give her, Catherine devised a plan. It was a simple one, in truth, but in order to successfully complete it she would have to share it with her most trusted and most talented lady-in-waiting: Madame Antinori.

She picked up a small silver bell from the beautiful oak-wood table and rang it. A few moments later, Madame Gondi appeared before her.

'I wish to speak to Madame Antinori,' said Catherine. 'Tell her to join me in my apartments immediately.'

Raymond de Polignac stood in front of Sebastiano di Montecuccoli in a cell which stank of sweat and urine.

It had only taken a few days to turn that so-called gentleman, once so handsome and well-groomed, into a human wreck with dirty hair, black-rimmed eyes and a shirt of cambric linen that though once white was now spotted with dirt in several places.

Montecuccoli's hands were fastened in shackles, his wrists scraped raw by the steel rubbing against his skin, and yet the self-styled count had not entirely lost his treacherous aura and mocking look.

They will vanish soon enough, thought Raymond de Polignac.

'Monsieur Montecuccoli,' he said, 'I don't know if you realize how difficult your position is about to become.'

The Count of Modena raised an eyebrow.

'And why is that, Captain Polignac? Have you made any progress in this personal crusade of yours against me? Since it is a fact that, to this day, I am held in this cell in a completely arbitrary manner and without...'

The words died in his throat as Polignac held up the valise he had brought with him.

'Do you recognize this?' asked Polignac. 'Do you

remember where you left it? You, *monsieur*, may have no idea what happened, but I can assure you that I will not stop until we have got to the bottom of this story. Answer my question: do you recognize this valise?'

Montecuccoli looked at him in amazement. He clearly hadn't been expecting Polignac to appear bearing such an article. How the hell had he got his hands on it?

'I don't understand,' was all he could say, his expression now a little less arrogant.

'I am sure you do not,' said Polignac laconically. 'In any case, answer my question.'

The Italian clearly decided that there was little point spinning it out.

'Those are my initials.'

'You are referring to these?' asked the captain, showing him the inside of the valise where the initials S and M were visible on a pocket in costly gold embroidery.

Montecuccoli nodded. What choice did he have?

'What's the matter?' urged Polignac. 'Have you lost your tongue of an instant?'

'Not at all,' snapped the Count of Modena in exasperation. 'It's mine. It's mine, I recognize it!'

Polignac threw out his arms.

'Finally! Was it really so hard to admit? Now,' he continued, 'do you know what this suitcase contained?

Shall I remind you of it? Come, don't be shy, take one of those two glass bottles that sparkle inside your valise.'

Almost mechanically, the Count of Modena did as he was told.

'Very good, *monsieur*. And now I ask you: precisely what dust does that little bottle in your hand contain? You do want to tell me, don't you?'

6

Nostradamus

An increasingly worried expression on her face, Madame Antinori watched as Catherine spoke frantically and without pause.

'You see, Francesca, I brought you here because I know that, by accident or by luck, you and I share a passion...'

Madame Antinori swallowed hard as an increasing unease took hold of her throat, seizing it in an iron grip.

'I am naturally referring to astrology and the arts of the occult.'

The lady-in-waiting began to deny it, but Catherine cut her off.

'Do not attempt to contradict me, firstly because I have irrefutable proof of your interest in the matter, and secondly because you have nothing to fear. Indeed, with your knowledge, you are the ideal person to accomplish the mission of the utmost importance which I am about to entrust to you. You know, I suppose, the city of Montpellier, do you not?'

'Yes, my lady.'

Catherine nodded. 'Very good,' she said. 'That makes things all the easier.' She went over to her bookcase and extracted a voluminous tome, beautifully bound in leather and with the title engraved in gold on the first page. 'Come closer,' she said to Madame Antinori as she put the book down on the desk. 'Do you recognize this?'

'The Tetrabiblos!' exclaimed Madame Antinori with an expression of amazement.

'Yes, Ptolemy's quadripartitum opus. Have you had the opportunity to browse its pages? This is the book that for perhaps the first time lays out the scientific foundations of astrology and establishes its principles, so that the most magical and supernatural aspects make way for a rigour and discipline which, for we lovers of the matter, are to say the least providential. Now,' Catherine continued, 'believe it or not, there is a man here in France who, by adopting the foundations of these texts as his own, is developing a vision of the cosmos and of how nature, through its own laws, can have a decisive influence upon human life.'

'I do not think I am familiar with his name,' murmured Madame Antinori.

'Naturally, especially since despite his genius he does

everything possible to make himself invisible to the world. And yet my interest in the subject could barely fail to allow me to appreciate the virtues of such an individual. For this reason, *madame*, I ask you to find him and to bring him before me. It does not matter how long it takes and it does not matter if he runs away to seek refuge even at the ends of the earth. You will give him a letter in which I summon him to court, granting him my protection provided he offers me his knowledge and advice for the benefit of my person. Have I explained myself?'

'Very clearly,' said Madame Antinori, her voice more confident now that she knew there was nothing to fear. 'And what is his name?'

'His name is soon told: Michel de Nostredame. Though I believe it is actually a name that his father chose to conceal his Jewish origins from the world. But to me this is of little interest. In fact, to be candid, it is of no interest to me at all. What matters is what I have heard about him, namely that he is able to shape and sculpt the wonders of existence. For this reason, Madame Antinori, I ask you to follow my instructions and to set off in search of this unique individual, and not to return until you have found him. But if I know you, I know that you are not lacking in ways to convince a man to follow you, not to mention that the person requesting his presence is no ordinary woman.'

Madame Antinori gave a curtsey.

'As you wish, my lady. I thank you, rather, for the honour you bestow on me in entrusting me with such a delicate mission. I hope I do not disappoint you.'

'I hope so too.'

'I shall require a pass for safe conduct.'

'You will be provided with one. Now that you know the reason I called you here, you should prepare to leave: as soon as I have drawn up the letter for our Nostredame and the pass for you, you can set off on your search. I will provide you with a carriage and a couple of trusted men, and you will inform me of your progress on a monthly basis. I hope, of course, that your investigations will not take too long.'

'I will be ready when you call me.'

Catherine nodded, then with a wave of her hand dismissed Madame Antinori, who, after another curtsey, made for the door.

'*Madame*,' called the French dauphine.

Francesca Antinori stopped and turned once more to face her.

'Forgive my complete lack of gratitude.' And so saying, she removed from around her neck a small silver chain from which hung a tiny key. She went over to the bureau and opened a drawer, then took out a casket which she handed to Francesca Antinori along with the key. 'In here you will find what you need to live like a grand lady for at least a year, though of course I hope your mission will be accomplished much sooner than that. If by some ill fortune you have not yet been able to meet Michel de Nostredame and bring him to court at the end of this time, do not hesitate to inform me of your economic needs so that I can meet them on your behalf. And now,' she concluded, 'retire to your room. You will hear from me soon.'

Sebastiano di Montecuccoli's back ran red with blood, which sprayed onto the cold floor of the cell each time the soldier standing behind him gave him another lash with his whip.

Raymond de Polignac stood watching. He was growing tired of this obstinacy. He had asked Montecuccoli several times to confess his crimes, all the more in the light of what Lieutenant Sorel had said in his letter and of the possible trial that, in addition to the lieutenant, would have called as witnesses Madame de Lille, proprietress of the inn of the Falconer, as well as the apothecary who had identified the poison as arsenic.

Montecuccoli was at the limits of his endurance.

His hands were tied to a bar and he was struggling to stand. With a nod, Polignac ordered two pikemen to untie him. They took him down and sat him on a wooden chair, and the Duke of Modena slumped in exhaustion, his hands hanging by his sides and his hair, damp with sweat, falling over his forehead, as though to hide the hateful light that flashed in his eyes, which were now narrowed to slits.

Polignac hoped that he had weakened the man's resistance.

'*Monsieur*,' he said, 'I would take no pleasure in continuing; indeed, the sooner you confess your crime, the better it will be for all of us. Only then will I be able to end your torment. Please do not oblige me to order my men to begin again.'

Montecuccoli coughed and leaned forward, saliva mixed with blood dribbling from his mouth. The excruciating pain had made him bite his lips until they bled.

'Water,' he murmured.

Polignac nodded to one of the pikemen.

The count drank eagerly, and when he had finished, he nodded. 'I'll tell you everything,' he said.

'I'm all ears,' replied Polignac.

'My name is Sebastiano di Montecuccoli. And that valise belongs to me,' he sighed, as though that were all he had to say. But he was so exhausted that he could no longer remain silent, and he surrendered to the words which flowed out of him in a complete confession. 'I bought the poisons in the shop of a Venetian apothecary. I arrived in France in the company of soldiers of fortune led by Captain Renzo di Ceri, who fought for the crown. We were, though, defeated by the imperial soldiers. Some of us were captured and taken before Antonio de Leyva.'

'The governor of Milan?' asked Polignac. 'The one with ties to Charles V and the current general of his troops?'

'Yes,' confirmed Montecuccoli. 'With him there was Ferrante Gonzaga. They made me an offer: if I killed the King of France, not only would my life be spared, but they would make me the lord of two of the finest lands of Mantua and a grandee of Spain.'

Polignac gave him a sceptical look. 'And you believed such offers?'

'I was desperate, and had no other choice,' Montecuccoli admitted. 'If I had refused, they would have killed me.'

'So how did you actually do it, then?' asked Polignac, who by now felt he had Montecuccoli by the throat. 'There was the game of Royal Tennis, and then?'

'As I told you, after we played we were hot and Francis was very thirsty. We sent a page with two silver amphorae to the well near the dauphin's lodgings. I accompanied him. He drew the water and filled them, and when he placed the two containers on the edge of the well, he leaned over to look down and I seized the opportunity – I went over and dissolved the poison in the amphora on the right.'

7

The Interview with Henry

She was not, unfortunately, beautiful.

She would have given everything to be so, but she was not. She was intelligent, cultured, attentive and charming, but she was not beautiful. She had no golden hair or sapphire eyes, she had no high cheekbones or perfect nose – she might at best be considered interesting, she thought, as she looked at herself in the mirror, but that was all. Nothing more. How could she possibly seduce Henry? How could she tear him away from Diane? The woman was like a curse.

Hatred and patience were her watchwords, and she had stoked the fires of both since the beginning when she had first come to court. But now one of the two principles upon which she had based her conduct had failed her, and she could be patient no longer. Francis

I had been clear. First there had been her uncle, Pope Clement VII, whose wonderful idea of renewing his loyalty to Emperor Charles V had infuriated the French sovereign. And upon his death, Clement had also failed to pay off the debt of the promised dowry, which was the only reason the Valois family had allowed itself to become related to a family of Florentine merchants in the first place.

It had taken all of Francis I's self-control to accept that cruel blow and not have her repudiated for it.

And now this: the suspicion that she had killed his son to become the dauphin's wife and to take the bloody throne for herself.

As if that were not enough, she was unable to give Henry heirs. Which in all honesty was not surprising, given that he never showed his face in her chambers except fleetingly.

She was so angry that she didn't notice Henry entering her rooms, and only realized he was there when he was standing before her.

'Henry!' she cried in bewilderment. 'How are you, my love?'

She used that word because despite everything – despite his obvious infidelities and despite his shortcomings – Henry had always been kind to her, and Catherine was aware that his behaviour was an anomaly in that hostile and treacherous court which, with the exception of the king, and eventually of his son, had since the first day never wanted her there. And also because he was so handsome that she could not resist his charms.

She went over to him and took his face in her hands. She saw a strange light in his eyes, as if he were absent, unaware of what he was doing or of the reason that had brought him to her.

He sighed.

'What I feared has happened, Catherine,' he said bitterly. 'My dear brother has finally left us, and it's all my father's fault.'

'Why do you say that? You know full well that it isn't so.'

'Ah, wife, true it is – true indeed. If only you had known my brother before those tragic days, before the imprisonment, pain, loneliness and violence, perhaps today you would not speak thus.'

Catherine watched as the coldness of his gaze gave way to an expression of profound bitterness and frustration, as if what had happened was, in Henry's mind, presaged and inevitable.

'What do you mean? Explain yourself, I don't understand.'

Henry looked into her eyes and Catherine felt something cold penetrate her veins, almost as if cruel and ineluctable thoughts lurked in his soul.

'Francis was never the same after the imprisonment to which we were subjected in order to save our father.

He abandoned us for three long years into the hands of jailers who knew nothing of honour, and worse still, knew nothing of pity. It was hell, Catherine.' Henry paused and looked out through the window at the green August meadows, and the flowerbeds and fountains of clear water in the gardens that surrounded the castle. 'I remember the rats, as big as dogs, that came to gnaw cruelly at our feet during the endless nights. And then the beatings, the insults, the humiliations. Francis was the oldest, and the guards concentrated their attentions on him. One day they took him and undressed him, leaving him completely naked. I remember Francis crying while those worms laughed, telling him that he was nothing but a French sissy. And the more they insulted him, the more he cried, because he was afraid of what they would do. I didn't understand at first, but when I saw what happened – because they forced me to keep my eyes open – I cried too, more even than he. There was a colossal man among them, with long hair and a thick beard, as black as coal. He punched Francis twice, two punches that would have floored a bull. My brother fell to the ground and the man took him by the hair and forced him to get on his knees. Then he undid his breeches and…'

Henry's voice faltered and he could not continue.

'Why are you telling me this, Henry? Stop tormenting yourself with these memories. You're only upsetting yourself.'

Catherine walked over to her husband and put

her arms around him. He rested his face against her shoulder, but clearly had no intention of stopping.

'When it was all over, he slapped my brother again, sending him sprawling to the ground once more, and then, as Francis tried to get back to his feet, he kicked him while the other guards laughed. I didn't lift a finger. I was afraid. I stood watching. Like a coward.'

'You were a *child*, Henry. What else could you have done? It wasn't your fault...'

'Then that man urinated over him,' he interrupted her. 'It seemed to never end...'

Henry's voice failed again and he remained silent, struggling to hold back his tears.

Catherine was shocked.

She understood now how horrible it must have been for those two little boys to remain locked in the prisons of the castle of Madrid for three years. And she also understood the anger and resentment that Henry had always felt towards his father.

'My God, Henry. I hadn't realized what you went through. It must have been terrible, *terrible*. A child should never have to experience what you and your brother suffered. Never.'

Henry shook his head and broke free of her embrace.

'No, Catherine. You cannot understand. No one who hasn't experienced such horror first-hand can, and neither can my coward of a father, who left us at the mercy of those devils. Francis lost his mind that day, and he never went back to being as I once knew him. That imprisonment broke him forever, and he became a ghost of what he had been. His behaviour became incomprehensible, and even afterwards he surrounded himself with the strangest, most bizarre people. What happened a few days ago is simply the inevitable conclusion of a journey of pain which began a long time ago. It was my father who killed my brother.'

Catherine felt a sudden pang, as if those words had opened a wound in her chest. What her husband was saying was so awful that it frightened her simply to hear it.

'Henry, you... you *can't* say that. You can't truly think that.'

He turned, a sneer on his face.

'Oh really?' The disbelief in his voice sounded sinister. 'Do you have any idea what you're talking about, Catherine?'

'You are right, I do not know your sufferings, and I do not know what it means to have endured what you endured, this is all true. But I love you, Henry, and I am here to help you overcome this, if you will let me.'

But the dauphin shook his head.

'Catherine... it's not your fault. You have always been so kind to me and I... well, I am fond of you, certainly. How could I not be? But you must also understand that you arrived too late. Everything had already happened.

If I am not completely mad today, there is only one reason for it.'

When she heard those words, Catherine was afraid to ask what the reason was, as she sensed that it would make her suffer even more, but she summoned up her courage.

'Say what you have to say, then. Say it all, and hold nothing back. Be sincere with me, at least. I think I deserve that, Henry, don't you?'

He nodded.

'If I did not lose my mind after I returned from Spain, the credit is due to one person and to one person only.'

'Diane,' said Catherine. And the name emerged from her lips as if it were poison.

Henry looked at her.

'I am sorry,' he said, 'but it's the truth.'

'Very well, then,' said Catherine. The tone of her voice had changed, and now she was angry. 'I understand. I understand that you came to my rooms simply to humiliate me once more. Humiliating me outside them clearly wasn't enough for you. So now, please do me the kindness of leaving.'

He looked at her sadly. 'Forgive me, Catherine, I didn't mean...'

'Please, spare me your compassion,' she snapped. 'Leave immediately. If you ever decide to come back, you will do it because you wish to see me, to talk to me, to be with me. Not to speak to me about that whore, Diane of Poitiers.'

Henry blanched, and without adding another word, he left. As she watched him go, Catherine burst into tears. She wept silently, not wanting to be overheard or to appear weak. In her heart the pain grew along with the hatred, and while she tried to stop her tears, she swore to herself that she would have her revenge against that accursed woman.

OCTOBER 1536

8

The Square of Lyon

The square was teeming with people.

Each of its four sides was lined with *maisons à colombages* with half-timbered frontages, and it was dominated by the imposing facade of the cathedral of Saint-Jean, its squat bell towers flanking the sumptuous central rose window and the spire like heralds. A whole company of pikemen was arrayed along the perimeter of the square.

Captain Raymond de Polignac was smoothing his moustache as he waited to see the awful spectacle which, predictably, had attracted a crowd of thousands that now filled the square. Clad in a long blue coat, a glittering breastplate, boots with red parade bows and a cloak of the same colour laid gently over his shoulder, Polignac stood stiffly, his large-plumed vermilion hat slightly tilted forward so he could see without being seen. The hilt of his sword shone in the pale October sun.

At the centre of the square, four black horses, arranged crosswise, were tended to by the same number of executioner's assistants.

Raymond de Polignac shook his head. He looked over at Catherine de' Medici and noticed her frowning face. Considering the suspicions that had immediately fallen upon her, she must certainly have no shortage of worries, yet she maintained a seemingly unyielding pride and stared straight ahead, her gaze dazzling even though nothing about the rest of her appearance was particularly noteworthy. Not her brown hair, or her dull, slightly protruding eyes, nor her lips, which were too full, nor even her large nose, which certainly did not improve the overall picture.

On the whole, while she could not have been called ugly, neither was Catherine beautiful, and though richly dressed and accompanied by her ladies-in-waiting and servants, in comparison with the king's lover she was practically invisible.

Diane of Poitiers had dark-brown hair that shone like onyx. Her eyes were the colour of the night sky with delicate hints of cornflower blue, and the perfection of her face would have provoked even a man of the noblest principles to impure thoughts. Her magnificent alabaster neck and her immaculate, diaphanous skin, suffused slightly with a delicate pink, made her more sensual and desirable than any other woman in France.

A week earlier, the king had ordered wooden platforms and stands built to ensure the best possible view of the execution, and so Raymond now had both of Henry's women sitting in front of him. The two most important women in France – after the queen, of course, who sat next to the sovereign.

And yet, in her face one could sense Catherine's iron will. It must have been that, after all, combined with her uncommon intelligence, which had kept her at court until then. There had been more than one rumour that the king was about to repudiate her, but despite the gossip it had never happened.

While he awaited the arrival of the prisoner, Polignac looked around him.

The situation appeared calm. The peddlers were selling sweets and candied apples, and the *boulangeries* must have been working overtime to satisfy a clientele which had more than doubled for the occasion. Huge numbers of shepherds, peasants, woodsmen and tenant farmers had flocked in from the countryside to witness the execution of the dauphin's murderer.

And who could blame them? Though far from over, now that the war was going in France's favour, that execution had taken on the characteristics of an act of collective catharsis.

Sitting on his wooden bench, King Francis I looked

indulgently at his cheering subjects. At the end of the day, it had been a marvellous idea to ride the wave of this story of poisoning and make it public. Montecuccoli's betrayal and his work in the shadows as a spy for Emperor Charles V of Habsburg had made him the perfect scapegoat in the eyes of the people.

The crowd shouted loudly and the pikemen watched the square.

Suddenly, like an actor taking the stage on cue in some theatrical performance, the condemned man made his appearance. He arrived on a wagon with raised sides which was pulled by a pair of tired mules. Railing against him and whipping him mercilessly was the executioner's crippled aide, a hunchback who was lame in one leg and who was giving Montecuccoli such a quantity of lashes that it would be a miracle if he survived long enough to be tied to the four horses and torn to pieces.

From the centre to the houses and buildings on the perimeter, the crowd filled the entire square except for the four routes along which the horses would move. Even the most adventurous of the onlookers kept cautiously behind the wooden barriers, so as to avoid being sent to the next world by a kick from one of the black stallions.

Montecuccoli was taken off the wagon, and a chorus of insults and whistles filled the air. Men and women alike spat at him, and pelted him with rotten fruit and vegetables which also struck the executioner's aide. Seemingly heedless, the hunchback multiplied his efforts so as to make the distance that separated the condemned man from the place of his quartering an authentic ordeal.

Montecuccoli was the ghost of the youth he had been. His once-beautiful curls were now stringy and lank, his eyes were sunken, his face even thinner than before, and his cheekbones pressed out through the skin of his face as if the flesh had disappeared, leaving room only for the bones. He moved with difficulty, not only because of the shackles on his hands and legs, but because of all that he had suffered in prison.

Polignac was well acquainted with the treatment given to assassins, and even he himself had not spared Montecuccoli a whipping.

With his ragged clothes and unsteady gait, Montecuccoli trudged forward until, just as he was about to collapse, he was grabbed by the assistants of the executioner. The executioner himself – a tall, imposing man, dressed in black and with a completely bald head – removed the stocks and kicked away the chains, which rattled on the granite flags of the square. Then, together with his helpers, he began to tie the four ropes, each of which was attached to the pommel on the saddle of one of the horses, to the condemned man's arms and legs.

Montecuccoli was so exhausted that he did not resist.

To the great annoyance of the crowd, who had been hoping to see him beg for mercy, he did not squirm, did not kick out, did not shout. Instead he did nothing, and simply lay there like a rag doll.

After having tied the ropes to his hands and feet, each of the four minions pulled out a whip and struck the hind quarters of the horse that had been assigned to him.

The jeers and cries of the crowd were drowned out by the whinnying of the horses, and silence descended as all present stared at the awful scene.

The ropes grew taut as the horses began to advance, and Montecuccoli suddenly found himself lifted from the ground, his arms and legs being pulled in different directions. His veins standing out in relief against his pale skin, the Count of Modena screamed as he had never screamed in his life, almost as if his body were about to burst.

And then, indeed, it actually did.

Polignac glanced over at the royals. The king and his son Henry were staring at the scene.

Queen Eleanor of Habsburg and Diane of Poitiers, on the other hand, had looked away, turning their heads slightly and shielding their eyes with their hands.

Catherine, though, was watching. She didn't seem to be afraid.

'Remarkable,' thought Polignac. And for the first time he realized that he had begun to like the little Italian.

9

In Search of an Astrologer

Madame Antinori was tired, discouraged and afraid.

She had been travelling for two months now, and there was no sign of that accursed Michel de Nostredame. Or rather, she seemed to have some special talent for always arriving in the right place an instant after he had left it. Not to mention that each time she mentioned his name, she made herself more enemies than she would have believed possible. And incredibly quickly, if truth were told. For whatever reason, Nostredame did not seem to enjoy great popularity.

Why, wondered Francesca as she sat down at her desk, had the queen decided to entrust the thankless mission to her? If Catherine had so much faith in her, why not give her something more pleasant and rewarding to do?

Having to provide a monthly list of her ongoing failures was a recurring humiliation.

She shook her head, took up pen and inkwell and began to write, noting down on paper everything she had discovered in that most recent period. If nothing else, giving an account of the investigations she had conducted would help her to organize her ideas.

To Her Highness Catherine de' Medici, Dauphine of France.

Madame la Reine, as previously, I send you this monthly report of mine in the hope of pleasing Your Highness. I must warn you, though, that the news is, alas, not comforting.

As you suggested, I conducted my first search in Montpellier. Upon arriving in the city, however, I established fairly rapidly that Monsieur Michel de Nostredame had not actually been there for some years. Having obtained a bachelor's degree in medicine, he had left for Aquitaine, summoned, it seems, by a certain Julius Caesar Scaliger, personal physician to the Bishop of Agen. Before departing for that city I also verified another fact: I can confirm the Jewish origins of Monsieur de Nostredame, grandson of Guy de Gassonet, who converted to Catholicism towards the middle of the last century with the name of Pierre de Nostredame.

The reliable source of such information was a former professor of anatomy of Michel, a certain Claude de Montmajour, who fully satisfied my most profound curiosity on the matter.

And there is more. It seems that the name Nostredame was given to Guy de Gassonet by the then archbishop of Arles, Pierre de Foix. In any case, Michel's grandfather took his conversion very seriously, even going so far as to repudiate his wife, who had not renounced the allurements of Judaism.

Be that as it may, after hearing this news, I headed to Agen. After a long and somewhat uncomfortable journey (we were attacked by brigands and one of the men with whom Your Highness provided me as an escort was injured, albeit slightly), we finally arrived in Agen.

Here, though, things became even more complicated, not least because the city is in the grips of the plague. I will confess to being terrified by the sight of the carts full of corpses covered with black boils that split their flesh.

In this regard, I confess to Your Highness that I was on the verge of returning immediately to court because of the grave risk to my person, but fortunately for me, meeting Scaliger has dispelled all my doubts since, after having expounded to me at length upon several methods he considers infallible in curing the disease – methods which do not seem to have proved to be in the least effective, to judge by the piles of corpses I have seen in the city – he finally thought it appropriate to inform me that Michel de Nostredame had left Agen for Bordeaux. The reason for this departure, which has something of the flavour of an escape, is linked to the fact that Nostredame's wife and children had succumbed to the plague. Scaliger admitted that he did not know the precise circumstances of the tragic events since, after a period of friendship, his relations with Nostredame had deteriorated.

Without wasting another moment in Agen I will therefore head to Bordeaux, in the hope of not having contracted the disease.

With this, I believe I have said all that I wished to say and, in the hope of having performed well the task entrusted to me well, will take my leave.

Your grateful and faithful servant,

Francesca Antinori

She reread the text several times, then rolled it up, sealed it with wax and called for one of the guards who was accompanying her so that he could entrust it to a courier and have it delivered as soon as possible to Catherine.

Only then was she able to relax and reflect upon the good fortune which had accompanied her on that terrible journey, preserving her from the plague which was bringing France to its knees.

That thought brought her back to the war-torn countryside: when they were not actually burned, the uncultivated meadows had been reduced to mounds of whitish stubble or black and fuming expanses by the feverish and cruel retreat of Charles V of Habsburg's troops. And the cities were in no better condition: consumed by the plague, their populations decimated, their gates marked by crosses and prey to purifying flames.

Francesca feared for her person, of course, and the generous purse that her lady had given her was of little help. She shivered, and pulled the fur stole tighter around her shoulders.

Autumn seemed already to be announcing winter, and she hoped she would have better luck in the days to come. She had no intention of spending an entire year hunting down an astrologer who was most likely a lunatic and who seemed to be hated by everyone he encountered.

JANUARY 1538

10

Nightmares and Fear

Catherine saw the flames: blazing red, they were as high as the walls of Jericho. Horsemen clad in black armour advanced, cutting throats as they went, the steel blades of their swords flickering like lightning over the pink flesh of the Roman nobility.

She saw the Pope, locked inside Castel Sant'Angelo, trembling and sobbing like a child whose playthings have been stolen.

She saw Rome ravaged, prey to drooling *Landsknechte* hungry for lives to snuff out with their swords, its streets black with the smoke of the fires, regurgitating the dead and the wounded. The Tiber ran red with the blood of the city's children.

She found herself at Palazzo Medici in Florence, with a screaming mob outside the door. Her aunt, Clarice

Strozzi, held a knife to defend her from those who hated the Medici and stretched out clawed fingers to tear at the eyes of the womenfolk of that family of usurers and leeches.

Sunlight. They were alone: abandoned by Cardinal Passerini, by her cousin Ippolito, whom she loved so dearly, and by Alessandro, the bastard, whom she had believed her brother despite the curly hair and full lips which affirmed more clearly than a thousand words that he was actually the child of a nobleman and the wild graces of a Moorish servant.

The men and women of Florence separated her from her beloved aunt and led her to the monastery of the Dominicans of Saint Lucia, who would keep her there as a prisoner, walled up inside.

Catherine awoke with a start.

She was drenched in sweat, her hair plastered to her temples and her heart pounding so powerfully that it seemed likely to burst out of her breast at any moment.

It had happened again – that nightmare, which seemed to bring together all the darkest and most terrible fantasies of her childhood, had stolen her sleep. She looked at the red embers glowing in the wide fireplace. The room was atrociously hot. Kicking off the covers and bedsheets, she leapt up from the four-poster bed, put on her velvet slippers and stumbled over towards the large windows, flinging them open and letting the icy winter air caress her face. Fontainebleau was a marvel and the first flakes of snow were falling silently from the pearl-coloured sky, dusting the gardens with white. For a long time she breathed in the sharp, clean air, the bitter cold seeming finally to awaken her from her torpor of a moment before.

It was a liberation.

Suddenly, almost as if her body had regained consciousness only in that moment, she felt the cold, and closed the windows.

Fontainebleau: another castle, another move from palace to palace. But it was what the king wanted. Francis I was categorical on the matter, and anyone who complained about it would have him to deal with. Presence and readiness were fundamental, and not having them could cost you dearly. Catherine sighed as she thought about how much the king's coffers were being depleted on one hand by that eternal war and on the other by the construction of these magnificent residences.

But the beauty of Fontainebleau made up for all that: it almost helped her endure Diane, in a way, though she already knew that her patience would be severely tested that day. The king had decided there was to be a ball, and that meant sumptuous clothes and jewels, charming conversation, and dances – but also gluttony, orgy, betrayal and unbridled sex.

She tried to put it out of her mind. She would wait, as she had done all those years. Hatred and patience, just like always: hatred for Diane, and patience while she waited to bear a child.

It had been over a year since she had heard from her dear Francesca Antinori, and she had given up hope that the woman was still alive, just as she had surrendered to the evidence that she would never be able to bring the most powerful and gifted astrologer to the court. She had so many to consult, but none of them seemed able to soothe her fears.

Time was passing, and she still hadn't given the king an heir – though the absence of the now legendary Henry from the marital bed was obviously more than a minor hinderance to her conceiving.

She snorted in annoyance at the thought of what awaited her, then took up her copy of Niccolò Machiavelli's *The Prince* from her desk. She had made it her personal bible, and she had read it and reread it in an attempt to commit its wisdom to memory, since she knew that the ideas it contained would prove all the more useful to her in the future. Sooner or later, even Francis I would die. She hoped that would not be for a long time, especially as he was now her only protector, but the transience of life required her to make ready in any case.

After leafing through the pages she had consulted so many times, she decided that she would soon call her ladies-in-waiting to help her prepare for the ball. She must be irresistible enough to seduce Henry and take him to her bed. And just let that damned Diane even *try* to get between her and her husband: she would regret it bitterly if she did.

When she entered the beautiful ballroom, Catherine was wearing a diamond-studded gold necklace set with hazelnut rubies which had been a gift from her uncle Clement VII, while on her finger she wore the ring known as *en table* because of the exceptional size of the diamond set in it. The pearls of a precious choker gleamed upon her throat.

Her carefully styled hair, her diaphanous skin, the precious dress of blue brocade embroidered with threads of pure gold all exalted her fragile femininity. She looked extremely elegant, a marvellous, magnificent doll, and was preceded by eight pages and eight ladies dressed in velvet and silk.

Clad in white satin robes adorned with lilies, Francis I beamed with pleasure at the sight of her.

The lamplight danced on the spiralling volutes of the columns and the colourful frescoes, but when Catherine saw her bitter rival enter the hall at Henry's side and shoot her that usual disdainful look of hers, all of the splendour instantly melted away.

Catherine went over to her: she was tired of waiting

and hiding – it was time to put her in her place. When he saw her approaching, Henry chose to walk away, pretending to have to something very important to communicate to his father.

'*Madame*,' began Catherine, 'I see that you are radiant even today. I imagine that the constant presence of my husband in your apartments is the principal cause for this, despite your no longer young age.'

Her dark eyes flashing icily, Diane looked at her with cold hatred. She pursed her lips in a pout as adorable as it was irritating.

'You imagine rightly,' she said. 'And as for age, with all due respect, it does not yet affect a beauty which you will, in any case, never possess.'

Catherine could not believe her ears. Diane had never before been so impudent.

'How dare you?'

But apparently her rival was not yet done.

'Dauphine or not, you will always remain an Italian at the court of France, and the daughter of merchants to boot,' she continued. 'And as for Henry, he knows very well which bed to choose.'

'So you insist in your arrogant madness?' asked Catherine. 'I knew I had you as an enemy, and this is the proof of it. I will remember it when the time comes.'

'Your threats are completely wasted on me, my dear,' replied Diane contemptuously. 'And, in any case, your hopes of becoming queen grow fainter and fainter by the day.'

Catherine raised an eyebrow in disbelief.

'I am in no hurry. I hope rather that our good sovereign reigns for another hundred years.'

'It is doubtful that will be the case,' observed Diane with a cruel smile. 'And anyway, I would remind you that given your barrenness, he could easily repudiate you. Not to mention that I would advise you to prepare yourself for unpleasant news.'

The enigmatic phrase obtained the desired effect, and Catherine's eyes widened in uncomprehending shock.

'So you *don't* know?' said Diane mockingly. 'I would say not, to judge by how big your eyes have grown – far too big, given their unfortunate form…'

'I forbid you to address me in this way.' Catherine was furious and her pale face began to turn purple with rage.

'As you prefer.' Diane did not flinch. 'I must therefore deduce that you have overlooked one vital detail.'

'I do not understand.'

'That seems obvious to me.'

'I would therefore ask you to explain yourself,' snapped Catherine. 'And I demand an apology.'

'You will wait forever for the apology, because it will never arrive. As regards the news, though, I can give you a name and a surname: Anne de Montmorency.'

'The marshal?'

'Do you see that you know nothing?' said Diane, disdainfully. 'Montmorency is about to become Grand Constable of France. I certainly do not need to tell you how profound his Catholic faith is, and therefore how little inclined he is to tolerate magicians and astrologers – especially those of the Jewish faith. I believe he would not hesitate to judge them heretical. Do you understand now what I wish to say?'

Catherine's heart skipped a beat. Did Diane know about her investigations, or was she just guessing? She pretended not to understand.

'I have no idea to what you might be referring.'

Diane did not intend to let her off the hook so easily, however.

'Do not believe that he doesn't know what you read, my dear. Tread very carefully, therefore, because with a man like Anne at court it will be extremely difficult to leaf through the pages of certain authors. The king will soon become one of the fiercest champions of the Catholic faith, and it will be most inappropriate to nourish subversive ideas – especially for those who already have everyone against them.' And as if to underline her words, Diane sighed and pretended to be disconsolate. 'Well, don't say that I didn't warn you,' she concluded.

And without another word, she left. Though not before having shot Catherine a glare full of contemptuous superiority.

11

Towards an Edict

Anne de Montmorency could not understand how the king could admit the general commander of the pikemen to a meeting like that. It was the kind of thing that simply wasn't done, but he knew that since Polignac had conducted the investigation into the murder of the dauphin Francis with great zeal and skill, the sovereign dared do nothing without speaking to him first.

Because of his services, he had been directly promoted from captain to general commander of the king's pikemen, which explained the reason for all that glory.

It was said that the influence the man had over Francis I was second only to that of his favourite, Madame d'Étampes.

In other words, a great deal of influence.

But Montmorency had no intention of surrendering his position. As one who held the rank of Marshal of France, he was certainly Polignac's superior.

The king had called him to his apartments for the *affaire des placards* in order to consult with him and Polignac upon the decisions to be taken. The *affaire* was water under the bridge now, but in increasing numbers of French cities, new outbreaks of heresy were flickering like flames in the breeze – and flames like those could easily be turned into a conflagration.

Anne had very clear ideas about the matter, and as soon as he entered he wasted no time in expounding them: he explained exactly what action he thought was required.

'Your Majesty,' he said, 'the case of the *placards* was as regrettable as it was worrying. These attacks on the Catholic faith have already put us in a bad light with the Pope in the past, and now we desperately need his troops and his good graces in order to defeat the army of Charles V. I do not believe that we can wait any longer, and feel that you must write an edict against these brazen curs who now, with their *placards* and their insults, are acquiring a bravado which needs nipping in the bud before it is too late.'

Francis I looked at him with admiration and respect. Montmorency was perhaps his most skilled man of war: he had inflicted multiple defeats on the troops of Charles V, freeing Provence and taking back Artois.

Polignac, on the other hand, was a model soldier – a shrewd and intelligent officer who was above all trustworthy. That was something the importance of which Francis could not overestimate in a period when loyalty was so hard to come by that he occasionally found himself having to pray that God in his mercy grant him it.

The king was so tall and imposing that he was practically a giant, and he towered over his two most talented soldiers, but nevertheless he inclined his head, as though intent on paying to both the greatest possible attention.

'And what do you think, my good Polignac?'

Raymond stared at the king, then let his eyes meet those of the Marshal of France, who gave him an icy glare. Montmorency's eyes were as blue as mountain lakes, and his sparse red beard only made his narrow, gaunt face look even sharper, almost as if it were the attempt of some sculptor to fashion the definitive image of a warrior.

That being the case, Raymond tried to measure his words, even though it was an art in which he was not particularly well versed.

'If I may speak freely, Your Majesty, while agreeing with what the Marshal of France says, I must point out how delicate the situation with the Jews and the Protestants is. We certainly cannot authorize them to disregard the Catholic faith, but we must also be careful not to spark a war of religion. I doubt that we would be able to deal with any further conflicts, either in terms of numbers or in terms of economics, so I therefore would consider it premature to issue an edict against non-Catholic beliefs.'

Montmorency could scarcely believe his ears, and his agitation was such that he was barely able to restrain himself. His comportment made his profound opposition to what had been said clear, and he began clenching his fists as though fantasizing about leaping to his feet and clamping his hands around Raymond de Polignac's throat.

'Your Majesty, the advice offered by the general commander of the pikemen is completely inappropriate.'

The king raised an eyebrow.

'And why would that be, Anne?'

'It is soon said, my lord: we have waited long enough. Four years, Your Majesty, are an eternity, and even if it is true that in the meantime a good part of those responsible for the wicked deeds have ended up in the Châtelet and then been hanged or burned alive in the Place de Grève, it is equally undeniable that the Protestants prosper and grow stronger with each day that passes, and that the numbers of those in our beautiful France who are drifting away from the Catholic faith are on the rise. And this is dangerous, because it fractures and weakens the state, making it disunited and unprepared to face wars. Have you ever wondered why, although smaller in size and population, we are able to stand up to the empire of Charles V?'

'*Sacrebleu!* Because we are France, *that* is why! What kind of question is that to ask me, Montmorency?'

The marshal hastened to nod haughtily.

'Naturally,' he confirmed, 'but also because we are a united people, led by a grand sovereign. But if by chance that sense of unity should go astray, don't you too, Your Majesty, worry that France might find herself in difficulty? And that being the case, would it not be advisable to discourage such a possibility immediately? Deprive them of the right to citizenship in France, so as to crush the danger instead of bitterly regretting not having done so at a later date?'

Polignac tried to counter Montmorency's fiery words.

'Are you not perhaps exaggerating, Marshal? With all due respect as your inferior, I ask: wouldn't the issuing of an edict provide the perfect spark for igniting a religious conflict which might perhaps be avoided? After all, the fires that have blackened the sky and the cries of the hanged in the public squares may well have been sufficient to calm the waters, don't you think?'

But Montmorency did not welcome Polignac's thesis – far from it.

'Commander Polignac, I understand what you say, but the arrogance of the Protestants and of heresy more generally is spreading like the plague. We must not underestimate the problem. I would remind you that those outrageous screeds against the Catholic faith, against all that we hold most sacred, have appeared in Paris, Blois, Orléans...'

'Even on my bedroom door! In my castle in Amboise!' roared the king, who had suddenly become enraged at the memory of the events.

'Exactly,' said Montmorency with even greater conviction, reassured by the sudden flash of fury which, in a stroke, had brought the king over to his side. 'As if to challenge our sovereign,' he added. 'And besides, Polignac, wasn't it you yourself who unmasked Montecuccoli and had him condemned for the murder of the dauphin? Did you hesitate in that case?' Montmorency let the question hang in the air, then seized his advantage to conclude the discussion for all intents and purposes by adding: 'Your Majesty, you must issue an edict. Perhaps not immediately, but soon. We must show the heretics that the throne is strong, that Your Highness is a champion of the Catholic religion and that those who rebel will be burned alive.'

Francis I nodded.

'I think so too, Anne. I will give orders to my jurists to prepare the text.' Then, turning his eyes to Polignac, he added, 'I do not mean by this that you are wrong, Raymond – after all, the only thing separating your opinion from that of Montmorency is the question of the timing.' He paused. 'Very well, this too is done. You may take your leave, my friends.'

Happy with the outcome of the interview, Montmorency bowed and walked towards the door, followed by Polignac, but just as the latter was about to leave the salon, the king called to him.

'One moment, Raymond. I wish to talk to you further about something.'

12

An Unusual Assignment

Polignac turned around and walked back towards the king.

'I must speak with you of an important matter,' said Francis I, then stopped, as though choosing his words with care. 'It is an issue which is immensely close to my heart, since it concerns the most defenceless person at court. I will say more: the openness of your views and your prudence in tolerating creeds other than the Catholic faith make me believe that you would be the perfect man for this position which, believe me, is of no small importance.'

That introduction, so immensely cautious, sounded strange to the ears of the general commander of the king's pikemen, especially coming as it did from the lips of the sovereign who, more by nature than from his position, was not a man to beat around the bush. It must therefore be something he cared about deeply.

'I am listening, Your Majesty,' Polignac said.

'You see, Raymond,' the king continued, 'there exists in this court a person who is as dear to me as one of my own children, if not more so. I recognize them as possessing extraordinary grace and intelligence, yet nevertheless, their nature being what it is prevents them from receiving the support at court that they deserve.'

'Are you referring to the dauphine, Your Highness? To Catherine?'

'My dear Polignac, this is why I am so fond of you and have such immense respect for you: because you understand things immediately and spare me the effort of giving silly explanations. You are right, I'm talking about *ma fille*, Catherine.' And as though to underline that the situation was far from ideal, the king gave a sigh. 'You see, Raymond, the girl is treated unjustly: no one can blame her for being a Medici, for I am the first to cultivate a passion for intelligence and a love of art, and it is a fact that it was Catherine's ancestors who gave us geniuses like Filippo Brunelleschi, Leonardo da Vinci, Raphael Sanzio, Donatello and Michelangelo. Only a fool could not hold them in high regard and refuse to be grateful to them for what they have left us: Florence. And if it is true that the girl does cause me some headaches, it is equally undeniable that no one is doing anything to help her. That being the case, Raymond, here is what I want from you...'

Francis I cleared his throat. A page in blue livery embroidered with French lilies appeared, bowing so low that he almost prostrated himself to the floor as he offered the king a glass of Champagne wine. Francis absently took it and drained it in two gulps.

'Catherine is alone and helpless and, my word, she desperately needs to get herself with child,' he continued. 'Forgive my frankness. The fact that my son Henry has a relationship with Diane of Poitiers is of no help at all, but it is equally undeniable that Catherine needs to gain more self-confidence and attempt to have a child in any way possible.'

For an instant, an incredulous expression appeared on Raymond de Polignac's face. The king noticed it.

'*Sacrebleu*, Raymond, don't pull that face: I have no intention of asking you to do anything unsuited to your role as the second-best soldier in the kingdom. What I want from you is simply to put yourself at the service of the girl. Stand by her and watch over her, now and always, also and especially when I am no longer here.'

Polignac's face relaxed.

'Of course, nothing would make me prouder than to obey Your Majesty,' he said, 'and yet how can I help you? And, Your Highness, let me also ask: how can I become the bodyguard of Catherine de' Medici if I am the general commander of the pikemen?'

'That, my dear Raymond, is not a problem at all: you can certainly remain such and still do as I ask. I will appoint one of your lieutenants to replace you for as long as necessary. The thing is that Catherine is engaged upon a quest which, whether you believe it or not, I hope will solve this damned question of children once and for all. Don't ask me what it is – go and speak to her and you will find out for yourself. And after that, you are to do exactly as she asks you. Have I made myself understood?'

'Perfectly, Your Highness'

'So everything is clear?'

Polignac nodded.

'As crystal.'

'Very good, my friend. Well, don't make Catherine wait – go to the gardens.'

Without another word, the king dismissed the general commander of the pikemen, and for the second time that morning Raymond de Polignac bowed and headed towards the door.

Catherine was growing increasingly worried: after an absence of more than a year, Francesca Antinori had returned to court – but had returned empty-handed. Of course, she could not be reproached for it: she had done everything in her power to find out where that cursed Michel de Nostredame was hiding, but it had all been for naught, because the man had disappeared.

He seemed to vanish into a cloud of black mist each time Francesca was on the point of locating him. Perhaps he didn't wish to be found? Perhaps he was aware of her intentions and had no interest in offering her his work and his advice?

Catherine didn't know what to do, but she was convinced that without his help she would never be able to conceive a child. There was a curse on her, she was certain of it, and the only one who could remove the evil eye was Nostradamus. She had to find a way to make him come to court.

During the long trip Francesca had risked her life several times, and the soldiers in her service had proved to be completely inadequate for the task. And since the arts of Madame Antinori had proved insufficient, she needed a man who was capable of giving a woman like her the support she needed in a desperate undertaking of this nature: someone faithful, stubborn, courageous and ruthless. But such a man was difficult to find, and perhaps did not actually exist upon the face of the earth. His honour and his blind faith in the crown should surpass all his other virtues, since only in that case would he agree to leave on the orders of a woman in search of a magician, an astrologer, a scholar whom many would not have hesitated to define as a charlatan, and perhaps even a heretic.

So who to ask?

Catherine looked at the gardens, bare and glistening with dew: the winter light filtered through the bare branches.

She was about to go back inside when a tall man with long brown hair appeared before her. A soldier, clearly. And what was more, a handsome one.

Had heaven sent him?

He stared at her with eyes so green that his gaze resembled that of some ferocious animal, and yet in their martial rigour they harboured, too, a charm and a restlessness which hinted at the presence of a great spirit.

When she heard what the man had to say, therefore, Catherine felt almost that she would faint with gratitude.

'My lady, my name is Raymond de Polignac, general commander of the king's pikemen. By order of His Majesty, I am now at your disposal. Whatever you order, I shall do with a joyful heart. I know that you may have a mission for me. If you will be so kind as to inform me of its nature, I will be happy to undertake it.'

As she heard these words, Catherine closed her eyes and revelled in the joy that she felt. So the king loved her even more than she had ever hoped.

All was not lost, then. There was still much to play for.

And at the end of the day, Diane had not won yet.

DECEMBER 1542

13

The Changing World

The years had passed.

He hadn't even realized it, and yet it was so: month had followed month and now he found himself five years older. He had kept faith with his king and had listened to Catherine's instructions, and thus, after having fought at the front, he had now become the bodyguard of Francesca Antinori, a beautiful Italian half-witch who travelled around France in desperate search of an astrologer. Or perhaps the man was a necromancer. Or a charlatan. Or it might even be that Nostradamus – for so he called himself – was all three at once.

Over that time, Polignac had visited every corner of the kingdom in an endless peregrination, and day after day he had seen it dying a little at a time. It was a land consumed by hatred and violence, whose nobility of soul had been lost forever: the glory of war had been traded for a few coins, honour exchanged for betrayal and opportunism, love for sycophancy.

He had seen the flickering fires of burning churches and the dumb horror of entire families drowned in wells. He had heard the roars of brothers ready to tear one another apart because they were divided by religious belief, and the cries of women burned in the public square because they had been found guilty of heresy.

And the Catholic and Protestant churches fanned the flames of the lowest and most base instincts, turning men into fanatics and bloodthirsty beasts.

As he followed Madame Antinori, he had wandered through a countryside devastated by the plague, its villages reduced to piles of corpses buzzing with flies.

The Edict of Fontainebleau, issued by the king a few years earlier, had done nothing but sharpen the divisions and increase the agonies of a France which was now split into two and drowning in an ocean of resentment and superstition. On one side were the Catholics and on the other the Protestants, and in the name of the afterlife, the value of that everyday life which – for Polignac, at least – was far more important and worthy of being lived, was being lost.

Montmorency had achieved what he wanted, but at what price? Was it really necessary to tear France apart with a religious war? Wasn't what had already happened enough? He shook his head as he reflected on what a ferocious creature man was. And so foolish, too! Any excuse was good enough for killing one another: power, conquest, creed and language were nothing but pretexts, accidents in the journey of life which were bent to principles solely for the purpose of killing.

And yet, at the end, after five long years of searching, Polignac could finally say that he had succeeded: he had found Nostradamus! They had finally caught up with the strange and singular man who seemed to inhabit some distant, indefinable dimension of his own at the border between Franche-Comté and the Duchy of Burgundy, a land crushed by definition, and for this reason, ironically, a mirror of the entire kingdom, albeit on a reduced scale.

Nostradamus was there in front of him, right in that very moment. From the man's face, it was clear that there was something special and strange about him. He had immense charisma, partly thanks to his magnetic blue eyes but also because of the loping, slow and mesmeric way he had of talking and moving.

A heavy rain fell upon the commander of the pikemen, upon the astrologer, and upon the tired and fragile shoulders of Madame Antinori, who was wrapped in her shawl and fur in a desperate attempt to escape the cold. It was she who had led the company to success.

They needed to find shelter, so it was with no small

relief that Polignac soon afterwards sighted an inn, its lanterns filling the evening air with a milky glow. As soon as they had entrusted their steeds to the grooms, they hurried inside.

Madame Antinori was at the end of her strength. Several times Polignac had tried to send her back to the court, promising that he would continue the search alone, but she had always refused. Her tenacity was such that it both inspired and impressed him. He realized that for Francesca that mission had become her *raison d'être* – and on reflection, perhaps always had been.

After all, that man wrapped in his black kaftan, with his eyes like burning coals and his long forked beard of dark whiskers, was vitally important to the queen. Polignac had been away from Paris for an eternity, but even he had heard rumours about the possible imminent repudiation of the dauphine because of her imprudent and apparently incurable childlessness, and it was obvious that the end of the little Italian would also mean the end of her entire retinue. And so Madame Antinori had every reason to want that man at court.

Always assuming that he could be of help to them, Polignac thought.

Since he had agreed to come with them, Nostradamus had uttered not a word, but he seemed to have seen in Francesca someone he knew. Her presence had been fundamental, as Polignac was not at all certain the astrologer would ever have agreed to go to court without her. He had the appearance of a man who had suffered a great deal: those restless eyes contained a strange and inconsolable melancholy.

After speaking with the innkeeper, Raymond had rooms assigned to them and accompanied Francesca upstairs to hers. A servant was called. When Madame Antinori almost fainted as she washed her face, Polignac rushed over to support her, and the maid touched her forehead to discover that it was burning hot.

It was at this point that the man named Nostradamus entered the room. He demanded that the sheets of the bed and the blankets be changed, paying an extra coin for that incomprehensible luxury, and then dismissed the maidservant. In his hands he held a bowl: all he would say was that it was a preparation made from willow root.

He helped Francesca drink it, promising that he would come back the next morning with the same medicine. Once she had finished the decoction, he tucked her into her bed and placed a damp piece of cambric on her forehead to cool it. Then he blew out the candles and wished her good night.

All the while, Polignac remained on the threshold, watching in dumbfounded silence as the man went about his business. Nostradamus must have realized well before he and the maid that Francesca had a high fever. He was a doctor, after all, but his approach to curing the illness was different from any other that

Polignac had ever seen. Not that he had a great deal of experience with apothecaries or experts but, as an officer of the king's pikemen, he'd had the opportunity to appreciate the noble art of medicine on more than one occasion, sometimes first-hand.

Nostradamus demanded conditions of cleanliness at the inn which were decidedly out of the ordinary, and practically unthinkable for a place like that which, though certainly less dirty than others, now gleamed – or at least, Francesca's room did.

Once he had finished, he went back downstairs to the ground floor and into the dining room. Polignac did the same, and ordered a pitcher of Burgundy wine while Nostradamus stood motionless, staring at the red flames of the fireplace.

Polignac left him absorbed in his thoughts. The man had taken off his kaftan to reveal a black brocade robe edged in gold – a long heavy tunic that emphasized his broad shoulders and strong back. He had also removed his doctors' square hat, and his long black hair fell over his shoulders like dark tentacles. Leaning towards the hearth, he tried to absorb the warmth it gave off with his hands.

Outside the inn, the downpour had turned into a storm. Lightning flashed in the sky, and the thunder seemed intent on shattering the very earth.

Suddenly the door of the inn burst open, allowing in the rain, which flooded the entrance.

The two newcomers who strode in had thick moustaches and long, wet hair, and the armour they wore was unmistakable.

Landsknechte.

There was no doubt about it, thought Polignac: the formidable mercenary soldiers in the pay of Emperor Charles V and under the leadership of General Georg von Frundsberg, who had first routed Giovanni de' Medici, known as 'Giovanni of the Black Flags', before going on to sack Rome.

And that was only one of their awful accomplishments.

He hoped they weren't after a quarrel, but knowing their temper it was hard to believe they wouldn't start looking for it almost immediately. He hoped that the cold and the rain had taken away their desire to cause trouble.

Once they had removed their cloaks, they both shouted for beer and then went to sit at the table opposite Polignac's. As soon as the innkeeper brought the mugs, one of the two drained half of his on the instant then spat on the ground, running his hand angrily over his moustaches.

'*Das Bier... Scheisse, es ist zum kotzen.*'

The other laughed. Polignac did not understand what the man had said, but he realized that it could not be a compliment.

'This beer...' explained the *Landsknecht* who had laughed, addressing the innkeeper in halting French, 'is disgusting.'

'I have some Burgundy wine, if you prefer,' replied the innkeeper with admirable self-possession.

The *Landsknecht* shook his head as if the matter were intolerable, and then barked something in German to his companion, who, in response, spat again, and hurled his mug to the floor where it shattered into pieces.

Then with breathtaking speed and a harsh scraping sound, he drew his sword. Unsheathed, the steel blade glowed in the firelight.

'My friend doesn't want your shitty wine,' he said with a malevolent smile. 'He wants your blood.'

14

Blood and Wine

Polignac knew there was no time to waste.

If he did not act immediately and take advantage of the element of surprise, the situation would only become even more complicated.

With all the strength he possessed, he hurled his jug of wine at the *Landsknecht* who had unsheathed his sword. Then he swiftly drew his own, together with his dagger, and kicking his chair out of the way leapt forward towards the second adversary who, taken off guard, had still to pull his sword from its sheath.

The terracotta jug exploded into fragments against the first *Landsknecht*'s jaw, sending his head jerking sideways. One large shard cut into the man's cheek, opening up a deep gash from which blood gushed copiously, while the other pieces fell to the floor and the wine the jug had contained splashed everywhere, along with the man's blood.

The mercenary gave an agonised cry.

Polignac spun round to face the other *Landsknecht* and thrust his sword at the man's belly. This opponent, though, had been fortunate enough to be knocked off balance by his friend and fallen to the floor, sending Polignac's blade whistling through the air.

The general commander of the pikemen made a further two thrusts, but the *Landsknecht* dodged the first and, having drawn his sword in turn, parried the second. His companion meanwhile, moaning in pain like a whipped cur, was on his knees with his hands to his cheek as he tried to extract the large shard of terracotta from his flesh.

The sinister screeching the blades made when they crossed sounded like a gnashing of monstrous fangs. The German mercenary kept up an aggressive guard and, after fighting off Polignac's surprise attack, began to harry him with a series of slashes. But Raymond was ready for him: throwing chairs crashing to the floor, he parried a couple of lunges and dodged a downward cross, attempting to return the attack at shoulder height. But his opponent was quick to parry.

The other *Landsknecht* was still on the floor, but Polignac knew he must hurry or he risked having to face two opponents at the same time. He leapt backwards, leaving his opponent's sword to slash at empty air, then feinted a fourth attack on the man's return swing, parrying his blade with the blade of his dagger, then lunging at him with his sword. The steel ran the *Landsknecht* through from side to side and the man dropped his heavy Katzbalger,[†] which rattled to the ground.

It was at this point that Polignac heard atrocious screams coming from behind him.

He spun on his heel, leaving the *Landsknecht* to surrender his soul to the devil, and found himself looking at the most unexpected of scenes.

Nostradamus was standing there, his hand stretched out, palm upwards, while the remaining German mercenary screamed like a stuck pig, clutching with his hands at what was left of his disfigured face. He fell backwards again, his feet stamping madly on the floor.

Without waiting an instant longer, Polignac sank his sword into the man's chest, the blade slicing into the fabric of his jacket and through his flesh until it struck the wooden floorboards beneath him, pinning him to the ground like some giant insect.

There was an acrid smell in the air, not too strong and in some ways barely perceptible, but it was evident

---

[†] Also known as a 'lanzichenetta', the Katzbalger was the wide-bladed sword used by the *Landsknechte*.

that Nostradamus must have blown something into the face of the unfortunate mercenary.

What it might have been, Polignac had no idea; nor did he have any desire to ask.

'What now?' asked the innkeeper. He had watched the whole scene in silence, praying that the two *Landsknechte* would not smash up his inn, and now there they were, lying dead as doornails in front of him. 'What are we going to do?'

'You will make them disappear.'

'How?'

'The cellar,' said the commander of the pikemen.

The innkeeper's eyes flashed with inspiration. 'The barrels!' he exclaimed, with a hint of amused satisfaction. 'A splendid idea, *monsieur*.'

'Now,' observed Polignac, 'I feel rather tired, so I would therefore ask you to take care of things. Here are two *scudi* for the damage we caused to the room, and two more to keep your mouth shut. We will be leaving tomorrow morning. I expect an abundant breakfast.'

And so saying, Polignac threw on the counter four gold coins, which the innkeeper immediately seized with all the rapacious joy of a vulture.

'Of course, *monsieur*.'

He put the *scudi* in his apron pocket and went to work, taking the first body by its feet and dragging it towards the cellar.

After thanking him with a nod, Polignac left Nostradamus staring at the orange flames in the hearth.

15

Too Cold a Bed

There were tears in Catherine's eyes.

She was weeping silently, her wet pillow soaking up all the misery she was capable of feeling. Beside her, Henry lay staring at the magnificent ceiling, but in his eyes there was no hint of joy. It had been so long since he had visited his wife's chambers that he no longer remembered what it was like. And when he had been reminded, what he had seen had evidently left him unimpressed.

He sighed.

Catherine was curled up with her back to him and had no intention of turning around. She didn't know what to do: it was quite evident that Henry didn't feel in the least attracted to her. So evident that a wave of nausea rose up through her chest, filling her mouth and soul with such bitterness that she thought she would lose her mind.

It was all Diane's fault! She had subjugated Henry and kept him away from her, and now it would be impossible for them ever again to find one another.

For all those years, Henry had visited her only once a month, and sex between them had become a torture. The only reason he still came to her bed was that, despite everything, he didn't want to repudiate her and didn't want her to be turned out of the court for failing to fulfil her conjugal duties. If that happened because she was unable to get with child, though, it would be simpler: in that case no responsibility could be ascribed to him.

There was something deeply perverse and cowardly about his behaviour.

And that, of course, did not make it any easier for them to celebrate the joys of sex.

The pain grew worse, seeming to devour her insides like some ferocious beast. Catherine wanted to speak, but could not: in that bed of feathers and frost, an invisible curtain of ice separated her from Henry.

Though there was a fire roaring in the fireplace, she felt cold, but at least she managed to hold back her sobs. She didn't want him to see her in that state or to realize how profoundly his indifference hurt her. She would have given anything to make him happy because, despite everything, she loved him from the bottom of her heart. And yet she felt so awkward, so inadequate. In a word: ugly.

It had always been that way.

Catherine would have liked her eyes to be a brighter blue, and to be wider and more sensual. She would have liked to have a smaller nose and hair that shone like silk, instead of being as dull as cheap cotton. She liked her hands, and her breasts – if nothing else, they were certainly not small – but her legs were so robust that they gave her yet another reason for lamenting Mother Nature's work.

How could Henry be attracted to her? Even she couldn't stand looking at herself in the mirror. And her husband was so handsome! He had broad shoulders and was tall, and his beautiful black hair framed a regular face with elegant features.

And Diane too was a true splendour!

In comparison to them, the French dauphine felt even more acutely and undeniably her failure as a woman and as a wife.

She wanted to scream.

If she did not manage to get herself with child from her husband soon, the king would be unable to defend her.

Catherine was profoundly aware how long it had been since Francis I had warned her to get pregnant. More than six years had already passed since the murder of the French dauphin by Sebastiano di Montecuccoli: an eternity.

And Polignac had disappeared into that infinite span of time in search of a man that no one could find.

During those years, Catherine had wondered if Nostradamus were not perhaps nothing but a fantasy of her own sick mind – and if that were the case then there was no doubt that all was lost. And yet deep within her soul, she still nurtured the flickering flame of a timid hope, whose feeble light she safeguarded so as not to remain in the dark forever.

She heard Henry breathing deeply. He had fallen asleep.

With all the caution of which she was capable, she turned over in the bed. The dim glow of the hearth cast an amber light over the dark room and lit the contours of his face, bathing them in its half-light. Catherine looked at his black eyelashes, so long that they resembled those of a woman and yet in no way detracted from the masculine charm of his features – in fact only exalted their harsh elegance: the thin firm lips, the dark beard, the broad chest that rose and fell with each breath.

Henry was truly handsome. She wiped away her tears and promised herself that he would be hers. It didn't matter what she had to do, she would get him back again. She would make sure that he changed his mind: she would beg him to make love to her, she would become a whore if necessary, and she would do it for him.

Catherine knew that she only needed to regain her confidence in herself. At that moment she felt as if she were broken into pieces, but there were at least two good reasons not to give up.

The first was completely irrational: she felt within herself the certainty that she would soon hear from Polignac and Nostradamus, and even though she was aware that the sensation was a child of her mood, she clung to the thought with the stubborn strength of a shipwrecked man clutching a piece of flotsam. And the second reason was that time was on her side. Hatred and patience, she always repeated to herself. If she could survive that moment, she could, little by little, defeat Diane. Because beauty, after all, was nothing but a passing gift, and with the passage of time even Diane would grow less and less attractive.

For a fleeting moment, a smile formed on her face. There was still hope, she told herself as she watched him sleep. It was so pleasant to see Henry, who usually wore a frown, finally at rest.

She would change her destiny.

She knew that she would soon be able to govern the will of the stars, thanks to an extraordinary man.

It was only a matter of time.

APRIL 1543

16

A Spring of Flesh and Blood

When she dismounted, Catherine could not at first understand where the devil it was that her guest had agreed to meet her.

But, she thought, it had been she who had moved heaven and earth to have him at court.

And in any case, his arranging to meet her in the woods outside Fontainebleau castle was perfectly understandable: by doing so, the man who awaited her apparently intended to invite her to enter a different world and pay her respects to the ancestral forces of nature.

Catherine had not wanted a carriage, preferring to enjoy the horseback ride through the French countryside: the blades of green grass dishevelled by the breeze of April, the scent of awakening, the rich brown earth, the branches of trees bearing their first buds and leaves. The evening sun that painted the sky blood red.

Although Raymond de Polignac was on his own horse nearby, the place where Nostradamus had asked her to meet him nevertheless gave her the shivers. Catherine could not understand whether the dark and ominous edge of the forest was part of some peculiar plan of his: something inexplicable that the ineffable and mysterious man had in mind. Seemingly sensing the dismal atmosphere, her horse began pawing at the ground with its hoof. She stroked its muzzle as she tied its reins to a fence and whispered soothingly in its ear.

The sun disappeared behind the horizon, immersing the scene in the inky blackness of the night, and a glowing red light appeared nearby: Polignac had lit a torch.

Catherine went over to the wooden hut. Smoke curled upwards from its chimney.

She took a long breath and knocked.

No one answered, but the door creaked as someone pulled it open.

She went inside.

At first she could see nothing. The room, bare and spartan, was filled with a cloud of perfumed vapour which gradually dissipated. The air inside the old hovel was so stifling and humid that it took your breath away, and impregnated with essences so intense that they left you dazed. It was as if the walls themselves were of flesh and blood, pulsing with unknown life.

In the centre of the room was a table upon which a silver tray had been placed. Upon it stood a pewter cup, and in the cup was something that at first glance she could not make out.

Suddenly, a gust of cold air sliced through the warmth of the room, making the flames of the candles flicker for a moment: dozens of bright points of light appeared in the darkness like hellish eyes, seeming almost to be governed by some supernatural will – or perhaps they were simply sparks which had been drawn down the chimney by a backdraft.

It was then that she saw him. He was a man of portentous appearance, his black hair loose and falling rebelliously far below his shoulders. His long charcoal-coloured beard ended in two sharp points, and his eyes were the colour of silver, so pale that they seemed to sparkle in the light of the candles. His garb was a long tunic of black velvet and a cloak of the same colour. On his wrists he wore bracelets made of almost opalescent discs, and around his neck a long necklace of gems glinted in the candlelight.

Nostradamus stared at Catherine for a long time. There was something so profound and inquisitive about his gaze that she felt a thrill of fear and pleasure: it was as if a wolf were scrutinizing her at length – or better, penetrating her, taking her in some strange way that she would never be able to explain. She felt her thighs grow wet with amorous humours as she tried, but failed, to hold his gaze.

Silently, he raised his hands to the ceiling, and the wide sleeves of his robe fell down to his elbows, revealing sinewy arms.

It was then that Catherine saw.

In his hands, Nostradamus held some kind of object. Whatever it was, it was no bigger than a fist and was strangely shaped. It began to ooze a thick red liquid, weird threads of which dripped into the pewter cup.

In a low voice, Nostradamus began to chant and, as though awakened by some wild song, a chorus of muted barks began, as if the creatures of the woods around them had decided to join in with the incomprehensible words. Except that the animal noises weren't coming from outside: Catherine could have sworn that they were coming from beneath the floor. It seemed that the cursed house actually was alive, just as she had thought, or was at the very least inhabited by unspeakable creatures.

Nostradamus's voice was serious but well-modulated, somehow exuding an ancestral and enchanting sensuality that left Catherine completely devoid of will.

Terrified by what she felt and irresistibly attracted by an instinct that she could no longer control, Catherine sensed an irrepressible sensuality filling her veins with liquid fire. Her eyes widened as she found herself looking at something she could not understand.

Nostradamus handed her the cup and gestured to her to drink: his eyes were clear and enormous, glowing as brightly as the stars in the sky. Feeling as though her gaze were lost in those iridescent globes, Catherine was no longer able to govern her body. She raised the cup to her lips and drank.

The liquid was thick, and left an unpleasant feeling in her mouth. She knew what it was, and yet could not stop herself, continuing to drink until she had emptied the cup. She wiped her lips with the back of her hand, and when she withdrew it, she saw that it was smeared with blood.

Nostradamus did not stop his litany for a moment, and beneath the wooden planks of the floor the sound of the barking continued.

Someone tapped at the door, which remained shut, and she heard Polignac say something, a hint of powerlessness in his voice.

'What have you done do to me?' shouted Catherine at the man she had had brought before her.

But Nostradamus gave no answer.

The chanting continued as did the monstrous howls, which grew louder and louder until Catherine clapped her hands over her ears.

Nostradamus continued to stare at her.

'Do you want to go and see?' he said. 'Are you truly

sure? I ask you this, because if you accept, you will not be able to go back.'

Catherine felt strange, excited. Her nipples were as hard as arrowheads, and she was overcome with a burning so intense that her vulva was flooded with humours. She ran her tongue over her lips without understanding why, and touched herself between her legs – she felt an irresistible urge to be penetrated.

'Go and look, if you really want to.'

Catherine opened the door she saw before her and heard the growls, or whatever they were, suddenly become more intense.

In the floor in front of her was an open trapdoor. She went and stood over it, and felt the air fill with a sour, musky smell.

Her head spun and she feared she would fall, but with incredible effort she managed to keep her feet and, consumed by the desire that set her thighs aflame, hoisted up her robe and started down the stairs.

The barking increased in intensity as she descended. She proceeded carefully, and when she reached the foot of the stairs, she saw a faint light illuminating what looked to be a sort of stable. The stench of dung filled her nostrils, and the air was full of the damp panting of the mating beasts. She saw a sort of iron cage, and inside it a beast with grey fur that was savagely mounting a she-wolf, clawing at her and biting at her neck with its white fangs, its manic thrusts making the female howl with pleasure.

Catherine could not believe what she was seeing. Nor what she felt.

17

Protect Love

'I tell you, that woman worships the devil! She professes to be a Catholic, but the truth is that she has made a pact with the fiend, and the messenger of those blasphemies is the man that she brought to court: Nostradamus is a minister of Satan. Please, Your Majesty, believe what I say, be on your guard. That little Italian will be the ruin of France.'

Diane of Poitiers was beautiful that day, and she employed all of her charms, and all of her eloquence, to convince the king of the truth of what she said.

Francis I snorted: he loved Catherine, although he had to admit that her eccentricities certainly didn't help her. She could be forgiven the lack of progeny, for which Diane was nevertheless responsible, but her surrounding herself with astrologers and magicians was a madness that only fed the slanders and hatred towards her. But then, on the other hand, he thought, it had been he who had allowed her to carry out her plan, by putting a man of the talent and courage of Raymond de Polignac at her service. If he was honest, though, he didn't feel able to condemn her.

'Come, Diane, you are too harsh on the girl. And please remember that you are speaking about the dauphine of France, so I would therefore ask you to show a little more respect and deference. One day, whether you like it or not, that young woman will become queen, so you would be wise not to say anything which you might later regret.'

Diane of Poitiers nodded, but maintained the brazen confidence which the king found of no small annoyance: firstly because, by temperament, he far preferred women who were sensual, mysterious and lascivious, but who were also more given to playfulness and laughter. And also because, even with her dazzling beauty, Diane always presented herself as inviolable and inscrutable. Good God, the woman was so intense that Francis I was afraid she was about to declare war on him!

'I will treasure your advice, Your Majesty. But on the other hand, I am obliged to note that this line of conduct risks encouraging practices which border upon heresy, and that would be highly unwise if it is true that the Pope—'

'*Sacrebleu, madame!*' thundered the king. 'I know

what is good for France without the need of your advice. The fact that you possess some influence at court thanks to your noble birth and your friendship with those intolerant Catholics of the House of Guise and with Anne de Montmorency does not give you the right to suggest policy to me. Note that out of common courtesy I avoid commenting upon the way in which you exercise your influence over Henry, not to mention that showing excessive intransigence towards the Protestants risks on the one hand consigning the country to yet more religious war and on the other, alienating the few allies that we have managed to assemble against that scoundrel, Emperor Charles. I have already issued an edict – do not ask me to do more!'

Diane's face flushed bright red, but she was forced to swallow her anger. By appealing to all her self-control she managed to rapidly moderate her tone and to assume an expression that, although not contrite, did at least display a certain modesty.

'I meant no disrespect, Your Majesty. Only it seemed appropriate to point out the expectations the Catholic cabal nourishes…'

'Are you threatening me?'

Diane's large, beautiful dark eyes opened wide in feigned astonishment.

'Threaten you, Your Highness? I would never dare! Quite the opposite, and evidently the fault is mine that I am unable to explain myself. I am simply trying as well as I can to warn you about the dissatisfaction which is mounting among the ranks of the nobles of the Catholic faith – a faith which you too share.'

The king made a brusque gesture with his hand as though to shoo away that torrent of words.

'Very well then, I shall consider myself warned. But as I said at Montmorency some time ago, I have already had at least a hundred Protestants hanged and quartered in the Place de Grève following the *affaire des placards*, and I must protect my alliance with the German princes. Not to mention that with the Turks, who are certainly not of the Catholic faith. And as for the Pope, who declares himself to be our ally, I would remind you that he is nothing but a two-faced Janus who has made an agreement with Charles V. And we know very well the amount of men and resources those damned Habsburgs possess, without even counting those *Landsknechte* butchers. If it were not for Scotland and the princes of Germany, we would be nothing more than a colony of the emperor by now. I should instead thank the Ottoman Porte, whose janissaries almost razed Vienna to the ground. Do you understand now why I cannot appear to be too pro-Catholic, *madame*? Because, if that were the case, I would suddenly find myself *alone* against an empire!'

Diane nodded – but she had not yet finished.

'Of course, Your Majesty. But to return to Catherine…'

'To return to Catherine,' the king interrupted, 'you,

Diane, will make sure that you leave your lover, my son Henry, some time to attend his wife's bed, do you understand? Don't think I haven't noticed the way that you monopolize him, seducing him like... like some *maîtresse*! I doubt that Catherine will ever have children if she is never given the possibility to lie with her husband,' the king continued while his interlocutor blushed with shame and anger for the second time that day. 'You will be the one to encourage him to return to his wife, do you hear me? I know that half the court is already wondering about whether I will one day repudiate Catherine, but I can tell you now that I have no intention of doing so. I instead expect that she will soon succeed in giving Henry a child, despite you and all your accursed Catholic cabal, Guise and Montmorency first among them! So see to it that you do your part. Have I made myself clear?'

Diane was astonished. The king had never spoken to her that way before, and she realized that, contrary to her intentions, she had gone too far and had weakened her position.

The king noticed, but felt no pity.

'And now, please be so kind as to leave me. Our interview is over.'

'But you don't understand! He is on her side, there is no doubt of it!'

Diane was furious. Her beautiful face was flushed with anger, and her black eyes flashed like an animal's. Henry looked at her with an expression somewhere between fear and worship. He was twenty years younger than her and owed her everything, and her charm and authority had a powerful hold over him. He had grown up, certainly, but in his mind Diane remained a sort of necessary presence – a woman for whom, if necessary, he would have given his life without a moment's hesitation.

'We're in danger, Henry! Your father hates me because he is manipulated by that whore Anne de Pisseleu, who has no intention of losing the power she has acquired thanks to her arts of seduction. She considers Catherine much less dangerous than me, so the fact that Italian dwarf hasn't even got pregnant has now become *our* problem!'

Henry couldn't follow her – in what way had Catherine's sterility become their problem?

'I don't understand how that could be damaging to us.'

'Then I will explain it to you!' his lover shouted.

'I can always repudiate her...' Henry insisted.

'That is where you are wrong! Your father will not allow you to!'

'I doubt that.'

'Do not doubt it, because your father is king! And what is worse, he adores Catherine. How this is possible defies my understanding, but he is fixated upon that merchantess, despite her poverty and her being as fertile as a field of rocks. And yet he is, and that is not all – the more I attack her, the more he defends her! So please, Henry, go back to her and see that you get her pregnant.'

'But I love you,' said the dauphin, his voice trembling with anger and frustration.

Diane realized that she must use another tone if she wished to obtain what she wanted.

'My dear, adored Henry, if I ask you this, I do it for the sole purpose of protecting our love. No one loves you more than I, and I have no intention of sharing you with anyone. What I ask of you is to do as your father says in order to strengthen our position. You cannot yet do what you wish, and will not be able to as long as he is the King of France. And so, if it is Francis I's will that Catherine stay at court and bear children, then you must obey him. I will know perfectly well that what you do is no affront to me but a sacrifice to which you submit in order to guarantee our survival at court. If you have descendants, the king will have no objection to our relationship, as it will not compromise the greatest of your obligations. You must understand that appearances need to be kept up. I certainly will not deny what I feel for you, but we cannot allow the purity and sincerity of that feeling to be polluted by suspicion and slander – we need to maintain decorum.

There will be no harm done. Indeed, by demonstrating your wife's fertility and assuring her lineage we will protect the passion that binds us. Do you understand now why I ask this of you?'

Diane was so beautiful and spoke in such a sweet way in that enchantingly husky voice of hers that Henry would do anything for her – even make love to his wife in the bridal bed if necessary. In truth, he had nothing against Catherine, but she was so insignificant compared to Diane, who gazed at him now with those big eyes of hers, as dark as the night sky. Her small white bosom heaved against her bodice, rising and falling with her breathing, her perfectly styled hair, her thin, elegant lips and that vivacious gaze of hers all bespoke an immeasurable royalty. How could any man resist her? And among the many suitors she could have taken to her bed, she had chosen him! The younger brother, the one the king – who doted only on his eldest son – ignored.

What magnificent revenge it had been to make the most beautiful woman in France his own – she who had loved him with sincere passion ever since he had been entrusted to the clutches of his Spanish jailers. She who had eyes only for him, even when he was too young to have a favourite. She who had supervised his education, who had encouraged him after his defeats and celebrated with him after his victories.

And then, suddenly, Catherine had come along and

ruined everything. But there was nothing to be done about that.

'I will do as you say,' he concluded with a sigh, and the bitterness that filled his voice was so sincere that Diane was almost moved.

'Kiss me, Henry. Kiss me with all the passion you have.'

The dauphin did not wait for her to repeat her request: he embraced the woman with whom he was so hopelessly in love and set to devouring her lips, kissing her as if it were the last time – as if he feared he would never see her again. His darting tongue forced its way between her lips, and Diane's did the same to his, then, mad with passion, he tore off her dress and bit at her dark nipples, prey to an overpowering desire.

She let her beautiful hand move down to his groin, and with feverish gestures she unbuttoned his breeches and grasped his member. He was so strong, and so full.

Henry moaned.

She began to masturbate him, and Henry abandoned himself to her caresses.

Diane bent down and took him in her mouth.

To Henry it felt as if he were admitted to heaven.

18

Sulphur and Evil Spirits

Raymond de Polignac could not fathom what had happened. He was more than willing to defend the future queen on every occasion that presented itself, but he needed to be in a position to do so.

What Catherine had been through the previous night remained a mystery to him, as did the reason why the door of that old house at the edge of the woods had not yielded to his shoulder.

Nostradamus made him uneasy, and for a very simple reason: though he could not have described or identified them, Polignac was certain that dark forces lodged within the man. The general commander of the king's pikemen was afraid of nothing, but he had no idea how to comport himself if faced with the supernatural. And he was almost certain that it was evil spirits and the supernatural which had been behind the events of the night before.

Of course, he had been careful not to report anything to anyone and had continued to do his duty as he had promised his king long ago, and he in any case admired Catherine for her pertinacity and the inexhaustible courage she displayed. Despite the criticisms, allusions and offences she was forced to endure because of what some saw as her original sin of simply being Italian, she continued onward, cultivating an ironclad discipline and an admirable capacity for endurance.

But it was undeniable that something had changed in her, and probably forever.

Nothing clearly perceptible, except in her attitude, but it nevertheless conferred upon her a new charm. In a word, Catherine had become more beautiful. She seemed to have acquired a sensuality that had previously been completely denied her. But now, as he watched her approach, he saw in her eyes something wild and daring that he could not remember ever having seen before.

He was sitting waiting for her in the parlour where she spoke with the most trusted members of her entourage. It was accessed through an almost invisible door which was cut into a niche in the wall.

Polignac had enjoyed the favours of the future queen since he had succeeded in a task which for five long years had seemed impossible and had brought Nostradamus before her.

He was happy, of course, because he liked the determined and intelligent little woman.

'Thank you for coming, *monsieur*,' said Catherine when she arrived, with that odd accent of hers: there was something so wonderfully imperfect about her. 'What would I do without you?'

'*Madame*, I am happy to see you looking so radiant – if possible, more radiant than usual. But I confess that I am still confused about what happened last night.'

'You need not fear, Monsieur de Polignac, nothing happened that need worry you. Trust me.'

'I do, my lady. So much so that, as you will certainly remember, even yesterday I did not allow myself to utter a single word and limited myself to bringing you safely to your rooms in Fontainebleau.'

'That is true, and that is exactly why I am so fond of you, Monsieur de Polignac. Your discretion and loyalty are a rare and precious – I would almost say *unique* – gift, given the times we live in.' And as she uttered those words Catherine could not hold back a smile.

'You have no idea how much your good opinion of me pleases me, *madame*.'

'Monsieur de Polignac,' said the dauphine, her expression suddenly changing, 'if I asked you for an opinion, would you be honest with me?'

'Do you doubt it, *madame*?'

'In truth I do not, my valiant friend. I simply wished

to tease you affectionately. The mere fact of your having brought Nostradamus to me means that I owe you my life. But that does not change the nature of my request, and so I expect a frank answer to what I am about to ask you.'

'And that you will have, Highness, have no doubt of it,' said the commander of the king's pikemen, making an elegant bow as though to emphasize his words.

Covering her mouth with her hand, Catherine gave a silvery laugh.

'For goodness sake, my good Polignac, there is no need for all that! You truly are a textbook soldier.' Then suddenly her amused tone vanished and she became serious again. 'Tell me honestly… what do you think of Madame de Brézé?'

Polignac raised an eyebrow. He had not expected a question like that, nor did he have a particularly precise opinion of Diane of Poitiers. He was a soldier, after all, and even though he had recently given up the battlefield to serve Catherine de' Medici and his king, he remained one. He cared nothing for gossip or rumours, and therefore as for Diane, he knew only what everyone knew, and was not particularly happy to have to admit that to his future queen.

'Honestly?' he asked.

'That is what I asked of you.'

Polignac could not suppress a sigh. 'I know what everyone knows, *madame*.'

'And that is?' Catherine clearly had no intention of letting him skirt the issue.

'Well, you know what they say…'

'No I do not. You tell me!'

'Very well. Diane of Poitiers is the favourite of Henry, Duke of Orléans and Dauphin of France.'

'You mean, my husband.'

Polignac raised his hands in resignation. There, he thought – now I have got myself in hot water.

'You asked me, Highness…'

'I know what I asked of you and I appreciate your candour. What else?'

'What do I think of her?'

Her eyes flashing, Catherine nodded.

'Well, I think that she is a cold, calculating, ambitious woman. She is a friend of the constable of France, Anne de Montmorency, and of the House of Guise. She is so embroiled with the Catholics that she is practically a fanatic, and would go to any lengths to favour the Guise family.'

'That is so, my brave Polignac. And how about the Duchess of Étampes?'

'The king's favourite?' This time the general commander did not wait for confirmation and continued with his reflection. 'Well, she is something else entirely.'

Catherine looked amused. 'What do you mean?'

'*Madame*, I certainly don't have to tell you. The Duchess of Étampes greatly prefers Calvinists and

Protestants in general. Not a day goes by without some so-called poet, under her careful direction, composing some filthy ditty about Diane of Poitiers. I believe that if we continue in this direction, with the favourite of the king and the favourite of the dauphin crossing swords with each other – and moreover in the name of religion – we run a serious risk of dragging the country into the abyss of war.'

'Do you believe that it might come to that, Polignac?' asked Catherine. It was quite clear though that she already knew the answer and had asked him to speak for the sole purpose of informing him what the situation actually was. And the situation was precisely that, because on the one hand there was the king and his favourite, who was tangled up with the Calvinists and Protestants, while on the other there was his son Henry and Diane of Poitiers with the Catholics, who were aiming directly for the throne and could not wait for Francis I to give up the ghost and clear the way from them.

And in that dispute over the throne of France, Catherine, aspiring queen and betrayed wife, played the same role as Margaret of Navarre, the current queen: a woman left to rot alone in a corner. It mattered little that Francis I was a pleasure seeker and his son a melancholy young man riddled with doubts.

But something suggested to Polignac that things would soon change.

'Stay with me, Raymond, because whether you believe it or not, I will manage to take what is due me.'

Polignac gave Catherine a questioning look. He had never considered abandoning or disobeying her, so he wondered what her cryptic words meant.

What was clear to him was that the future queen wanted something from him.

'Give me your orders, *madame*,' he said. 'You will have no cause to regret it.'

19

Passion and Vendetta

Henry couldn't have said precisely what, but he was certain that something about Catherine had changed.

The way she looked at him, to begin with. She seemed almost to be devouring him with her eyes.

The perfumes that filled her room seemed to bend his will. He had gone there through a sense of duty, but now he found himself desiring her. She was his wife so there was nothing wrong with it, but it was the first time it had ever happened.

Hardly had he kissed her on her forehead, as he always did, than she began to undo her nightgown. It was made of light, soft linen, so thin that her pale, full breasts were visible through it. Henry was not indifferent to the sight.

Catherine seemed possessed by wild desire. She held herself against him and caressed his member, then withdrew her hand, took up a goblet and drank, so eagerly that a few drops remained on her lips and ran down her chin to her neck. In the shadows her skin, tinted purple by the dim light of the burning candles, looked magnificent.

Henry moved closer to her.

'Drink, my love,' said Catherine, offering him a goblet of champagne. Henry took it and drank the icy cold wine. It tasted delicious, and once it was drained he felt a pleasant sense of light-headedness. Small, delicate hands explored his chest.

He found himself in the large bed with Catherine biting his nipples and twining his thick chest hair around her slender fingers. Then she licked him with a studied, lascivious slowness that increased the pleasantly dazed state in which he now languished.

He let her do it.

Catherine did not hesitate and continued to lick him, moving lower down until she found his member, which was already erect. She caressed it and kissed it, taking her time, and prolonging for as long as possible the sweet torture that intensified his desire.

God, how good she had become at it!

It was as though the clumsy girl of a short time before had suddenly turned into a woman who knew all the arts of seduction, even the most forbidden.

The thought was a fleeting one, as rapid as a beating of wings, and it disappeared in an instant. Henry revelled in the sensations, the first drops of semen emerging from his glans as Catherine continued sucking at him deeply. He took her by her brown hair and pushed her head against him, feeling his flesh tense with pleasure and burning desire.

He forced himself to wait. He wanted her to give him everything he had waited so long for, and when he was satisfied, he took off her nightgown and put her beneath him. She was small, and her skin was beautifully soft and velvety. He caressed her gently, then brought his hand to explore the most hidden of her treasures. He felt its moist, soft lips open to welcome his strong fingers.

He moved his index and middle finger in a circle, lingering long in that tiny cathedral of pleasure. It was a delightful profanation and he had no intention of stopping, at least until Catherine began to moan so loudly that the hoarse sound of her voice became a powerful and irresistible aphrodisiac. He felt his turgid member grow tense in preparation for the spasm.

It was then, when he was so aroused that to do otherwise would certainly have made him lose his mind, that he penetrated her.

Catherine seemed to have lost all inhibition, and the sensation was so intense that it barely seemed possible to him.

Unable to resist any longer, he came inside her, and Catherine felt the liquid flame explode within her body.

Unseen, a cruel smile spread across her face.

Her vendetta began at that exact moment, she promised herself.

20

The Prophecy

Nostradamus looked at Catherine with those blazing ice-coloured eyes of his.

The dauphine knew that the revelation would be shocking, one way or another. She had blind faith in this man, who seemed to belong to a world so dark that it cast its shadow everywhere he looked.

The atmosphere of the room in which she found herself was lugubrious and oppressive: dark curtains at the windows prevented the pale sunlight of spring from filtering in, and strange alembics and transparent glass jars full of powders and herbs crowded the finely crafted wooden tables. Swaying lazily and elegantly on his long legs, Nostradamus moved through the twilight ochre-coloured glow of the coloured lanterns that filled the room like a spider on a web, the dark kaftan which he always wore giving him the appearance of a giant bat.

The smell of the incense and the other perfumed essences in the braziers was mystical and arcane, as though intended to better reconcile the senses with some otherworldly vision capable of travelling beyond time and space and the known dimensions, and suspending the judgements of a rationality that, in matters of prediction and prophecy, had no rights of citizenship.

Catherine observed him more carefully: there was in him the strangeness of the ferocious animal – of the beast that, though apparently calm, awaits the hesitation of its prey to strike. A feline, a bird of prey, a creature of the dark capable of governing unknown forces and who the dauphine desperately needed.

As he turned his inquisitive eyes upon her face and stared at her, Catherine again felt herself penetrated, as though his gaze dug into the deepest recesses of her soul.

'Finally, *madame*,' he said, 'you are pregnant. You are with child, I can already see it. All it took was to encourage your own instinct to flow, perhaps with the help of a couple of well-played tricks in addition to the natural seductive force that dwells within you. The force you had never wanted to free and which you yet possess, as powerful as the Florentine blood that flows in your veins.'

Her amazement at hearing such statements was such that for a moment Catherine was as though struck dumb. So it had been neither magic nor enchantment nor charm, but she alone? Becoming something she had never thought she could be?

'But how?' she objected. 'It was you, with the mystical power...'

'Of what?' he interrupted her, looking amused and incredulous, his voice now grown gentle and almost tender. 'Do you really believe that the scent of some sandalwood from the East and a bit of wolf's blood can work a miracle if you don't believe it yourself? You must have more confidence in your beauty! It is great and powerful and waits only to be unshackled. Do not be afraid to show yourself for what you are, because by hiding that you only wrong yourself and those close to you.' Nostradamus paused and gazed into the air, thick with heady scents, before settling on her face again. 'But you came here today for another reason, did you not?'

Catherine had the impression that those large eyes with their long eyelashes were capable of exploring the innermost furrows of her mind, and it would have been foolish of her to not only think that she could prevent it but also to deny its inevitability. Nostradamus read her as easily as some infernal lutenist reading the melody on the sheet music before his eyes.

'You are right, Monsieur de Nostredame, it is so.

What I had learned about you is perfectly true, I see: nothing can be hidden from you.'

'Nothing that your eyes have not revealed before your words. And believe me, Your Majesty, it is far better to hear what the eyes say than to follow the boring melody of the lips. Useless, treacherous, mocking or cruel, words are a very poor currency with which to pay one's interlocutor. They mean nothing, and are merely the echo of a forger's trick. And a poor forger at that. That forger is destiny, who so enjoys deluding us that she can determine the fate of events which hang in the balance and yet elude us, unless we contemplate them in silence with all the attention of which we are capable. Let the French sovereigns trust in the deception of the word, but you, who belong to a lineage of men and women who gained power instead of inheriting it by divine right – and believe me, never was there a fiction more ingenious and at the same time more pathetic – well, you cannot limit yourself to relying upon the five senses. You can and must look beyond. Always keep this in mind.'

And so saying, Michel de Nostredame sat down upon a bizarre high-backed chair and invited Catherine to sit down in front of him. Between them was a rectangular mirror, its edges reddened with some scarlet liquid which might have been blood. The moment she did as she was asked, the future queen saw that the astrologer's chair was set at the centre of a double concentric circle drawn upon the floor – a ring of pale wood which stood out from the dark planks.

She dared not ask any questions.

Nostradamus drummed his fingers upon the worn wooden arms of the chair, which ended in two wolves' heads, took a deep breath, then closed his eyes and, as if remembering a passage from some ancient book, began to recite unknown formulas in an incomprehensible language. The words which emerged from his mouth sounded as fierce as fire and as sweet honey.

Suddenly his eyes opened wide, and he read his response to the future queen of France from the smooth, perfect surface of the mirror.

'*Madame la Reine*, you will give birth to a baby nine months from today. You will give the child the name of Francis, and he will be lord of this kingdom. The current king will die sooner than expected, however, because of the illness which has long been undermining his health. A life for a life, as is always the case in the circle of existence.'

Catherine's heart skipped a beat. She was pleased to hear about the announced birth, but upset at the thought of the loss of a great sovereign and the only true friend she had ever known.

'Are you sure?' she asked in a faint voice.

'I have questioned the stars several times and I continue to do so. I know the king's date, place and time of birth, and thus have had no great difficulty reconstructing his astral chart. Believe me, therefore, when I tell you that in a little over four years' time, Francis I will die. Only now do I see that you are here because his absence will cause confusion and uncertainty. From these derive conflicts and conspiracies which will bring chaos upon the whole of France. Do not ask me to be clearer because I cannot. Only prepare yourself for this tragic event and be ready when it happens: you will need all your strength of spirit and your courage to emerge victorious. But if you know how to favour these virtues, which are so strong in you, then you will reign over France one day – one day still far away, but from that moment on, you will be queen for a long time. I do not know if this will bring you joy or torment, perhaps both, but it remains an ineluctable reality. It is only a matter of waiting.'

At that point Nostradamus fell silent and his eyes seemed to return to normal, no longer oscillating and liquid like those of a reptile. He seemed suddenly very tired, as if the few moments he had spent gathering prophecies from the memory of the stars which seemed to flow across the surface of the mirror had exhausted him.

Catherine didn't have the courage to reply – the revelations had left her absolutely speechless. She was so shocked that she asked herself if it was actually worth knowing the future in advance. Was there any advantage in precognition, or did those revelations do nothing but show her human misery and all the inadequacy of a race that perhaps deserved nothing better than to die out to make way for more honourable creatures?

'But then,' Nostradamus went on, 'I doubt that I am the first to reveal such facts to you, since there are plenty of astrologers and fortune tellers in your court... Or perhaps I am wrong?'

'No one else has been so precise, *monsieur*,' replied Catherine. She sat for a moment raptly observing the bluish swirls of smoke that rose from the braziers in front of her, composing forms both extravagant and restless – as restless as she herself was after what she had heard. 'I confess that your words have upset me and so I will take my leave, but first I wish to thank you for your services.' And so saying she took off a ring upon which shone an emerald the size of a hazelnut. 'This is for you, Monsieur de Nostredame,' she said in a voice that still trembled with emotion. 'And now, if you permit me, I intend to retire and rest. I need to reflect upon these revelations.'

'Your Highness, you need not ask for my permission,' replied Michel de Nostredame without hesitation. 'You are the future queen of France and may do whatever you wish. But the fact remains that in four years' time, King Francis will die.'

As she watched him speak, Catherine felt a strange sensation.

It was as though, despite the serious expression on his face, some hidden part of Nostradamus, deep within himself, were laughing in the coarsest way possible.

JANUARY 1544

21

Birth and Death

The child looked up at her with deep, sincere eyes. He was a delightful little thing, and when he yawned and clenched tiny fists which were no bigger than coins, it seemed almost that his charming face might break. His little hands were covered with wrinkles so pretty that Catherine was moved at the mere sight of them.

'Francis,' she told him, 'how sweet you are, my love, and how beautiful you are and will become. Soon you will be able to walk and to ride a horse, and then I promise you that we will go together to see the woods behind Fontainebleau, and you will lose yourself among the green leaves of the trees and the blue of the sky.'

Francis' skin was so white that the large flakes of snow which fell silently outside the window looked dull in comparison.

Eyes wide open on the world, he worked his plump little legs.

Catherine smiled. She had only been a mother for a few days yet already she wanted to give Francis a brother or sister. She felt full of hope and joy – sensations to which she was no longer used. It was as though all that time spent at court waiting to see her virtues recognized but in reality only rarely managing to have them even accepted had dried up her humanity and happiness one drop at a time.

But now that white creature, that soft little bundle who from time to time gave some funny cry, had changed everything. She wrapped Francis in a warm, comfortable blanket, lifted him to her chest and held him close to her.

His breath was sweet and his little heart beat wildly. The life in him was so strong and so overpowering that it thrilled her. She went over to the window and watched the snow fall on the French countryside, which promised the little creature so much.

And yet as she looked at the icy winter and the flames in the hearth gave off their pleasant warmth, she thought of her husband who, after having rejoiced over the birth of the child, had returned to war. Henry was absolutely determined to lead his men on the battlefield himself. It was not just a sense of duty, but something more like a mission – a vocation, almost.

Catherine admired the dedication and valour he

demonstrated in his endeavours, and thought that France was lucky to have a leader like Henry, but his constant braving of danger frightened her, especially now that he had become a father.

She sighed.

If nothing else, with Raymond de Polignac alongside her husband and with Michel de Nostredame studying the course of the stars, she felt more secure. Would she be able to outwit destiny? She was not sure, and in her heart of hearts doubted it was possible, but she at least nurtured the hope that by knowing future events in advance she might be able to avoid the most tragic and disastrous of them. Nostradamus was her eye upon the future and Polignac her eye upon the present, and with two such talented servants, she was certain she would manage to protect herself and all those she loved.

Or at least that was the hope she would fight for.

Raymond de Polignac was doing his best. As he had promised Catherine, he had stayed with her husband for the last year, and Henry was courageous, fought well and feared nothing, not even the melee. With his lean, robust body, he always prevailed over his opponents, but his need to constantly prove his worth in battle was becoming truly exhausting.

In any case, there was little they could do against the imperial troops of Charles V. The dauphin dreamed of routing them and driving them back to the Netherlands, but at the moment there was nothing more unlikely: they had just taken Cambray and were now preparing to spread out over in northern France.

The accursed *Landsknechte* who were in the ranks of the imperial army were less soldiers than bloodthirsty beasts, and they left a dark trail of death and pain behind them. Even at that moment, while Polignac and a patrol of French pikemen held out on a half-gutted bastion near La Fère in Picardy, those savages were massing right in front of the outpost, their numbers increasing by the day.

The only hope they had of stopping them was that it was now winter. The snow was deep and the temperatures so harsh that their opponents' hands froze to the barrels of their arquebuses, fusing with the metal so that the flesh was torn off in shreds when they pulled them away. Perhaps the cold would at least slow them down. But what was true for them was true also for the French, and it was worth remembering that the *Landsknechte* were perhaps more accustomed than they to the harshness of the climate.

As the wind whistled around the hills, Polignac racked his brain for a way to get the dauphin to safety.

The only real possibility was to attempt a sortie immediately, since retreat appeared to be the only way forward. He and his men needed to act quickly, though, because the imperial troops were growing more and more numerous and threatened to outnumber the pikemen. They would soon surround them, and at that point it would be almost impossible to get away.

A few moments earlier he had spoken with his men in order to prepare a plan of action. They had recovered some of the arquebuses of their dead companions in order to load them with gunpowder. In recent times the arquebusiers had been growing more numerous within the ranks of the pikemen, and now made up half of the company.

They had spent what felt like an eternity loading the guns, but at least it meant they would be able to give themselves covering fire. In this way, they could run at breakneck speed down the path with the hope of avoiding being shot by the *Landsknechte*, earning themselves a minimal possibility of success.

It was certain that those bastards would try to shoot them down like thrushes, and obviously it would have been much better to wait until dark, but the risk was that by then it would be too late. For that reason, taking advantage of the steel-grey sky, the snow and the icy wind, they had devised that precarious and uncertain solution.

Polignac looked at the jagged line of enemy tents which stood out black against the snowy knoll, and saw there were now also a couple of makeshift shacks and a line of arquebuses ready to spit fire from behind a sort of barricade made from debris and pieces of rotten wood. Here and there, shadows moved about in the cold of the winter afternoon which was gradually turning into evening: a few more moments and it would be time for them to race down the path.

Him and the dauphin of France.

It had been a serious mistake to remain with the rearguard, but no one had dared contradict His Highness. Henry II had taken leave to visit his wife to celebrate the birth of his firstborn – and also, according to the gossips, to visit his favourite – and they had all hoped that he would remain in Paris for a while at least, but instead he had managed to return to the battlefield to once again flaunt his valour in a way so bold that it verged upon idiocy.

So now there they were.

Polignac looked at Auger: one of his eyebrows was interrupted by a scar and he wore a great moustache on his angular face. The keen gaze of a kite lurked in eyes as dark as sin itself. He scratched his jaw. Giraud too stared back at him just as intently, awaiting his signal.

'Your Highness?' asked Polignac. 'Are you ready?'

Henry nodded. His face was tired and his skin red with cold, but he was not lacking in determination.

He had three loaded arquebuses on his back, as did Polignac, since once they reached the end of the descent, they would need to turn around and provide covering fire for their companions' retreat.

In front of them on the other side of the valley, all was silent.

'Now!' said Polignac, and the dauphin began to run. Polignac followed him, keeping pace, and as soon as the path began to descend towards the forest he slipped in among the foliage in the hope of making himself a less easy target, but the path soon returned to the open and, predictably, a musket ball whistled past him, raising a spume of snow where it struck the ground.

Above them, Auger and Giraud opened fire. There were loud bangs, and scarlet flashes filled the cold afternoon air while white smoke rose from the arquebus barrels. Another volley of shots followed, but this time a musket shot at them from the knoll ahead, hissing just over Polignac's head. It hit the trunk of a pine tree, raising a pinwheel of splinters of bark and filling the air with a smell of fresh wood.

More shots and again the rumble of thunder, and then a cry from directly above them. Henry kept running and Polignac kept pace with him. He had the terrible feeling that something bad had happened to Auger or Giraud and he would have liked to go to their aid, but in the middle of the white snow, without even a tree for shelter, that would have only risked getting himself killed too.

He headed for the line of pines he saw a few yards in front of him, and in that moment heard another volley unleashed against them. He dived for safety just as the musket shot hit the ground, raising a spray of icy fragments.

Polignac found himself among pine needles, and in the time it took him to get into a kneeling posture and take up the heavy arquebus, he was in position. They were safe now. He heard footsteps in the snow and realized that someone was coming down from above – exactly where he and the dauphin had just arrived from.

He pointed the arquebus barrel towards the knoll in front of him and pulled the trigger. The pan opened, the fuse took light and there was a blue flash of sparks as it rapidly burned itself out and the shot ripped through the air like thunder, the weapon recoiling as powerfully as a mule kicking out with its hoof. Polignac threw the discharged weapon to one side. He doubted that he had hit anyone at that distance, but it didn't really matter: all that mattered in that moment was to provide covering fire to prevent their opponents from shooting. He slipped another of the arquebuses he was carrying from his shoulder while Henry, the barrel of his weapon propped on the resting fork, opened fire at the *Landsknechte*.

There were more sparks, another crack of thunder and another puff of white smoke, and in the meantime Polignac heard the laboured breathing of those who were descending the path.

He had just time to fire his third shot when he saw

Giraud appear at the beginning of the stretch of path which was not protected by the tree line. Henry fired almost immediately after him.

At that very moment a musket ball struck the French pikeman in the back.

A scarlet blot spread across his jacket. He thew up his arms and then collapsed onto the snow.

'*Merde!*' cried Polignac.

Giraud lay motionless upon the white ground. There was nothing they could do for him. He was dead. Of Auger there was no trace. In all probability the cry they had heard earlier had been him. For an instant, Polignac watched as the snow around Giraud turn red.

'Let's go,' he said, more to try to rouse himself from the numbness which had descended upon him with the soldier's death than to Henry. He got to his feet. 'Are you injured?' he asked.

The dauphin shook his head, and they started off down the path again. By now they were sheltered by the branches of the trees and the forest was growing thicker.

And in that moment, they heard something. Voices, muffled by the tangle of the branches and the snow that covered the ground.

Polignac and Henry froze. They were the voices of soldiers.

And they weren't speaking French.

22

Horsemen

There couldn't be many of them: Polignac had heard no more than three or four voices. They were getting closer, though, and he could hear the muffled sound of the horses' hooves on the snow. They were warily advancing together.

He hid under the branches of a pine tree and waited. He was at Henry's side, just as he had promised and as he would always remain for as long as Catherine ordered it. For him, loyalty and honour were not simply virtues; they rather represented the principles of a moral code which informed his vision of the world.

They breathed silently as they waited, clouds of vapour dancing in the air. For an instant, the scent of the forest seemed to break the tension. The sky had grown clear, and the golden light of the dying sun filtered between the pine needles.

A bow and arrow, thought Polignac. If only they had a bow and arrow! But at least they still had an arquebus each.

'What shall we do?' whispered Henry.

'Your grace, in another situation I would opt for staying silent and waiting for them to pass, but they have horses and, *Mort-Dieu*, we need them. They are the only chance we have of getting out of this situation alive. Judging from what I can hear, though, I fear that there are more than two of them. We will have to use the arquebuses and try to be accurate. If we succeed in putting a pair of them out of action, perhaps we will manage to prevail over the others.'

'But they will hear us…'

'Doubtless, but with the horses we will go faster and we will be able to lose them in the thick of the forest.'

Henry nodded. While they waited, they reloaded their weapons. Polignac opened the pan and filled it with powder. He checked the serpentine and inserted a new fuse, then loaded the coarse gunpowder into the barrel. Finally he inserted the pellet and drove it down as well as he could with the tamper rod. Then they cautiously emerged into the open and selected a shooting position. The sound of hooves was rapidly approaching: the soldiers would be upon them in a few moments.

Polignac lit the fuse and listened to the sizzle as it

burned away to ashes. Suddenly, white smoke rose from the arquebus and there was a red flash as it fired at the exact moment the first horseman appeared. The pellet hit him in the face, smashing through his forehead and skull and sending a cloud of blood and brain matter splashing onto the snow and the bark of the trees.

There was a cry of rage, followed immediately by a second bang, and another knight fell to the snowy ground after Henry's shot had taken off half of his face.

Without waiting another moment, Polignac launched himself against the remaining two horsemen who were coming up the path. One of them had lit the fuse of his weapon, which sparked with festoons of light and then discharged. The pellet missed Polignac by inches and smashed into the trunk of a tree, sending up a cloud of splinters. The other horseman had not been as quick-witted and his palfrey circled in the snow, neighing and puffing out clouds of vapour.

Drawing his sword, Polignac jumped at the opponent who had just fired at him and brought his blade down in a merciless arc that sliced open the man's leg.

There was another scream of pain as the man dropped the Reitschwert which he had just managed to extract from its sheath and fell to the ground. Polignac watched him bleed into the snow then, for good measure, planted the Reitschwert in his throat. When he saw the situation, the fourth opponent fled without delay.

Polignac leapt up onto the back of one of the riderless horses, and Henry did the same.

'*Allez!*' shouted Polignac. 'And let's keep clear of the path.'

And without another word he raced off into the thick of the woods, followed closely by the dauphin.

MARCH 1547

23

The Death of the King

Even the sky had grown dark. Threatening clouds had gathered to cover the heavens and seemed ready to fall upon the towers of the Château of Rambouillet.

An angry rain, its drops as large as silver coins, poured down violently as the day finally made way for an accursed night.

In the largest chamber of the castle, by the light of lamps and candles, Francis I fought his last battle – the most important battle of all.

His face was hollowed out with fatigue and large dark spots covered his chest. He breathed with difficulty and his body was wracked by repeated fits of coughing.

Henry and Catherine knelt at his bedside, listening to his last words.

Despite the pain and the bitter awareness that he was on the brink of death, the king still felt some happiness: he had made peace with his son, and knew he was with Catherine. In recent years he had argued more than once with Henry over his passion for Diane, which he had more or less openly opposed, but it had been fruitless. And moreover, how could he demand his son change his behaviour when he himself had been subject to the will of the Duchess of Étampes?

He wanted to tell Henry not to make the same mistake as he. The dauphin stared at him bitterly, his gaze as gloomy as ever but now also tinged with melancholy for the separation that was finally coming and which, deep in his heart, he did not want, despite everything.

The King of France cleared his throat and spoke in a faint voice.

'Henry... I'm not long for this world... as you know... and I realise that I haven't always done what I should have for my children...'

The dauphin tried to reassure him. He felt he owed him that.

'Don't worry, Father,' he said, his voice almost breaking with emotion. 'All is forgiven, you know that.'

At a certain point in his life he had come to hate his father, but when he had seen him looking so old and tired and realized that time had passed its sentence, he knew that he had wasted years of his life on a feeling which had done nothing except fill him with hatred and resentment. He felt ashamed of himself.

'I leave a country at war with our old enemy,' said Francis, his voice coming with difficulty. 'But I know you will be able to defend France. Honour your wife, and beware of false friends...'

Henry completed his thoughts for him in his own words. 'Don't torment yourself, Father, you are already tested enough. Catherine will be by my side and will help me to govern in the best possible way.' And so saying he took his bride's hand.

Francis smiled. 'Catherine, *ma fille*, I entrust him to you... you know how much faith I have in you and in your intelligence. Do not disappoint me, my dear...'

Catherine wanted to speak but could not find her voice. The emotion was so great that the sobs she was managing to hold back had frozen into a lump in her throat, so she remained silent, looking at the good man who had loved her so much and who had always defended her against everything and everyone.

Against the suspicions that she had murdered his eldest son, against the gossips who claimed she was a heretic and a lover of the devil, against Diane of Poitiers who had stolen her husband, and against those who hated her simply for being Italian and the daughter of a merchant.

Francis had been a generous king. In many ways he had been the father she had never had, her own having died a few days after her birth. For this reason and for many others, Catherine was infinitely grateful to him. Her gaze spoke clearly of the inner turmoil she felt at seeing him depart forever.

His body had been rotting for some time now, and as the dark spots had spread over his skin he had grown weaker and weaker until for the last few days he had not even been able to rise from his bed.

In a sense, she was grateful to God for the knowledge that he was near his end. If that was the way that he would have to live, he might as well finally have peace.

Francis almost seemed to read her thoughts. He gave her a look full of profound affection, and then closed his eyes.

'Now let me rest,' he whispered, folding his hands over his chest and seeking the most comfortable position. His face relaxed and took on an expression so calm and peaceful that if Catherine had been forced to choose a word to describe it, she would not have hesitated to call it 'blissful'.

A smile seemed to pucker his lips, and then he died. Henry looked at him tenderly and reached out to touch his father's forehead for one last time. Catherine felt the first tears streaming down her face as she wept.

DECEMBER 1550

24

Mandragola

They had arrived together with the first flakes of snow on a small cart pulled by a pair of exhausted mules. They were led by a singular man with piercing, mocking eyes, astride a limping old nag. They wore strange hats and ragged but gaudy robes, ate fire and knew how to juggle. They wore masks and disguises, knew the scripts of entire dramas by heart, and were masters of all the charms of invention: they were acrobats, actors and tightrope walkers, a company of madmen and dreamers, whose leader was as eccentric as he was charming.

The company of actors was a blessing, and when she had learned that they were Italians, Catherine had clapped her hands with joy.

She had ordered the leader of the company to be

brought before her and soon found herself facing a man with long grey hair and intense green eyes.

'What is your name?' Catherine had asked.

'Mercury,' the man replied without blinking, an amused smirk beneath his thick, well-groomed moustache.

'A messenger then?' asked Catherine, playing along.

'Precisely. As well as a protector of thieves and swindlers.'

'I hope that you are neither one nor the other.'

'Only occasionally. But as we are at court, I shall work hard not to give in to my weaknesses.'

'And you do well to do so,' retorted Catherine, who appreciated his spirit but not enough to allow him to overly indulge his tongue, 'or you will risk finding a nice noose around that skinny neck of yours.'

The man nodded.

'Now, Master Mercury, what do you have in your repertoire?' asked Catherine, scarcely able to conceal her impatience.

'Majesty, I confess we are spoiled for choice. Seneca, Plautus and Terence as regards the Latin theatre, Aristophanes and Menander as regards the Greek classics. But lately, being Tuscans like Your Majesty, we have also decided to pay our respects to some of our fellow citizens.'

The queen's eyes flickered.

'To whom do you refer?' she asked, raising an eyebrow.

'I have been told Your Highness has a certain fondness for Niccolò Machiavelli,' the man said, as though reading her thoughts. 'Have I been misinformed?'

Such was her happiness at hearing this news that the queen could barely hold back a cry of disbelief.

'Truly?'

'Absolutely.'

'Do you know that your words give me great joy?'

'Frankly, Your Majesty, that is exactly what I had hoped.'

'It appears that I am an open book to you, Master Mercury.'

'Highness, I am an actor. Understanding people's characters is my job.'

Catherine smiled. 'True,' she admitted, 'and you seem to me most talented at your work.'

'I do my best.'

'Very well, then. Do you think that in a couple of days you would be able to perform Seneca's *Medea*?'

Mastro Mercurio looked shocked, to say the least. It was only an instant, but that was long enough for her to see that he had been expecting no such request. The chief of the company of actors suddenly realized that it was *she* who had been reading *him* like an open book.

Catherine smiled. 'You are an actor, Master Mercury, but your face cannot hide your surprise.'

The actor could not hold back a grin. 'Frankly, Your Highness, your request leaves me lost for words.'

'The question troubles you, Master Mercury?'

'Not at all, Your Majesty.'

'Very good, because I have other orders for you.'

'Your Highness, I await your commands.'

'Very well. I desire that during your preparation of Seneca's *Medea*, you *pretend* to be rehearsing the *Mandragola* of my beloved Machiavelli.'

Mastro Mercury looked surprised for the second time.

'And why, Your Majesty?'

'You will be paid to carry out my orders, Master Mercury, not to discuss them,' concluded the queen.

The actor nodded his acquiescence to Catherine's wishes.

'I was just about to propose it myself, Your Majesty. As you may have guessed, we prefer the comic to the tragic, and Machiavelli's text is one of our favourites. It has a freshness and a rhythm that few other recent works can boast.'

'Very well, then, so it is decided. You will rehearse a performance of *Mandragola* so that these Frenchmen who criticize us so much may change their minds.'

Mastro Mercury heard the hint of resentment in the voice of the queen but, as was proper, remained silent.

'At this point, I intend to give precise orders. Madame Gondi?'

An elegant lady appeared in the salon. She must have witnessed the interview and overheard the entire conversation, thought Mercury, possibly hidden in some niche or passage that had escaped his gaze.

'Madame Gondi, thank you for coming so quickly. You are to ensure that Master Mercury's company are given lodgings. They are to have at their disposal accommodation and a hot bath. You will reserve a hall of the building so that they can rehearse for a performance which will take place two days from today. You will have the salon prepared in accordance with Master Mercury's wishes. Have I explained myself?'

'Perfectly, Your Highness,' confirmed Madame Gondi. She had a warm, soft voice like velvet which Master Mercury liked very much.

'And now,' concluded Catherine, 'take your refreshment and then get to work immediately, Master Mercury. If I remember correctly, the *Mandragola* is a marvellous text but a very demanding one.'

And so saying, without waiting for him to reply, the queen dismissed Mercury, who gave an elegant bow then turned and left the room.

The actors would pretend to rehearse Machiavelli's text, but on the day of the show they would perform *Medea*. Catherine smiled to herself. That small stratagem would prevent Diane from knowing what Mercury and his company would be bringing to the stage. Diane had an encyclopaedic knowledge of theatre – almost as encyclopaedic as Catherine's own. And Diane *was* Medea: the barbaric usurper warrior, thirsty for blood and for power. Catherine intended to insult her in front of everyone but without the public realizing: apart from her and Diane, none of the court was particularly fond of theatre. It would be a bitter surprise for her rival.

After the king's death, the bond between her husband and his favourite had grown even closer. 'Indissoluble' would not be too soft a word. Catherine had been able to do nothing to prevent it, and in fact the accursed triangle of relationships which she had been forced to accept had actually proved itself to be functional, albeit in a perverse way. But that didn't mean that she didn't hate Diane.

In truth, she had never detested her more.

If nothing else, thought Catherine, *Medea* might make the accursed woman choke on her dinner.

Polignac had ridden for a long time as he followed the unmarked carriage. Catherine was certain that for some time Henry and Diane had been consummating their love away from court in some place of their own whose whereabouts was unknown to her.

Identifying the precise location of their amorous encounters would not give her any pleasure, of course, but if nothing else, it would put her soul at peace, and so, in order to please her, Raymond de Polignac had followed the king like a shadow.

He took no pleasure in doing it. In fact, if he was

honest, he hated himself for it – he had never wanted to be a spy.

Polignac sighed.

Before the carriage had entered the village of Écouen and continued to the castle gates, he had stopped his horse and slipped into an inn for a quick meal, then had gone up to his room and had drawn the appropriate conclusions. He knew perfectly well that the castle of Écouen was owned by Anne de Montmorency, the current constable of France, who had risen to power under Henry II. Polignac had been surprised: he had known of the agreements Diane had reached with Montmorency and with the House of Guise, but it was evident that their circle of power had become increasingly narrow and unassailable if the constable had even made himself guarantor of the carnal congress between the king and his favourite by putting at their disposal one of his own residences.

With this new knowledge, Polignac had finally lain down, falling asleep quickly owing to the fatigue accumulated during the ride that day.

Henry gazed at Diane's face. How beautiful she was! The years passed and yet she lost not even a smidgeon of her charm: her perfectly styled brown hair, her skin as white as alabaster, her eyes as black as a crow's wing, that haughty look of hers.

He went over to her with the intention of covering her with kisses, but Diane waved him off with a smile.

'Be patient, Henry. I have to tell you something that cannot wait.'

The king did nothing to hide his disappointment.

'Diane, I came as soon as I could, you must believe me.'

'But I do believe you! It is simply that a situation is developing at court which worries me and I wish to inform you of it.'

'What do you mean?'

Diane sighed. 'Is it possible that you do not understand?' she asked with a hint of annoyance.

Henry stared at her, wordlessly urging her to speak.

'She is becoming dangerous again, Henry.'

'Who?' he asked in exasperation.

'Catherine, of course. Who else?'

The king shook his head.

'Come, Diane. You exaggerate.'

'Not at all,' she snapped. 'Is it possible that you cannot see what is right before your eyes?'

'And what is it you think I should see?'

Diane laughed. How naive the king was, she thought. But she was also charmed by his candour: his way of openly admitting without any kind of subterfuge that he had no idea what she was talking about won her over every time. She saw again in him the boy she had loved since he had been taken to Spain to serve the time of his father's imprisonment. In a sense, nothing had changed since then: she was still the mother he had never had, and he was the son she had always dreamed of. That play of tensions between them was even more erotic and seductive than the sex.

Diane's reaction annoyed Henry. He accepted her influence and manipulation, often without realizing it, but he was not willing to be openly mocked. He was still the king.

Sensing his irritation, she immediately adopted the most accommodating of tones.

'Henry, you know as well as I do that Catherine is in some ways our best ally. She hates me, of course, but she is intelligent enough not to challenge me. Not openly, at least. She knows that without your father's protection we could annihilate her and therefore, despite the suffering our love causes her, she accepts it in the name of a greater good.'

'France?'

'Power, Henry. Although at the moment she is at a disadvantage, Catherine knows that she can count on our support because we consider her less harmful than other possible pretenders. If you or your father had repudiated her, another bride and another queen would certainly have arrived, and God alone knows whether she mightn't have been worse than the one who currently sits at your side. Despite everything, Catherine plays along with us and obeys you. What really matters is that she continues to behave in this way, as otherwise things might become problematic. And it is precisely for this reason that I am going to ask you to make yet another sacrifice.'

Henry didn't like the sound of that at all, but since he had no idea what Diane was talking about, he gestured for her to continue.

'You must get her pregnant, Henry...'

'Again?' interrupted the king, who could scarcely believe his own ears. 'She's already had four children...'

'I know!' cut in Diane. 'And that, my love, is our guarantee. You must climb into her bed and do as I tell you. Again and again, and again if possible!'

Henry was speechless.

'Very well,' he said eventually. 'In that case I imagine that you will be pleased to hear that, in all likelihood, she is already pregnant.'

Diane's reply took him by surprise.

'Perhaps I have not explained myself. You must ensure she is pregnant all the time! You say she is already with child? Magnificent. But as soon as she gives birth you will have to do it again. Do you hear me? On the one hand this will guarantee you a good lineage, and on the other it will keep her from playing any power games.'

The king was stunned.

'But I have just told you that she is most likely expecting another child!' he shouted.

'Are you sure?'

'I think so.'

'Ah, you *think* so?' asked Diane, her eyes blazing. 'We must be certain! And as I told you, as soon as she gives birth to one child, you must get her with another.'

She wasn't joking, he realized.

'She must become like a baker's oven, do you hear me?' Diane shouted, and this time the sculpted, faultless beauty of her face betrayed a cold and terrible rage.

The king felt his blood freeze in his veins.

25

The Deception

Everything was ready.

The stage had been set up just as Master Mercury had requested. The queen had allowed him to assemble his cast in the ballroom. The proscenium faced the large wooden fireplace, richly inlaid with gold, which was surrounded by a litany of wonders; the stuccos of the Italian school which were the work of Primaticcio who, on Catherine's suggestion, Francis I had brought to his court together with Rosso Fiorentino; the large wrought-iron chandeliers loaded with flickering candles; the enchanting coffered ceiling, covered with friezes and decorations. All this composed a collection of architectural wonders that made the room an authentic treasure trove of magnificence and luxury.

Chairs upholstered with blue velvet and golden lilies

and with finely carved backs had been arranged in long, orderly rows in front of the proscenium, and tables carefully laid with refined elegance for a brief lunch before the performance.

Catherine had indulged another of her great passions: the culinary art. For two days she had carefully been giving precise instructions to her cooks, some of them from Mugello, and to the pastry chefs, so that nothing would be left to chance.

The tables the waiters and pages had prepared were covered with damask tablecloths which were perfumed with clover water, and upon them were placed small silver trays filled with sugared almonds and fennel seeds to multiply the aromas.

But what most amazed the assembled nobles was the first course: an exquisite frozen cream of bright yellow and intense orange – a delightful mixture of ice and soft, sweet substances, enriched with a syrup of oranges and lemons. It was a true delight, flavoured with the finest ingredients grown in the gardens of Florence and brought specifically for the occasion.

The creator of this delicacy was one Bernardo Buontalenti, whom Catherine had called to court as a master pastry chef. And the dishes that followed it were just as successful. It was an extraordinary lunch, during which etiquette was followed to the letter.

But the real *coup de grâce* for the noblemen and noble ladies was discovering with what skill the queen made use of the strange little trident-like object that they had been astounded to see her extract from her own personal casket almost as if it were a relic.

'The fork,' she said, as some of the ladies gave faint cries of amazement. Catherine fell silent and with consummate theatrical skill let the surprise hover in the air for a moment. 'It seemed appropriate to me to introduce this interesting piece of cutlery, which made its appearance at Venetian dinners thanks to the merchants who imported it from Constantinople to the tables of France. Believe it or not, this extremely useful little tool is the protagonist of a famous painting which my great-grandfather Lorenzo, known as "the Magnificent", the lord of Florence, commissioned from Sandro Botticelli, a famous Florentine painter.'

A chorus of wonder arose.

'For this reason,' continued Catherine, 'I decided to do something amusing and equip each place with a fork, with which you may easily bring meat or vegetables to your mouths.' And so saying, Catherine speared an artichoke heart.

'How *wonderful*,' exclaimed Anne de Montmorency, who, in imitation of the queen, speared a piece of meat. He raised it to his mouth with surprising ease and then elegantly speared another while still chewing upon the first. '*Madame la Reine*,' he said, 'I must confess that you have an extraordinary talent for cooking. This duck *à l'orange* is a veritable breath of paradise.'

Catherine smiled, hiding her pleasure behind a joke. 'Come, Anne, we all know *your* talent at skewering your enemies.'

Her joke hit its mark, and Montmorency exploded with loud laughter, all the other guests immediately following suit.

The king applauded his wife and complemented her on the sumptuous meal. Sitting by his side, Diane of Poitiers shot her a look full of resentment and envy. It only lasted a moment, of course, but it was enough to make Catherine confident that she would be guaranteed an even better result with the performance which was to follow.

Amid amiable banter and artful conversation the lunch continued until, after the fruit and the dessert had been served, it was time.

The king sat in the front row between Catherine and Diane of Poitiers. Behind them sat the court nobles.

When Medea appeared on the stage, her hair a dishevelled mass of black locks, her clothes ragged and her nails as long as the talons of some barbarous and betrayed queen, invoking the fury that would lead her to kill Creusa, Creon's daughter and the betrothed of Medea's own beloved Jason, Catherine looked at Diane and, for once, rejoiced.

Apart from Catherine, only Diane knew enough

about the theatre to notice the changes that had been made to the play. Almost none of the other spectators were aware of them. This made Catherine's joke even more effective and cruel, as though it were some kind of intimate dialogue between her and Diane, completely removed from the possibility of anyone else's understanding.

At the sound of the flood of curses hurled by Medea at her lover, the face of the king's favourite grew stony. Diane betrayed no emotion, but Catherine knew her well enough to know that, deep within, Madame de Brézé was boiling with rage. Her thin lips, usually curled into a contemptuously lofty pout, were now drawn back into an almost imperceptible grimace that made her mouth look like a knife wound.

Catherine felt a sense of triumph. While the tragedy continued and the story unfolded in all its violence, Diane would certainly be identifying herself more and more with Medea, the queen who had sacrificed everything to have the man she wanted at her side yet who saw herself ultimately replaced by an inexperienced and foolish young woman, of whom she vowed to rid herself, to the point of consummating her revenge by sending Creusa a poisoned robe and tiara that killed her amidst atrocious torments.

It was just before the final scene that, unable to bear any more, Diane stood up, knocking over her chair.

She glared at the queen with furious eyes and, in

silence, Catherine held her gaze. Neither of them made a sound, but all present witnessed the scene taking place.

Without a word, Diane stormed away. The king, stunned and shocked to see her so enraged, got to his feet and followed her, and the audience too stood, the nobles unable to understand how the performance could have had this effect.

Some of the ladies muttered in annoyance at the interruption, while several nobles were prompted to criticize the play, following the obvious disgust they had seen in their king's eyes.

It was then that Catherine was overcome by a sudden, stabbing pain. She had won, of course. But she had also lost. And she had lost badly – Henry had not hesitated for a moment to follow Diane and humiliate her, his wife.

It was certainly not the first time it had happened, but that fact made it no less painful. Quite the contrary – it was the demonstration of how much more important to Henry Diane was than she would ever be.

In that moment, however, she couldn't allow herself to cry, so she forced back her tears. Later, in the privacy of her apartments, she would have ample time to despair, but for now she must appear blameless, and so she gave no sign of anger or suffering. Her face hardened and she avoided the sly glances of Anne de Montmorency, who studied her eyes in search of shadows or fear but saw only firm resignation. That was the face Catherine would present to the world, at least until things changed, and Montmorency realized it immediately and turned his attention back to the stage.

Without another word, Catherine walked out, leaving the court in the sumptuous salon room looking at the interrupted scene.

26

The Devil's Mortar

Michel de Nostredame's face always spoke volumes, and what he did not say in words could be intuited from his eyes. Catherine always found herself trembling before him, terrified by the sensation that she was not ready to learn his prophecies, and yet also consumed by an uncontrollable desire to know, her mind imprisoned in the disquieting oscillation between the two.

As soon as she had entered the ruined old house on the edge of the forest, that godforsaken place to which Nostradamus periodically summoned her to communicate his predictions, she had been immersed in its eerie atmosphere.

When she opened the door, the crackling orange flames of the fire burning in the fireplace flared up and seemed almost to scream for an instant as the icy wind blew into the room.

That night she smelled a delicate aroma of roses – a sweet scent which, however, faded away into a rotten reek, as though the petals had been pounded in the devil's mortar.

But it wasn't that which captured Catherine's attention. Rather, it was the mirror that for some reason stood above the fireplace. It was the same one Nostradamus had used during her previous visit. And once again, its sides appeared to be stained with blood. Catherine couldn't hold back a shudder.

Someone must have removed the table and the furniture, because the room was empty and the double circle of light wood was even more clearly visible, standing out against the darker beams of the floor.

At the centre of the double concentric circle was Michel de Nostredame. Dressed head to toe in black, with his long double-pointed beard, he greeted the queen with a nod and pointed to the mirror.

Catherine looked at its smooth, transparent surface, and waited. Michel de Nostredame sighed.

'I have summoned you at this time of night because I have read in the mirror what I feared, and I did not want to delay even a moment. I could not…'

For a moment the great astrologer seemed to hesitate, as if seeking the most suitable way to express himself. This terrified the queen, who knew all too well with what facility Nostradamus was usually able to choose his words.

'Please, Michel, tell me the truth,' said Catherine, her curiosity and despair driving her to urge him on. 'Do not fear, I will know how to face what you have to impart to me.'

'Majesty, judge for yourself.'

And so saying, Nostradamus began a murmured litany whose meaning Catherine could not initially understand. Gradually, though, she realised that his words were an invocation to the angel Haniel. The astrologer's voice, initially subdued and so deep that it seemed almost a rumbling, became bolder and clearer, and as his chanting grew louder, Catherine increasingly felt her grasp upon reality begin to slip.

The fumes of the incense, the words pronounced by the deep voice, the blood at the corners of the mirror which seemed to coagulate into four names... Catherine watched entranced as the transparent surface, so large and so perfectly smooth, seemed to dilate until he vanished into it.

In his place an angel appeared, followed immediately by a lion, its muscles straining under a thick, shining mane. A battlefield, littered with dead and flooded with blood. And then Catherine saw the lion behind the golden bars of a cage. Something seemed to pierce its eyes, leaving it on the ground, lifeless.

It was then that the vision disappeared, as if the mirror had shattered into pieces.

The spell or illusion, or whatever it was, seemed to break. With a violent flash of light, the fire flared up in the fireplace, its flames stretching out into long tongues, only to turn, in an instant, into ash and embers, almost as if extinguished by a single gelid breath from some giant.

The light grew weaker, the torches seeming dimmed by revelation, and the room fell into shadow. Nostradamus, his voice seeming to come from the deepest recesses of the earth, spoke.

'The young lion will prevail over the old in single combat on the battlefield, and in the cage of gold its eyes will be pierced, two wounds in one, to then die a cruel death,' he recited.

Catherine gasped as she felt a pang in her heart as if the blade of a knife had cut it in two.

She did not understand the words Nostradamus had spoken, but she somehow felt a sort of instinctive understanding of the prophecy that shook her deeply, and such deep pain and sadness that she wondered how she would ever survive the night.

'You must protect Henry: he is the lion who wins in battle, but he must fear duels in closed spaces. Protect the king, or he will die with his eyes pierced by a blade. Today I saw his end.'

Catherine was on the point of fainting and she grew

pale as the blood drained from her face. Her vision blurred and everything around her became indistinct.

She heard nothing more, only the voice of Raymond de Polignac from far, far away. His strong arms held her, and rocked her gently.

Then there was only darkness.

SEPTEMBER 1552

27

The Last Days of Summer

They were the last days of summer.

Fontainebleau shone with the warm colours of September, and fragments of light danced like pearls in the clear water of the pond. The garden was an intense, almost blinding green, and the pure blue sky seemed full of promise and hope.

It had been a difficult summer, spent in solitude with only her children for comfort. Henry had left for war again, with Polignac at his side, and in that moment they were consolidating positions in the North. Only a few months earlier, Henry had triumphantly entered Metz on Easter Sunday without even having to fire a single shot. Previously, Nancy and Toul had also fallen, and the same had happened in Verdun. The strategist behind those victories was Francis of

Guise, a true hero of France as well as the protégé of Diane.

And so also of Henry.

Catherine sighed as she gazed at the gardens of Fontainebleau. It was Francis I who had created that marvel and who had not hesitated to involve her in its realization.

She missed him.

Her children and she were having breakfast in the pavilion in the middle of the carp lake, and she was trying unsuccessfully to teach them the use of the fork, just as she had done with the rest of the court some time before, though with greater success.

Francis I had built the pavilion for boat trips and, of course, for lunches and breakfasts, so as to enjoy the liquid magic of the water during those moments of conviviality. The view was magnificent.

With them there was also Diane who, with diligence and skill, supervised the education of the sovereign's sons. Catherine hated having her around but could do nothing about it. After the death of Francis I, the woman's power had grown enormously. Not only was she the favourite of Catherine's husband, not only had she acquired mind-boggling incomes and appanages and not only did she dictate political policies; she also intended to keep control over Catherine at all costs, even influencing her relationships with her children.

Many times Catherine had thought of rebelling but she had always backed down in the end, sometimes accepting and sometimes enduring the intrusion of her rival.

Over the past two years, though, Diane had shown herself to be attentive and thoughtful towards her, working hard to build a sort of silent triangle in such a way that, through mutual concessions and favours, she, Henry and Catherine could protect themselves and coexist, holding absolute power and keeping out all those who were not Guise or Anne de Montmorency.

Ironically, her coldness and her ruthlessness had melted away to reveal a sudden and inexplicable sweetness towards Catherine's children – Diane, who had never been a mother and who enjoyed a reputation as an ice maiden.

Catherine watched her as she helped little Francis sit up straight at the table. Diane was just as keen on etiquette as she was.

Francis had big sad eyes and was somewhat sickly and rather ill-tempered, and his short blond hair and fair skin, combined with his surprising thinness, gave him a somewhat emaciated look. He never missed a chance to play some cruel joke on his sisters: only a month before he had set fire to the pigtails of Elisabeth, who was so beautiful, with her long, thick auburn hair which, despite her brother's misdeed, was now growing back even thicker than before.

Catherine found making Francis behave himself a challenge, but with Diane things were different.

'Prince,' she said, looking at him crossly with a pout as if he were beyond all hope, 'your manners leave something to be desired.'

Francis stared at her in surprise, his eyes betraying a flicker of regret.

'Really?' he asked, trying to show restraint.

'And you even dare ask me? Look at what you have done to your brioche!'

Normally, Francis would have burst out with one of those coarse laughs of his, but instead he fell silent.

Elisabeth, on the other hand, struggled to hold back her laughter. 'Francis, your mouth is all dirty!' she teased him. She could not understand how her brother could have made such a mess of himself: the prince's lips were completely covered with sugar and jam.

'Come, prince, you cannot remain in this state. What would your father say if he saw you like this?' Diane knew perfectly well how to play upon Francis' feelings, and managed to shut out his mother as if she were not present and as if she herself were the Queen of France instead.

The child had boundless admiration for his father, so the effect of Diane's words was as powerful as a slap in the face.

Catherine observed her son while he picked up a napkin and did a careful job of wiping his face until it was once again clean. When he had finished, the boy shot Elisabeth a fiery look for having dared to make fun of him.

His attempt to threaten her did not escape Catherine's attention.

'Francis, I warn you: don't you dare hurt your sister, either now or later when I am not here to see,' she said. 'I will not let you off so lightly this time.'

In her arms, the queen held little Charles, who looked up at her with big eyes and a mischievous smile on his lips, which were smeared somewhat with milk. He gave a little gurgle and his big dark eyes stared into his mother's, seeming to shine only for her.

Madame Antinori had arranged magnificent dahlias in the centre of the table, and all around there were small garlands of white and red berries. Despite her efforts, though, the white Flanders linen tablecloth had become a battlefield thanks to Francis, who had strewn it with quantities of crumbs, jam and cream.

But now, after being rebuked by Diane, Francis looked almost worried, and Catherine was annoyed because it only underlined the fact that her son recognized Diane's authority. If truth be told, he wasn't the only one, but that knowledge did little to alleviate the pain. The Duchess of Valentinois had managed to make him behave himself. Henry had given Diane that title as a gift, along with the most beautiful castle of all: Chenonceau. What an affront that had been to her!

Catherine looked away as, without uttering a word, Diane gave her a triumphant smile.

She needed Henry so, and hoped desperately he would come back. She knew that even if he did, it would only be to see Diane, but later, at least, he would visit her. She hoped he was safe. He was a great soldier, but she feared for him.

Suddenly she began to feel as if she were suffocating. The pavilion became oppressive, and her mind was filled with Nostradamus's prophecy.

The sensation only lasted a moment, though, and then she was herself again. In her heart, she prayed that Raymond de Polignac would protect the king.

Madame Antinori seemed to sense her moment of difficulty. 'Is everything all right, *Madame la Reine*?'

Catherine nodded. She had no intention of giving Diane the satisfaction of seeing her upset – it already happened far too frequently. She tried to master her emotions.

'Do you like the plum tart, Claude?' she asked, looking at her younger daughter, who was staring at the water of the lake with her sister.

'Yes, Mother,' replied the child. Her hair was fairer and thinner than that of her sister and she had a plump face. She wore a magnificent dress of light linen.

Catherine stroked her daughter's head.

Elisabeth approached her. 'Mama,' she asked, 'can I hold my little brother in my arms for a moment?' And as she asked, her big brown eyes widened. She was such a sweet child that Catherine agreed. When she took him in her arms, little Charles gave a cry of pleasure.

While her sister held him, Claude kissed him on the forehead. 'You will be king one day, Charles,' she said.

Francis glared at her as if she had taken the Lord's name in vain.

'How dare you?' he shouted. 'I shall be the king when our father has gone, do you understand?' And so saying he got up from the table, raced over to his little sister and pushed her out of the pavilion.

'Francis!' shouted Catherine.

But Francis took no notice of her. Blinded by anger, he grabbed Claude by the throat, almost shoving her into the waters of the lake. 'Take it back!'

'Francis!'

Catherine saw that Diane remained motionless and she hated her even more for it. The rage that was rising within her felt as if it would suffocate her. She realized Madame Antinori was too far away to help, so she hoisted up her dress and raced towards the children as fast as she was able, despite the clothes hindering her movements. She had to prevent her son from doing something terrible.

Francis had raised his arm and was about to hit Claude. Her eyes wide with shock, Elisabeth was staring at the two of them.

Catherine managed to grab the boy's arm just in time to stop him from hitting Claude.

'What on earth do you think you're doing?' she thundered. 'Hitting your sister who is younger than you? A little girl? Shame on you!'

Francis looked at her with eyes full of hatred and she pushed him away. Claude clung to her and burst into tears, then, as if to emphasize what she had said before, the little princess turned to her brother and to Diane.

'One day Charles will be king, whether you like it or not.'

Her words left everyone speechless.

Catherine was afraid, yet at the same time she felt a profound and irrepressible joy. She loved her children deeply and without exceptions, but Francis was becoming a puppet in the hands of Diane, just as Henry was, and that fact, so evident and incontrovertible, caused her to suffer.

As inexplicable as it was, Claude's little rebellion had given her strength, as though she had succeeded in giving voice to her own frustrations through her daughter's words.

Of course, she did not really hope that Charles would be king, because that could only happen if Francis died, and the very thought terrified her.

But she was certain that, in a different world, Charles would have made a better ruler than his father.

28

Letter from Metz

Catherine pushed desperately, but the child did not want to be born.

She could barely breathe, and her body was dripping with sweat.

Never before had she suffered so much during a pregnancy. She felt swollen and huge – ugly, monstrous even, like some obscene cathedral of flesh.

With blood-stained hands, Madame Gondi begged her to breathe deeply and to push with all the strength she possessed.

The screams that emerged from Catherine's throat sounded barely human. It felt as though the pain were tearing her apart.

She turned to Madame Gondi and saw that she looked worried. During the previous deliveries she had always managed to remain calm, even in the most difficult situations, but this time it was different. Something was going wrong, she could feel it inside her, almost as if the life which had budded within her had done so for the sole purpose of devouring her from within.

She tried to speak but was not able, and then another stabbing pain tore an inarticulate sound from her – the bestial scream of a wounded animal. Without realizing it, she found herself weeping. The burning sensation in her loins was intolerable. It was as though someone were sticking hot knives in her lower back at the height of her kidneys.

'Just a little more effort,' whispered Madame Gondi, in a sort of chant, but Catherine was starting to fear that she was repeating it simply because she had no idea what else to say. Perhaps she believed that those words would act like some sort of talisman.

She pushed again, with all her strength.

'I see it, Your Majesty,' cried Madame Gondi, but Catherine couldn't tell whether the expression on her face signified jubilation or terror. 'Keep going, Your Highness, we are almost there!'

Catherine appealed to all her remaining energies and tried to push again. The pain was now unbearable, and the child imprisoned inside her felt as if it didn't want to come out.

Then finally, when all seemed lost, she saw Madame Gondi put her hands between her legs.

But when she raised the child, dripping with blood, she let out a gruesome scream.

Her hips aching from the birth, Catherine looked up. And what she saw chilled her to the bone.

Her heart was beating wildly and she awoke with a start in a pool of sweat. She had fallen asleep in her armchair. Had it been a nightmare? When she saw the unopened envelopes sitting upon the desk, she remembered.

Madame Antinori had given her her letters. None was them was from Henry.

The disappointment had been exhausting. Feeling weak, she had sat down to rest, and the golden warmth of the sun's rays filtering through the curtains must have lulled her into a deep sleep.

She was still upset by the nightmare. She tried to push away the worries that lurked in her mind and cancel the chilling images of the monstrous child which had been born from her belly, but to no avail.

She was pregnant. Again. She could take no more of it.

She was happy to be able to give birth to children, but at the same time she hated seeing her body swell and bulge, making her look even uglier than she already felt. She wanted to weep.

She went from one pregnancy to the next without having the opportunity to interest herself in the affairs of the kingdom. She had lost count of the number of days she had spent in bed those last eight years.

She was comforted by the thought that Diane was growing old and that sooner or later she would have her revenge. Catherine still loved Henry, despite everything – despite the fact that he was a puppet in the hands of that evil, unscrupulous woman who was so totally devoted to power that she had forever given up the possibility of becoming a mother.

Diane had made her own body a weapon: to seduce the king and embody, through her femininity, the very magnificence of the realm. To enjoy the fruits of the extraordinary wealth she had accumulated in those years, she had transformed herself into a fortress.

Admired and feared, she was an icy beauty who gave herself to no one except the king and who had no lovers or friends, and it was her very unattainability which had earned her a reputation as the most attractive and powerful woman in France.

Catherine would have gladly scratched her eyes out if she could have, but instead she was tied to her, because Diane had managed to involve her in a tacit agreement: for as long as she was Henry's favourite, no one would raise a finger against Catherine, as Diane would protect her as one corner of the splendid *ménage à trois* she had managed to create.

She felt bitter bile filling her mouth: she was disgusted with herself.

Rising from her chair, she went over to the desk and picked up the unopened letters. As she looked through them, her gaze was drawn to one in particular, which bore the king's pikemen's seal and was written in an orderly and elegant hand.

Catherine tore it open and began to read the contents.

Your Majesty,

I write to you as Charles V's army is setting up its cannons, carts, tents and barricades to besiege Metz. First of all, I confirm to you that I am at the king's side at all times of the day and never abandon him, just as you ordered. His Majesty is in excellent form, his morale is high and he trusts that he will be able to keep the city.

This would be an unprecedented coup and would open to France the route to Upper Germany and therefore the Netherlands, thus delivering a serious blow to the power of Charles V, not to mention the threat posed to Thionville and Luxembourg. In short, without boring you further, suffice it to say that maintaining dominion of the stronghold of Metz is a strategic objective.

The real reason I am writing to Your Highness is, however, another.

I feel I must inform you of a situation which is developing. The king has decided to entrust the defence of the city to Francis I of Lorraine, the second duke of

Guise. Why do I write to you about such a fact, Your Highness? What makes it of such special import that it merits such a long and tedious letter? It is soon said.

Firstly, though, I should clarify that I have no wish to question the military qualities of the Duke of Guise. I can, however, see the danger in giving him such power, and I regret to say that it is certainly the first step towards limiting and reducing the authority of the constable. Anne de Montmorency is an excellent warrior and a skilled politician, but it is clear that, through the hands of the king, Diane of Poitiers intends to move him away from the spheres of power and replace him with the younger and greedier Duke of Guise.

In principle there would be nothing wrong with this, except for the fact that Francis is a man completely devoid of scruples and of a barbarous and bloody cruelty.

In recent days, for example, he has had five entire districts of the city razed to the ground and burned down no fewer than forty churches and cathedrals, turning Metz into a plain of ash.

Do not misunderstand me, Highness – these are necessary measures in this kind of situation, especially if one wishes to resist the kind of siege to which Metz will be subjected. But what terrifies me – and I do not use the word lightly – is how these measures were taken. Innocent people have been killed, women have been raped and, even worse, Guise displays an unparalleled religious fanaticism. There is the light of madness in his eyes: he rejoices in his heart whenever a Protestant church is razed to the ground or devoured by flames.

A man like Guise has no intention of stopping: it is perfectly clear that he considers this first assignment of his as the beginning of a perfectly planned rise to power. Of course, it may be that Charles V prevails, even though I would not wish that for our France. But I tremble at the thought of what Guise might do in the event of victory.

Our king, who is a brave and just man, is as charmed by him as everyone else.

Madame la Reine, I know perfectly well that what I am telling you is not only troublesome but also dangerous, but you have always asked me for sincerity and fidelity, so I have once again tried to obey.

In any case, the king will soon return to court and you will be able to see for yourself the truth of my words.

My wish was simply to reassure you of your husband's health and to alert you to those who may wish to cause you trouble in the future.

I felt that this news could not wait. I am, as ever, ready to obey your every disposition and command.

Your servant always,

Raymond de Polignac

Commander General of the King's Pikemen

When she had finished reading the letter, Catherine was appalled. Had Diane truly acquired such power? Was Henry in no way able to keep her decisions in check? If it were really so then, by God, France was lost.

She hoped she was wrong, of course. She hoped that Raymond de Polignac was exaggerating, perhaps to make sure she realized the severity of the situation.

But inside she sensed that was not the case. Not at all. Madame de Brézé's star shone high in the French firmament.

And Catherine promised herself that she would do everything in her power to extinguish its light.

APRIL 1558

29

Notre-Dame

The bride and groom had reached Notre-Dame after passing through triumphal arches and beautiful gardens. Catherine had worked her hardest to prepare the most beautiful wedding France had ever seen.

Escorted by some forty knights in livery, Mary Stuart, Queen of Scotland, and Francis II, Dauphin of France, had arrived in the square of Notre-Dame where they had been greeted with cries of jubilation, while pageboys and fools recreated the atmosphere of a village fete, drawing in the onlookers and encouraging them to shout their praises of the future king.

Preceded by a group of musicians, the spouses had entered the cathedral through a gigantic pavilion, arrayed with infinite pomp and decked out with blue curtains of Cypriot silk embroidered with the golden lily of France.

Mary and Francis crossed the central nave and knelt before the main altar, the Queen of Scotland's train covering at least twelve yards of the cathedral's marble floor as Notre-Dame sparkled in the rays of light refracted through the multicoloured Gothic windows.

The tall naves seemed infinitely high, and between their slender and magnificent columns, all of Paris held its breath as the Cardinal of Lorraine performed the sacred rite.

Far from the front rows, Raymond de Polignac observed the scene just as he had twenty years before in Lyon.

This time, however, the occasion was a completely different one.

Time had lightly streaked Polignac's moustaches with white and his thick brown hair with silver, but in every other respect he might have been said to be indifferent to the ravages of the passing years. His body was still lean, his eyes lively and his martial clothing impeccable.

But in those two decades he had experienced the thrill of ascending to the highest ranks of the army and the bitterness of dismissal following the historic defeat they had suffered in Saint-Quentin thanks to Montmorency. Anne had even ended up a prisoner in Ghent with his four children, suddenly becoming, despite himself, the protagonist of one of the darkest pages of French military history.

Polignac had been in the game and had lost, but things had not gone too badly for him, by and large. At the end of the story he had become what, in essence, he had already long been: a bodyguard – a soldier in the service of the queen. Henry II had long since stopped taking him along as he once had, fearing that through him Catherine would be informed of his and Diane's plans, and the defeat at Saint-Quentin had provided the perfect pretext for his dismissal. And so it had been. He was no longer the general commander of the king's pikemen but simply the personal guard of the queen who, for his services, had rewarded him with a small county in Picardy, a title, and an honest salary of ten thousand *scudi* a year.

So all things considered, Polignac had come out of it all rather well.

He looked at the young Mary Stuart, Queen of Scotland and now the dauphine of France. With her snow-white skin, long blond hair and deep eyes as dark as wild honey, she looked nothing short of magnificent in her ivory-coloured dress, her supple regal neck adorned with the most sparkling jewels. Standing at her side at the foot of the altar, Francis cut a poor figure in comparison. A couple of years younger than her and clad in a cyclamen-coloured satin robe, precious lace around his neck, he was so thin, weak and emaciated that he looked like a parody of a man. The king – and even more than him the Duke of Guise – had brought forward the ceremony because they feared for Francis' health.

Polignac snorted. Mary was a dazzling light, and behind her, her four Scottish ladies-in-waiting composed the corolla of a flower of incomparable beauty: Mary Fleming, Mary Beaton, Mary Livingston and Mary Seton. A little farther on, the captain of the guards, Montgomery, watched the glorious scene like a raven of ill omen.

And then of course he saw the king and Diane, glowing in a blue robe studded with pearls and diamonds yet forced to hide the wrinkles that spread mercilessly across her tired, power-hungry face like a spider's web beneath a thick layer of white lead. A mask of youth consumed by power that, though perfectly applied, was in any case pathetic.

At least to Polignac's eyes.

In the midst of her children, Catherine sported a long dark robe of splendid blue. The little Italian was still waiting, Raymond thought: with patience and determination she was waiting to finally rule the kingdom. The successes he had enjoyed during the disastrous war, which had culminated in a peace that tasted of defeat, had brought Francis of Guise closer to the queen, who had demanded that her husband wage war against Philip II, emperor of Spain, in the desperate hope of reconquering Italy and her beloved Florence.

That had not been the case, precisely because of the terrible defeat suffered by Montmorency at Saint-Quentin. But then, in an unexpected reverse of fortunes only two months ago, Guise had wrested Calais back from the British with a surprise siege, forcing them into the waters of the channel and becoming a national hero so powerful that his opinions almost outweighed those of the king.

When Henry had managed to make peace with Philip II, Guise, disappointed by this turnaround, had begun to look to Catherine as a possible ally. Both, in fact, believed that peace had come too soon.

Polignac did not look favourably on the nascent friendship between the two but was forced to surrender to the realities and, in the name of fidelity and honour, had remained at Catherine's side despite nurturing no particular sympathy for the duke.

While the Cardinal of Lorraine, who was the brother of Francis of Guise, proceeded with the ritual, Polignac observed Henry: the king repeatedly cast fleeting glances at the most beautiful of the ladies in the bride's retinue.

He did not know her name but she was truly splendid: blue eyes and a head of thick blond hair like a sea of wheat in the sun. She wore a long light-blue robe which showed off her figure and her high, shapely hips. Even seen from behind she was of a breathtaking beauty, and far more sensual than Mary Stuart.

As he studied her carefully, Polignac was struck by the feeling that this girl would cause France and Scotland more than a few headaches.

As if to confirm his thoughts, she turned for a moment and cast a furtive glance at the king.

In her eyes, Raymond de Polignac saw a flash of light that announced the arrival of a storm.

30

Elizabeth MacGregor

As soon as he had seen her, Henry had desired her more than any woman he had ever seen. Even Diane faded in comparison to her unbridled beauty.

He had told himself to forget about her, and had prayed that he would succeed, but it hadn't worked.

Henry was desperate to find her, despite the fact that he didn't even know her name. And damn it all, that detail excited him even more. He was tired of Diane, and as for Catherine... well, he had done his best. They had ten children. He deserved respite.

At the same time, he had to confess to himself that the situation terrified him, especially since the girl was even younger than his son's wife.

But he was the king. Had he forgotten it? He could do whatever he wanted, and he certainly didn't need to ask anyone's permission. No matter how beautiful she was, that girl was nobody.

The problem was that he had no idea how to go about it. She had set his blood afire, though, that was certain, and she had known it perfectly well too! The looks she had given him that morning at Notre-Dame during the ceremony had been unmistakable, and she had continued to cast them at him until a few moments before the sumptuous feast which had been given in the halls of the Palais de Justice. It was as clear as day that this young Scot was provoking him in a wholly brazen way.

As for the feast, Catherine had outdone herself. She had a natural talent for organizing memorable receptions and entertainments, he had at least to give her that. But then, after all, hadn't the Medici shaped their fortunes with the receptions they put on?

During the banquet, where one incredible course had followed another, surprises had been revealed which were nothing short of extraordinary: ships completely inlaid with pure gold had sailed across huge sheets of silvery cloth which had been specially sewn for the occasion in order to simulate stormy seas, with teams of operators working invisibly behind the scenes to make the simulation as realistic as possible.

But Catherine had made sure to include room for symbols and allegories in that extraordinary performance. On each ship, a prince completely dressed in gold had been ready to invite the great queens of the court aboard: Catherine de' Medici, Mary Stuart and then the queen of Navarre and the princesses Elisabeth, Claude and Margaret. Each had joined her prince, and for each of them it had been a happy journey of life, accompanied by luxury, splendour and the purest glory.

A triumph!

But now, after the banquet, after the revelry, after the rivers of wine and skewers of meat, Henry wandered like a ghost in the middle of the night, a cold sweat upon his brow. He was exhausted by his emotions and even more so by the crapula, and had therefore been walking the corridors of the building with some friends in a sort of drunken delirium. A little at a time he had lost sight of them all: one had gone to linger with the ladies, another had preferred to play cards, and thus Henry had found himself in an empty corridor while his wife, the queen, had retired to her apartments.

He walked up stairways and through salons. Almost everywhere, noblemen and noblewomen lingered in bawdy conversations fuelled by champagne. Some, more drunk than others, took their ladies into dark corners, where they coupled like dogs.

Tired after the long day, his head fogged by wine, and lulled by that atmosphere of dissolution, the king was traversing yet another salon when a beautiful woman suddenly appeared from an alcove. She had long blond hair, and behind the black mask she wore he could see deep-blue eyes.

Was it really her? Could fate truly be so munificent? He decided there was only one way to find out. But it was the woman, however, who made the first move.

'Could we for one night and one night only not be who we pretend to be?' she murmured in a mysterious voice as she came towards him. In spite of the excellent French she spoke, a hint of foreignness suggested a harsh, cold northern accent. To the sovereign, her husky voice seemed ripe with promises, and he found it irresistible. For once, fortune appeared to be on his side.

'I could ask for nothing more marvellous, *madame*,' he replied, his voice sounding distant in his ears as if he were listening to someone talking in the room next door.

The woman came closer still.

'Very well then,' she whispered in his ear. 'I suggest that you follow me.' And so saying, she led him through the corridors of the Palais de Justice until, spotting a secluded salon, she entered.

The king followed, closing the door behind him and turning the key in the lock.

The woman licked her lips and smiled. The king approached her and made to remove her mask, but in a languid, provocative voice she said, 'I beseech you, Your Majesty, do not take everything from me now, otherwise what will I have to offer you in the days to come? I want you to look at me in this way all night. With my mask on. I promise you that your chivalry of today will be rewarded by the ardour of tomorrow. My voice has already confessed to you who I am, and I have been looking forward to seeing you from close by all day long.'

Her bold words had the desired effect: they excited Henry even more. This woman took his breath away, and as she spoke he felt the blood stirring in his veins.

'Please,' murmured the king in a voice hoarse with desire, 'give me at least a token of your love.' He knew that it was certainly not love which had them in its throes, but he enjoyed acting out this parody of courtship.

Biting her lower lip with wild abandon, as though his request had convinced her to concede something more than she had planned, she approached him and her mouth brushed against his.

The king let out a groan of desire. He made to grab her, but the woman sealed his lips with a finger then whispered in his ear: 'Do you really wish to know my name?'

'Nothing would give me more pleasure right now.'

'Very well then. My name is...' And as she bent her head forward, she pulled the king down to sit in an alcove and confessed. Henry felt her tongue flicker against his mouth and heard a name he would never forget. 'Elizabeth MacGregor.'

Immediately afterwards her lips went to the king's throat and kissed him passionately. 'Let us make an assignment to meet in a secret place,' she continued. 'I desire you so.'

'More secret than this?' Henry was incredulous. And impatient. The exquisite torture to which she was subjecting him was both sweet and cruel. On the one hand, he wanted more, while on the other the voluptuous expectation of what was to come consumed him. The girl was truly a talented seductress.

'This is the Palais de Justice, Your Majesty – here, even the walls have ears.'

The king sighed. 'You are right. Where and when will I be able to see you again, then?'

Elizabeth seemed to consider for a moment, and the wait almost drove the sovereign out of his mind. She rested her head on his chest then she gave him an inscrutable look. Her blue eyes sparkled in the warm glow of the candles and the black lace of the mask contrasted starkly with her alabaster skin.

The King of France was ecstatic. It had been a long time since he had felt such desire, and in that moment he was certain the time to take a new lover had come.

Though after all that had happened, even the most faithful man would have been assailed by doubts.

'At the apartments reserved for Mary Stuart,' she said, 'in three days' time.'

Lost in the fragrance of her perfume, Henry closed

his eyes, indulging in the blissful feeling its aroma gave him. For an instant his head spun, almost as though he were in a waking dream, so that he hardly noticed Elizabeth was leaving.

When he opened his eyes again, he saw the divine creature disappear behind the curtains.

He stared at the shadows. She had vanished just as mysteriously as she had appeared.

Deep in his heart he could scarcely wait to see her again.

31

France and Scotland

The ceremony had been a great success. Paris was enamoured of the newly-weds.

Polignac knew how important that was. Henry's constant wars, to which the queen herself and even his favourite had urged him in recent times, and the wanderings between palaces and castles, from Fontainebleau to Chenonceau, had almost risked driving a wedge between the people and their sovereigns, and that was something which could not be allowed to happen.

Raymond de Polignac had left the Louvre early, and after having taken Rue Champ Fleuri had arrived at the Rue Saint-Honoré, in front of him the magnificent church with its imposing bell tower. In the square outside were stationed the hawkers selling skewers of roasted meat and wine, beggars, jugglers, hucksters, prostitutes: all kinds of people, who had been crowding Paris since first light that morning.

Polignac had proceeded along the great street, turning into Rue d'Orléans and then making his way to the loggia of Beauvais, where numerous butchers' stalls were concentrated. The smell of slaughtered animals filled the air and blood covered the floor. There were several vendors selling freshly made sausages.

Polignac looked at the pieces of offal, the salted hams and the cold meats, and decided that a hearty breakfast would be the perfect thing for the appointment he had made. Especially considering the person he was supposed to be meeting.

Without wasting any more time, he therefore entered an inn which bore the sign of a black boar and looked for a table, choosing one in a corner which gave him a view of the entrance. The smell of food filled his nostrils, immediately making his mouth water. Despite the hour, the inn was already rather crowded. He saw a couple of Protestants intent on confabulating in a corner – they were immediately recognizable from the black garments they wore which made them look like crows. A little farther on, an old whore was deep in discussion with a man who, despite making every effort to appear a gentleman, on closer inspection could only be a pimp. He wore a cherry-coloured doublet, but the fabric was of poor quality, as anyone used to dealing with laces and fine fabrics would immediately have realized. A couple of idlers – probably students, and probably drunk – were playing dice. Polignac sat down. It was early, and he quickly identified the man he was waiting for as soon as he walked through the door.

When Gabriel de Lorges, Count of Montgomery and Captain of the Scottish Guard, made his entrance, Polignac was already sipping a glass of excellent Burgundy wine. He waved the captain over to join him.

As the man approached, Polignac smiled at the sight of his elegant brown doublet and the sword poking out from under his light cloak like a metal tail. Montgomery reminded him of himself twenty years ago.

'Montgomery,' he said, 'what a pleasure to see you. Forgive me for having brought you here but I needed to speak to you far from indiscreet ears.'

'On the contrary, *monsieur*, it is I who thank you. By inviting me here, you allow me to enjoy one of the finest breakfasts in Paris. Even though I imagine that was not the reason for your summons.'

'You imagine well, my young friend. However, no one will prevent us from combining business with pleasure, so please sit down and enjoy a glass of this magnificent burgundy.'

Polignac uncorked the bottle and filled Montgomery's glass with the intense ruby-coloured wine.

His guest sat down without further ado, and from a buxom serving wench Polignac ordered a pigeon pie, stuffed eggs, salted ham and fruit. Then he began to speak.

'Captain Montgomery, it will not take me long to tell you what I must. Whether you know it or not, at one time I too was in the service of the king, the father of our good ruler, Henry II. Conspiracies and betrayals were then the order of the day, just as they are today. We might almost say that the French court thrives upon them, so what I am about to tell you will come as no surprise to you and certainly, even if it is not entirely known to you, it will at least have reached your ear.' Polignac paused for a moment when the food was brought to the table. 'They are wonderfully expeditious here,' he said with barely concealed enthusiasm. With the passing of the years, a good breakfast every now and then was a luxury that he allowed himself more than willingly.

'I am listening,' said Montgomery while he served himself, commenting 'Delicious' as he bit into a stuffed egg.

'It truly is,' Polignac agreed, sampling the ham. 'Now, it will be clear to you that Francis, Duke of Guise, is on the warpath. He not only promoted the marriage between Mary Stuart and the dauphin of France, but is doing everything in his power to convince Henry to take up the Catholic cause. Not that the king is ill-disposed in this matter – his religious beliefs are not in question. But the defence of the Catholic faith is not enough for

Guise – he wants fanaticism. I suspect that he is even planning to bring over to his side she who more than any other could have been the last bastion to defend the power he is acquiring.'

'Diane of Poitiers?' asked Montgomery, raising an eyebrow.

'The king's favourite?' Polignac shook his head. 'No, my friend. I am alluding to the queen herself: Catherine de' Medici.'

'Do you have proof of this?'

'I do not. But I will tell you one more thing: nobody loves that woman more than I.'

'Really?'

'Exactly so.'

'Then forgive my brutal frankness,' said Montgomery, unable to hide his incredulity, 'but why the devil are you telling me all this?' The young man was so surprised that he had frozen with his food halfway to his mouth.

'Because I fear for the life of His Majesty.'

'Are you sure of it?'

'As sure as I am that you are here sitting before me.'

'I see.'

'No, you do not see, Montgomery. And it could not be otherwise. You are young and you have not seen the half of what I have, but you are a valiant soldier and your mission is to protect the king's life.'

'If you called me here to remind me of the obvious…' said Montgomery.

But Polignac cut him short. 'Double the guards on duty. Let the king always have someone by his side. Act personally as his bodyguard, and let no one else replace you. For a long time that was my role, but after His Majesty suspected that I was acting against his interests, he sent me away. How wrong he was!'

'That's not what people say.'

'*Mort-Dieu!* And what is it that people say?'

'That the reason for your departure can be found in your conduct at Saint-Quentin.'

'What "conduct"?'

Montgomery shook his head.

'Monsieur de Polignac, whether you believe it or not, I hold you in high esteem, as do many other soldiers. But Saint-Quentin...'

'It was a bloodbath, I can tell you that,' Polignac interrupted. 'We were trapped in a gorge and being torn to shreds by the imperial troops. Anne de Montmorency, may God bless his soul, fouled everything up, despite what I and many other better officers than I told him. He wanted to prove to everyone what he was worth, and he forgot the most basic rules of prudence. Anyway, it's not me that we should be talking about now. I have reason to believe that His Majesty has become infatuated with one of Mary Stuart's bridesmaids. This in itself does not represent a danger, of course, but I fear that Francis of Guise wishes to exploit this turn of events to his advantage. I do not yet know how, to tell the truth, but if something happened to our good sovereign, he would not find it difficult to control a king with barely more than fluff on his chin and a foreign queen who has only just turned eighteen. And if he had Catherine on his side, it is obvious what would happen.'

'What?'

'A religious war! That is precisely what Guise is hoping for. Needless to say, his goal is the Bourbons. Antoine, King of Navarre, and his brother Louis, Prince of Condé, are fervent Protestants. Worse still, they boast royal blood, and their descendants would have a far more effective claim to the throne than the Guise family, who in reality are nothing more than the advisers of a child king. In this sense, the Bourbons are the only ones who could redress the powers at play, but Guise intends to destroy them, I am sure of it.'

'Because of their beliefs?'

'Precisely, my friend. As I say, you will certainly be aware of how enthusiastically Louis has embraced the Calvinist faith, thereby becoming one of the heads of the Protestant Hydra.'

'Naturally. But it is equally true that Antoine has no idea what consistency and courage are. In short, the brothers do not seem to me to be particularly united. The Reformed and the Bourbons do not seem to me to represent a serious problem for Guise.'

'Do not forget that Admiral Gaspard de Coligny

is also with them. And in confirmation of my worst suspicions, what you say is not what I have heard.'

'Really?' Montgomery looked sceptical. More wine was poured.

'It seems rather that the Bourbons are thinking of putting together an army, and intend in all probability to kill the Guises and overthrow the Valois.'

Montgomery's eyes widened.

'Yes,' confirmed Polignac. 'They are so sick and tired of the Guises' repeated crimes that they intend to put an end to them. They loathe them with a deep-rooted hatred, both because of what they have seen and because of what they have been told. I myself saw Francis of Guise hang innocents and raze entire villages to the ground.'

'What do you suggest we do?'

Polignac sighed. 'If a religious war hasn't broken out yet it is only because Henry and Catherine haven't lost their heads. But if it weren't for Henry, I wouldn't bet a fig on the future of our beloved kingdom, and an *amour fou* could be a mistake for which we would pay all too dearly.'

'And so?' asked Montgomery, who was beginning to distinguish the threads of the dark plot the Guises had woven.

'Do what I told you. Never lose sight of His Majesty. Never. For any reason. Make sure of it yourself. And where you cannot go, send your most trusted man.'

'What about you?' asked the captain of the Scottish guard.

'I will try to prevent Catherine from getting too close to the Guises. There is a lot of good in her, and I don't want those bastards polluting her heart.'

'You think a great deal of her.'

'Of that you may be certain. What other queen would have tolerated what Diane of Poitiers has done to her with such nobility and courage? And who do you think is behind these machinations with the Guises? Diane of Poitiers again. Only now the matter has got out of hand, and a miscalculation like this risks costing us all dear. Therefore we must do all we can to avoid a tragedy.'

And so saying, Polignac raised his glass.

'To France,' he said.

'To France,' Montgomery replied.

'And that Scotland may not be its grave,' concluded Polignac with a hint of bitterness in his voice.

32

Danger Approaches

Polignac had been waiting for Catherine to receive him in the antechamber of her apartments.

That day she wore an elegant pearl-grey silk dress, its colour conferring a special light upon her eyes.

Despite the passing of time, Polignac always found her regal and suffused with an inner grace that never failed to make her attractive to him.

He esteemed her so profoundly that over the years his admiration had grown into desire, but he attempted to repress what he felt behind a curtain of loyalty and obedience. In his eyes, dedication was the closest thing to swearing his eternal love to her that he could allow himself.

That love had been born in him little by little over the years, as if he had become aware of it slowly. But in that moment his feelings were completely irrelevant. There were far more serious problems to deal with, and Polignac had the distinct feeling that Catherine was going about things the wrong way.

He wanted to tell her so before it was too late, but the queen seemed to give much more credit to the prophecies of that accursed court astrologer Nostradamus, relying on his clairvoyance rather than paying attention to Polignac's warnings, which she tended to dismiss as the fantasies of an old soldier.

An old soldier was certainly what by now he was. But that was precisely why he could smell in the air, even more clearly than before, the odour of conspiracy.

And Francis of Guise, the man who had propitiated the arrival of that young girl dressed up as Queen of Scotland, was certainly plotting something criminal.

'Your Majesty,' Polignac told her when he faced her, 'your elegance is second only to the unparalleled beauty which dwells in the dignity and pride that belong to you.'

Catherine gave him a dismissive wave of her hand. 'Come, Monsieur de Polignac, you flatter me, you are too gallant. Rather, do you have any news for me? To what do I owe the pleasure of your visit?'

'*Madame la Reine*, I have come to share with you my fears,' said Polignac mysteriously.

Catherine did not fail to note the worry in his words and immediately replied with a hint of wit. 'I have the impression, my good friend, that having regaled me with such noble compliments you are about to give me bad news.'

Polignac seemed to hesitate.

'Your Majesty, I apologize for what I am about to tell you...'

'Does my husband have a new lover? Is this what you fear, *monsieur*? Because, as you well know, such a fact does not represent a problem for me. I told you once before, if I remember correctly, though it was a long time ago: with me you may speak freely.'

Polignac nodded, but her answer did not make the task any easier.

'Your Highness, I have reason to believe that one of the women in the service of Mary Stuart has illicit feelings for the king.'

'"Illicit feelings"? Good heavens, Polignac, you speak like a priest! I repeat: do you really believe that given all I have been through, I would be troubled by the thought of a new flame? Get to the point, damn it, I command you!' And so saying, Catherine stared straight into the eyes of the old soldier.

'Very well, Your Majesty. I saw the king exchanging inappropriate looks with one of Mary Stuart's bridesmaids.'

'One of the four Marys? The girls in the Queen of Scotland's retinue?' Catherine betrayed a hint of surprise in her voice.

'Not exactly. I have made inquiries, and I believe her name is Elizabeth MacGregor. As you rightly say, she is only a young girl, but one who is reckless and unscrupulous enough to confuse our king even more.'

'I have always liked you, Monsieur de Polignac, because you have always been sincere. And you have always had this kingdom much more at heart than I, my husband or his favourite do,' said Catherine, uttering the last word as if it were a synonym for 'whore'. 'I know of your doubts about this marriage.'

'Your Majesty, there is much more,' observed Polignac.

'Really?'

'It is said that the Guises had Mary sign a secret document – a charter which states that in case of death the kingdom would be theirs.'

'What are you talking about?' The grotesque conversation was becoming dangerously calumnious.

'I am telling Your Highness,' insisted Polignac, 'that Francis of Guise has had his lawyers draw up a contract by which, in the event of the death of Mary Stuart, the kingdom of Scotland would fall into their hands. I am not referring to the marriage agreement formulated with the representatives of the Scottish Parliament, do you understand? I am talking about a second contract.'

'I've heard tell of it. Only rumours, of course, but not even I know what to expect. You are right, however:

it is clear that such a document would give the Guises immense power.'

'But above all, although we are only making assumptions and have no proof whatsoever, what I want to emphasize is how potentially terrible the situation is: Henry discredited by continuous romantic adventures, the dauphin Francis in such poor health that his own doctors advised him to get married before it was too late. Forgive my words, *Madame la Reine*, but it is so and you know it. Mary has been tricked by the Guises. What will become of France, Your Highness? Because if Guise really does intend to carry out such a plot, we can imagine where he intends to lead the kingdom.'

Catherine looked at him with a questioning expression upon her face. Did the implications escape her too?

Raymond de Polignac shook his head. '*Madame la Reine*, I beseech you, keep in mind what I have told you: beware of the Guises. Their purpose is to get their hands on the throne, exterminate the reformers who are growing in number every day in the French countryside, and drag the kingdom into a nightmarish religious war.'

Catherine stared gravely at Polignac.

'*Monsieur*, if what you say is true, then we would be lost.'

'Precisely.'

'But I cannot base my actions upon mere suspicions.'

'I realize that, Your Majesty.'

'In any case, I know how to verify the truth of your statements.'

'How, Your Highness?'

'That is my business, *monsieur*. But I thank you once again for sharing your concerns with me.'

'Your concerns are mine. They coincide, do you see? Here,' he added, extending his hand. 'This is my arm: it has always been at your service, *Madame la Reine*. You can grasp it, lean upon it, or tear it off and feed it to the hounds, as you wish.'

Catherine couldn't hold back a smile.

'How melodramatic you are, Monsieur de Polignac. But then, that has always been your style, and it is a style that I have never found unwelcome. I will therefore see if your suspicions are well founded. Until then, we wait.'

And so saying, Catherine dismissed her bodyguard.

Polignac gave a rapid bow and walked towards the door.

33

The Pactum Sceleris

In light of the marriage which was to bind Mary Stuart to her son Francis, in the recent past Catherine had ordered an architect she trusted, the Tuscan Paolo Bruni, to make some modifications inside the Louvre. Modifications of which the king was unaware.

As well as the renovation of several salons and balconies and the decorations in the wing of the Pavillon du Roi, the project actually served to provide the queen with a series of secret 'observation points' which allowed her to be always informed about everything that happened inside the Louvre.

And where her eyes could not reach, those of her spies and her ladies-in-waiting, carefully chosen for their comeliness and talent as conversationalists, could. With honeyed words and subtle allusions, they were able to snatch compromising information and confidences from nobles, politicians and ambassadors.

It was from one of these infamous observation points that Catherine was now spying upon her husband, the King of France.

She saw him in one of the rooms reserved for Mary Stuart's retinue. The woman who stood before him was certainly the most attractive of the ladies who had accompanied the Queen of Scotland.

What she saw wounded her for the thousandth time, but her heart, which had already been wounded so often, had grown accustomed to the pain. Catherine knew she should hate him for what he had done, yet she couldn't. Rather, she directed all her rancour at his conquests: they were the corrupters and whores in her eyes, while Henry was innocent and, despite everything, deserving of her love. Yes, he was weak, but he was ultimately an innocent.

She watched for a long time, and committed to memory every part of the awful scene which might be to her advantage.

And the clear advantage was the damage that it could do her eternal rival, Diane of Poitiers, who was certainly unaware of what was happening and ignorant of the fact that Henry was replacing her with a younger beauty. That infatuation could truly be a blessing for Catherine and for France: finally she could counter Diane's power, finally Diane would no longer be so sure of her control over the sovereign, and finally even the power of the Guises whom she supported so virulently could be reined in.

She returned to her rooms and brooded over her love for Henry and her inability to hate him. It would be wonderful if she managed to succeed, but Catherine knew she had completely lost all dignity and restraint. Henry was still so handsome, and that he had fathered children with her at all had been an act of great devotion on his part. Catherine nurtured that sick belief with such dedication that she would never be able to change her mind. And anyway, to judge from what she had seen, perhaps for the first time in all those years, the unhealthy relationship between her, Diane and Henry in which she had been trapped seemed destined to collapse.

Elizabeth MacGregor had no power. Of course, the king could make her his new favourite, but she was and would remain a Scotswoman.

But if Diane caught them in the act, thought Catherine. Well, then there would be fireworks.

Francis I of Lorraine, Duke of Guise and Peer of France, stood in his castle at Mayenne on the banks of the Loire. After attending the wedding of Francis II of Valois to the young Mary Stuart, he had decided to take a few days off before returning to court.

He wore a splendid black velvet doublet and on his

head a *tocco* of the same colour. A white lace ruff gave a further nuance of refined elegance to his clothing, and his pointed red beard made his face, already sharp, even sharper.

In front of him, clad in cardinal's purple, sat his brother, Charles of Lorraine. He too was lean and wiry, and in his pale eyes there was an uncommon determination.

Each of them sipped sauvignon blanc from a crystal goblet.

'*Parbleu*, we cannot wait any longer,' Francis was saying, 'the occasion is too tempting to allow it to slip through our fingers. Francis is just a little boy, Mary is young and Scottish. If we could only make things uncomfortable for the king...'

'Patience, my brother. The moment of our victory approaches, I feel it. Everything you say is true, and I agree that Henry's death now would be an act of providence, but on the other hand, we can afford to wait. After all, your victory at Calais has launched us up to the heights of Olympus.'

'Not high enough, it seems, given that, despite his ineptitude, Montmorency still manages to hold the position of Grand Master of France through his son,' said Francis, angrily hurling his goblet to the ground, where it shattered. 'And that despite the fact that he only watched the siege of Calais and neither planned nor participated in it.'

'Damn it, Francis, control yourself,' said Charles in exasperation. 'Our time will come. Thanks to Diane of Poitiers the situation for us is far more favourable, and all the pawns are now moving into place.'

'I'm tired of waiting! Time passes, and I must be content with a title and a couple of shields. And I challenge anyone to say that the recent successes of this accursed state are not my doing. We take Calais back, and what does Henry do? He decides to make peace with the emperor. Can you credit it? It doesn't make sense! We should have sunk our blade deep into that accursed Spain.'

Charles nodded. It was hard not to agree with his brother, but the time was not yet ripe.

'You are right in everything you say. And what is more, I believe that Diane has now had her day, and that her star is in decline while Mary Stuart's is rising. And let us not forget Catherine. I believe that she still has much to contribute to this story. In the last campaign she was, in some ways, our best ally.'

Francis gave his brother a puzzled look.

'Charles, let's be clear: if Catherine supported the war against Philip II to the point that she asked the families of Paris for the money needed to get the army back on its feet, the reason is that she believed that fool Henry could recover Italy and Florence. In that situation our desires coincided, but I do not believe at all that she is openly in our favour. She is looking after her interests, that is all.'

'That is all, you say? Well in my opinion, that is an epochal change. Of course, I agree that Henry is a hard cliff to climb, but one way or another we will succeed. You know perfectly well, I'm sure, what people are saying...'

'I certainly do not. What *are* people saying?'

Charles gave a grin.

'That Nostradamus foresaw the death of the king.'

'Ah.'

'And that the queen set a man to watch him day and night so as to protect him.'

'Monsieur de Polignac?'

'Exactly.'

'*Parbleu*, I remember him well! But he was relieved of his position.'

'Indeed.'

'And so?'

'And so the king is vulnerable.'

'Are you suggesting something?'

'Not at all, brother. I am simply saying it's easier for an accident to happen if the king is not protected.'

Francis looked at him incredulously. 'And are we to entrust our rise to prophecies and bodyguards?'

'Far from it. We will rely on our faith in God and his infinite goodness, in the hope that he will one day reward his faithful servants.'

'Charles,' said Francis, then paused to emphasize what he was about to say. 'You surely can't believe that

I will be satisfied with a statement like that. I know that you have something in mind, so explain yourself clearly.'

'If you weren't my brother, I'd think you were threatening me.' But this time Francis did not reply. 'Very well, then,' Charles continued, raising his hands in surrender, 'I will be more explicit, if that will make you happy? You see, my brother, as you surely know, there are some incredible beauties among the ladies of Mary Stuart's retinue.'

Francis began to guess what his brother was about to say, but was struck by the odd undertone in his voice.

It would have unnerved anyone. It even unnerved him.

'In particular,' continued Charles, 'there is one young girl who is so extraordinary that not even a paladin could resist her. I know what you are about to reply, but believe me when I say that this young woman is so attractive that she has had no difficulty in making a breach in the heart of our sovereign. And the point, Francis, is that Diane still knows nothing about it.'

Haughtily, Charles took another sip of sauvignon blanc from his goblet while his brother waited for the conclusion of his monologue.

'As you may have already guessed, Elizabeth MacGregor – for this is the maiden's name – has already approached the king and bestowed upon him attentions which have captured his interest, if you understand me.

So far, careless of the danger, he has met with her inside the Louvre, but now the masterstroke will be to have Henry join Elizabeth at Saint-Germain-en-Laye.'

'And you are intending to summon Diane there too?'

The Cardinal of Lorraine nodded.

'Precisely. To ensure that she catches Henry *in flagrante*. You can well imagine the storm that such an event will trigger. But if I know Elizabeth well, her arts will be such that she will remain etched in the king's heart long enough to weaken Diane's position.'

Francis seemed to weigh his brother's words. The plan was impeccable, but there was one small yet simple doubt which he could not resolve.

'One detail of this ingenious project of yours is lacking... How are we to summon Diane?'

'You will take care of it,' replied Charles without a moment's hesitation.

'Really?'

'Certainly. And to do so, you will have a topic of considerable effectiveness'

'Which is?'

Without ado, Charles took a document out of his pocket.

'A letter, my brother – one even signed by the king.' And so saying, the Cardinal of Lorraine unfolded the blank sheet bearing the sovereign's signature at the bottom. 'Here it is, waiting to be written as we see fit. I think that a romantic tone would be best suited to a carnal congress, don't you agree? Without overplaying it, though, because if I remember correctly, Henry's manners are rather measured.'

The face of Charles of Lorraine was lit by a candid smile.

His brother, profoundly impressed by the simple effectiveness of the plot, waited to learn the final details.

Their trap would throw the entire court into chaos.

34

Elizabeth and Diane

It was Guise who had given her the letter on behalf of the king.

Diane could not understand why Henry had sent her that invitation through the duke, especially since in it he simply asked her to join him in Saint-Germain-en-Laye.

Consumed by curiosity, though, she had set off in a carriage. The journey had been quicker than expected, and when she had climbed out she had stared in enchantment at the Seine, which flowed impetuously by like a ribbon of liquid silver, its white foam crashing against the dark rocks.

As always, she was charmed by the majesty of the Château of Saint-Germain-en-Laye.

She saw the large Italian terrace, surrounded by a

balustrade and dotted with carved stone vases, from whence one could see all the surrounding forest. Supported by its thrusting buttresses, the impressive Gothic vault loomed above.

The evening was sweet, and the air mild and full of the fragrances of spring.

It was the perfect occasion for a courtly encounter, thought Diane – and also for something more. It had been a long time since she had been able to share a moment of intimacy with Henry, and Saint-Germain-en-Laye seemed to provide the perfect setting for their idyll.

She sighed, because the days of passion seemed so far away. She knew that Henry loved her and that she had nothing to fear from Catherine – the mechanism she had managed to develop over the years had been repeatedly proven to work perfectly. Nevertheless, in the mottled sunset sky she seemed to see a blood-red stain of ill fortune colouring the heavens. She could not have explained what it was she felt, but her heart began to beat wildly.

She wanted to see Henry as soon as possible, to embrace him and sink into his arms.

Escorted by the royal guards, she entered the castle and asked to be led to His Majesty the King, but without being announced: she wanted to surprise him.

The servants seemed to hesitate so she slapped one

girl's face. The young woman put her hand to her burning cheek.

'Take me to the king immediately,' Diane ordered.

They walked along a couple of corridors and crossed the large ballroom before finally arriving in front of the door that gave access to the king's apartments.

There Diane found the captain of the Scottish guard, Gabriel de Lorges, First Earl of Montgomery, barring her way.

She could scarcely believe her eyes.

'How dare you, *monsieur*? Do you believe that I really intend to murder the king?'

The captain faltered. He seemed genuinely not to know what to do. He tried to make up an excuse, but it came out feeble and botched.

'Forgive my impudence, *madame*, but the king asked not to be disturbed.'

Diane seemed to weigh that statement for a moment.

'Impudence! Congratulations on your choice of words, Monsieur Montgomery, because believe me, it is truly accurate. Precisely for this reason you will now step aside and let me pass. I have an appointment with the king!'

'I understand, my lady, but believe me… If I say what I say it is because—'

But Diane cut him off.

'I have allowed you to talk too much, *monsieur*! Thank God only that I do not report the impropriety of your attitude to your sovereign. I can understand that you are tasked with protecting the king, but that fact does not justify such conduct: you should know who I am!'

'My lady, I know perfectly well who you are—'

'Very good,' said Diane, once again interrupting him, 'then move aside, *monsieur*.' And without waiting another moment, with a dramatic flourish of her arm, she turned the handle and opened the door.

That Scottish woman was indeed a gift from God.

The King of France had to admit it: the arrival of Mary Stuart had brought him something good.

Henry was taking Elizabeth from behind. Her buttocks, so pale and round, were pure globes of pleasure. He loved the feeling of her soft white skin, and he grasped at her firm, perfect backside as he penetrated her as if his life depended upon it.

'Yes, Your Majesty, yes!' moaned Elizabeth.

His head was bursting with the feeling of dominance that the sight of Elizabeth, her face buried in the cushions and her rump in the air, gave him, and at the sound of her words, he almost lost his mind.

He was on the verge of coming when a cry shattered the unrepeatable ecstasy of the moment.

At first Henry couldn't understand what was happening. All he knew was that whoever it was who had shouted was behind him. The feeling was as chilling as if someone had thrown a bucket of cold water on his back.

35

Surprise and Pain

Diane stood there.

She was weeping. In all the time he had known her, he had never seen her shed so much as a single tear, but now tears coursed copiously down her cheeks and the sight of them wounded him more than anything else.

He heard her sobbing.

'Don't stop, Your Highness,' murmured Elizabeth MacGregor in a voice hoarse with lust.

Diane felt as if she were about to lose her reason.

'Silence, whore!' she cried, and as the words echoed around the room, it seemed almost as if they were destined to remain there forever. As if the shame could be locked up and kept in there, hidden from sight.

It was only then that Elizabeth realized what was

happening. Her reaction, however, was quite the contrary of what one might have expected.

Instead of expressing remorse or shame, Elizabeth turned round, her bold eyes blazing. 'Who do you think *you* are to call me a whore?' she snapped, taking Diane completely off guard. 'Has age made you more virtuous? You're nothing but an old crone who took advantage of a little boy to try and steal the throne away from him and the Queen of France!'

Diane trembled with rage, like an old she-wolf about to pounce to defend her den.

'Quiet, Elizabeth!' ordered the king, who realized the gravity of the situation perfectly and saw how Diane's certainties were crumbling as she felt betrayed by the little boy she had raised. It was not the first time it had happened, of course, and Diane had been more than willing to turn a blind eye to antics in the bedroom as long as they were only the escapades of a young and handsome king. This, though – this was something completely different. He could see it in her flaming gaze.

'You and I know each other well,' she said with fury in her eyes, 'don't we, Henry? Because you were just a brat riddled with fears and nightmares when I taught you to face the dark. Do you remember? If you have today become the king that everyone respects, you owe it all to me. But apparently I erred, because before me all I see is a little man who is only too happy to flirt with a low Scottish courtesan. Believe me, you have all my contempt.'

Despite the disdain in her voice, Henry sensed Diane's bitterness, disappointment and regret. He was horrified by what was happening, but before he had time to open his mouth to speak, the Duchess of Valentinois had vanished as quickly as she had appeared.

He stood there completely naked, contemplating his own failure. He felt that he had lost a piece of himself. He had exchanged a great love for the pleasures of the flesh. Had it been worth it? Of course not, as he now clearly understood. But he understood equally well that the value of what is dear is only fully understood when it is lost.

He knew that at that point it would be extremely difficult for him to regain Diane's esteem and love. And it was her respect and her benevolence that interested him. More even than her love.

For a moment he felt once again like that child in the dungeons of the castle of Madrid.

Lost.

'Go away, you old witch!' shouted Elizabeth MacGregor to her departing shadow.

Henry felt a pang in his heart, because although he knew perfectly well what was happening, he could do nothing to avoid it. He was a child again, groping in the dark, desperate for a helping hand, a caress. And there was no one for him, no one at all. Diane had saved him and this was how he had repaid her. He was ashamed of himself. He trembled, his vision became blurry with tears and a feeling of nausea choked his throat. And the more Elizabeth railed against Diane's presence, still heavy in the air of the room, the more disoriented he became.

He sat down on the bed and bowed his head, his sweat-drenched hair falling forward like slimy snakes. He felt Elizabeth put her arms around him, but he pushed her away as violently as if her touch carried leprosy or plague.

'Let me be!' he shouted. 'Can't you see that you have just taken everything from me?'

Elizabeth seemed to hesitate for a moment then burst out in almost mocking laughter.

Henry couldn't bear it. He spun round and slapped her hard, his hand striking her pale, delicate skin like a whip. And then he slapped her again, and again, until the naked girl slipped out of his grasp and snatched up a small leather sheath. An instant later, a misericord dagger appeared in her hand, its sharp blade glinting in the candlelight.

'Try to strike me once more, Your Majesty,' said Elizabeth, brandishing the misericord and jabbing it toward the sovereign's chest, 'and God help me, I'll carve a red smile into your chest that will send you to the Creator!'

For a moment, Henry seemed to recover.

'Forgive me, Elizabeth, I shouldn't have...'

'But you did, didn't you, Majesty?'

Henry fell silent for a few moments, and then roused himself.

'I swear that it will not happen again.'

'And I am supposed to trust a man like you?' she hissed, her anger breaking through the facade of her courtly manners. 'I've seen how you treat those you tire of. But it won't happen to me, I can promise you that!'

Henry shook his head. 'There is no need,' he said. 'Now, leave this room or, believe me, I will not hesitate to kill you with my own two hands. I am the King of France, and even though I have made a grave mistake today, I have no intention of listening to the empty threats of a shepherdess.'

And so saying he stood up in all his formidable height. He was a robust man with a statuesque body and his eyes were red with rage.

Elizabeth didn't look too afraid, however. She was already dressing.

She slipped the misericord into a sheath inside her dress and then she too left the room.

Henry watched her go and thought to himself that she was truly beautiful, even now. Haughty and arrogant, but precisely for that reason able to capture a man's heart. He was the king and could have any woman, but that was a meagre consolation, especially after losing Diane and threatening Elizabeth, whom he had so unjustly beaten.

He was disgusted with himself. What kind of man had he become?

Francis of Guise had hoped that something irreparable would happen – something that broke the bond between the king and his favourite. Diane was still powerful and had to be moved out of the way. If Henry repudiated her, their room for manoeuvre would increase greatly. Catherine at least was certainly far less greedy and unscrupulous than the Duchess of Valentinois. Without Diane, Henry would feel lost, and Francis and his brother, Charles of Lorraine, would be able to carve themselves out roles as advisors to the king, who already esteemed them after the incredible victory against the English troops in Calais.

Now all they had to do was wait. Words would do the rest.

36

Margaret

'Margaret! Margaret! Where are you, child?' cried Madame Gondi desperately as she tried to find the girl, so flighty and already wise beyond her years.

There was no reply.

Madame Gondi was sure she had looked everywhere. Margaret certainly wasn't in her room and nor had Monsieur Bazin, her tutor, seen her. That morning, Margaret had not shown up for her Latin lesson. Monsieur Bazin had merely rolled his eyes with an expression full of resignation, aware that the terrible girl had embarked on another of her escapades.

Madame Gondi had hurried between the Pavillon du Roi and the library where Margaret loved to take refuge, filling her eyes with the wonders she discovered in the pages of books and manuscripts. She couldn't read perfectly yet but she was a quick study, thanks to her uncommon intelligence and lively curiosity. She harboured a stubborn vein of rebellion, however, that seemed to want to resist order and discipline in all their forms.

Could the little princess have dared break into her mother's apartments? She had repeatedly been forbidden to enter them unless Madame Gondi was with her, but nobody really believed that Margaret would obey.

Madame Gondi was not sure but, knowing Margaret, she believed that she had sufficient impertinence and initiative to explore that world to which she was so irremediably drawn.

Now that she thought about it, she remembered how much Margaret had always loved watching her mother while she put on beautiful clothes or had her hair coiffured by Madame Antinori.

In her eyes there would be a mixture of adoration and wonder, but also a pinch of envy, as if she wanted to grow up faster than nature permitted. She was a precocious girl, and at times Madame Gondi had the feeling that an adult woman was trapped in that pretty little body – an adult woman who could not bear to see herself still a child.

While she reflected upon her ward, Madame Gondi came to the door of the queen's apartments. As she entered the anteroom, she remained silent, listening carefully in the hope of hearing a noise, a squeak, a laugh.

Margaret was a happy child, full of contagious energy, and it was not uncommon for the rays of sunlight of a beautiful day to put her into a state of overwhelming enthusiasm.

And yet, Madame Gondi heard nothing. The antechamber was immersed in shadow, the curtains almost closed, and only a shaft of light filtered through. The environment had sunk into silence. She found herself in front of the door that led to the queen's rooms. She knew Catherine was out, and the queen trusted her blindly. She was the only person authorized to enter the apartments in her absence.

She felt in her pocket for the keys, but her fingers closed only on the shiny silk of the dress.

Where had she left them? Yet she remembered putting them in her pocket, as always.

Almost without thinking, she placed her hand on the golden handle and lowered it, and was stunned to discover that the door was unlocked.

Even worse was when she saw the state of Catherine de' Medici's apartments, lit by the sunlight which flooded in through the open windows.

The bed had been thrown into complete disorder, and an armchair had been turned over. On the floor were combs along with several books. She entered and, feeling something crackle beneath her feet, realized that she was walking on broken glass. A trail of shards led from the entrance to the bed. Someone must have dropped a glass. An open bottle lying on a side table dripped onto the floor.

Madame Gondi raised her hand to her mouth.

Who had dared do this? Had someone broken into the queen's apartments... perhaps in search of something? Rather than a thief, Madame Gondi immediately thought of one of the queen's many political enemies. A spy, a conspirator! But what need was there to create such havoc?

It was then that she heard the voice.

'You didn't expect that, did you, *madame*?'

There was a note of mockery in the words. She knew all too well to whom the voice belonged. Madame Gondi advanced further, and when she arrived in the make-up room she found Margaret there. Staring back at her from the mirror with indescribable impudence was the face of a little girl who was ever so slightly grown up, her eyes darkened with kohl, her lips painted red, her skin made pale with white lead. There was a child under that pathetic mask of seduction, but the effect was unpleasant, and the smudged make-up made her beautiful little face look eerie.

The scene was profoundly unnerving.

Madame Gondi raised her hand to her lips again, but this time she cried out.

'Margaret, what have you done?' she said, regaining control. 'Do you realize the mess you have made of your mother's apartments?' She looked towards the table and saw spilled powders and enamels in a miscellany of colours and shades covering the surface in a way that was nothing short of terrifying.

The queen would be furious.

'There is someone I must seduce.'

Her words sounded like an incontrovertible statement.

'What?' Madame Gondi didn't understand.

'You heard me.'

'How dare you say such things, Margaret! Do you believe your mother would approve?'

'We're not talking about her.'

'Was it you who...'

'Made this mess? Of course, who else?'

'Why did you do it?'

'Because the queen, my mother, thinks that I am too young for certain things.'

'Of course you are.'

'No I am not. I am a woman now.'

Madame Gondi tried to remain calm. She went over to the little princess and made to take her by the ear, but Margaret was quick to move out of her grasp.

'If I were you, I would be careful about what you do.'

Madame Gondi raised an eyebrow in disbelief.

'What? Do you intend to challenge me?' And so

saying, she smiled. But her amused expression died on her lips a moment later.

Margaret was dangling the lost set of keys before her eyes.

'If the queen knew how easily you lost these, I think your stay at the court might soon be cut short. I'm sure you agree, don't you?'

The little viper, thought Madame Gondi.

'And who is it you would like to conquer, painted that way?'

'My beloved older brother, Henry.'

'And did he convince you of such nonsense? Where is he now?'

'He's waiting for me. But I will never tell you where.'

With those words, Margaret returned her eyes to the mirror, gazing at herself as if she were a consummate seductress.

Madame Gondi was quick to grab her by the hair, and while Margaret screamed and wriggled wildly she took the opportunity to snatch the bunch of keys from her small closed fist.

Margaret kicked, almost growling, as bitter tears ran down her white-smeared face, making two long pinkish trails.

'Don't ever dare to threaten me like that again, Margaret,' said Madame Gondi in a voice trembling with rage. 'Neither you nor your wretched brother. Thank the Lord that I do not tell your mother what you have done. And worse, what you have confessed to me about your brother Henry!'

Margaret struggled and, in doing so, banged against a table and gave a grimace of pain.

'You're just a sad old woman, *madame*,' she muttered angrily in a venomous voice.

'Perhaps. But now this old woman is going to wash your face.' And without another word, Madame Gondi grabbed the princess by the hair a second time and dragged her to the bathroom. She immersed her face in cold water, rubbing it well, then dried it off with a towel.

Margaret seemed to have calmed down.

'You'll pay for this,' she said finally. 'Remember my words: I will make you pay for this one day!'

'I have no doubt of it.'

'I swear it,' continued Margaret.

'Until then,' replied Madame Gondi, 'you would do well to behave yourself and never try to steal my keys again. And if I find you playing with face powder again you will be punished. Have I made myself clear?'

'I will remember you.' Margaret had no intention of giving in. 'And I'll tell Henry. Sooner or later I will make you pay for this humiliation. You're nothing but an Italian peasant.'

'Very well,' said Madame Gondi condescendingly. 'Do whatever you wish. But now get out of here if you don't want your mother to find out what you've done.'

Margaret didn't answer her. She headed for the door of the queen's apartments then turned round to look at Madame Gondi one last time, her beautiful eyes seeming to glow white hot with rage. Then she disappeared.

37

The Last Time

Catherine hadn't believed it would happen. Not after what she had seen. And yet there Henry was in front of her.

He looked exhausted. And sad – so incredibly sad.

'Forgive me,' he said, 'for the harm I have done you. For not having honoured you as I should have. Now I understand how right my father was. How much intelligence there is in you and how much beauty in your person. I should have sought it out, but I was blind for a long, long time.'

She started to speak, but Henry had not finished.

'You are too good, Catherine, you have too big a heart for me. A heart that I could not hold in my arms. And I am sorry for that. But now I want to make up for my mistakes. I'm so tired of wasting my time and losing face behind women who aren't worth a quarter of what you are. I know that I cannot hope for your pardon simply by asking for it, but...'

Catherine sealed his lips with a kiss. She breathed with him. She wanted him to love her at that moment. There was nothing to explain, there was only the passion she felt for Henry.

Nothing else mattered. The world did not exist.

She took his hands, placed them on her face and abandoned herself to his strong yet sweet caresses. She needed them endlessly. She had been craving them for so long. So long that she barely even remembered them anymore.

She cried because she was happy.

'Is everything all right, *ma chère*?' murmured Henry.

'Love me as if it were the last time,' she replied.

He took her in his arms and gently rocked her. He was a big man, tall, with in his eyes a fearlessness that she loved. Henry was a fortress, his chest as impregnable as the wall of the Château of Chambord. She felt so safe when she was with him.

Her tears had dried now. She smiled and bit his nipples, making him moan with pleasure. She gave a silvery laugh. She was so happy, it felt as if she were flying when he lifted her and then laid her on the sheets of the bed, as white as snow. Golden rays filtered in through the window, bringing the blessing of the sun, as if spring itself wished to be a witness to that rediscovered love.

She let him take her tenderly. It was all so inexplicably beautiful. The way it should have been from the beginning. As if time had halted and decided to enclose them in a bubble, suspended and fragile yet out of reach of everything and everyone.

Henry moved slowly over her, and Catherine felt the delight of surrendering, of finally letting go, of not having to think about what might happen, because what was happening in that moment nullified everything else.

The room began to spin in a soft, sensual dance. Catherine wrapped her legs around Henry, her little feet resting on his buttocks, while, with a rocking movement which never seemed to end, he languidly penetrated her.

If only it could have gone on like that forever. She would have been the happiest woman in the world.

She sat astride him and felt Henry's wet, hot breath blowing delicately in her ears while his member filled her with liquid fire.

She felt a frenzy she had never experienced before, and grew impatient because she wanted even more. She rode him like a fury, like a little Amazon, and he indulged her thrusts.

Catherine felt him inside her, and finally he came. It was a flood of pleasure, and in that moment she had the orgasm of her life. She clawed at the white sheets and cried out, her body shaken by uncontrollable tremors until finally, overwhelmed by love, she collapsed into his arms.

JUNE—JULY 1559

38

A Heart in the Deluge

The day was hot and the sun an orange disk that blazed down upon the stands and balconies.

Paris was an oven and Rue Saint-Antoine a trail of fire. As wide as a square and well over two hundred paces long, its flagstones had been taken up in the days preceding the tournament and it had been covered with sand.

The joust had been organized for the celebrations of the treaty of Cateau-Cambrésis – a treaty which, all things considered, had given France much less than it had cost her.

Henry II had been obliged to return Corsica to the Republic of Genoa, and Piedmont to the Duke of Savoy. He had managed to keep Calais, of course – taken from the English by Francis of Lorraine, Duke of

Guise – and the marquisate of Saluzzo as well as the bishoprics of Metz, Toul and Verdun, which had been subtracted from the empire. But with the sole exceptions of Venice and Florence, the empire now dominated Italy unchallenged, and Catherine de' Medici's dream of seeing her land again was therefore shattered.

Gabriel de Lorges, Earl of Montgomery, had no idea why he had been put in that absurd situation which saw him competing against the king. It seemed to him absolute folly, but it was his duty and he had obeyed. His throat was parched and he would have been grateful for anything that prevented him from participating, but the king's foolish pride had driven him to compete – there, where he should never have been.

He had seen other horsemen leaving the field with broken bones, and therefore when he had spurred his mount at a gallop against his sovereign, he had done his best.

His best to lose the fight.

But his best had not been enough. Quite the contrary, in fact.

Because after being knocked off his horse by Montgomery's spear, the king now lay on the ground with a splinter of wood in his eye. Montgomery cursed himself as he reflected on the irony of fate: he, who was supposed to protect His Majesty, was responsible for the sovereign's being thrown from his horse and wounded. The splinter had broken off the lance when it had shattered in the impact against the breastplate of the king's armour. It was the kind of thing that happened all the time, but no one could ever have imagined it might fly through the gaps in the visor of his helmet.

Montgomery jumped down from his horse and entrusted it to two squires, then pulled off his helmet and ran over to the king. Two aides de camp had already removed Henry's armour and, not understanding exactly what had happened, were trying to dress the wound. Montgomery understood all too well, though. He heard the crowd roar. What had been the point of the king risking his own safety for a stupid question of pride? He should have insisted that the king not participate, but with Henry that was impossible. He had been acting strangely for a long time – ever since he had seen Diane emerge from that room he had allowed her to enter.

Montgomery realised that he had been a perfect fool.

Henry had not blamed him for what had happened, though: Montgomery was the captain of the Scottish guard, not his procurer.

Since that day, though, Henry had become a shadow of himself.

And all because of a woman.

What now? Montgomery might not be the procurer of Henry II, King of France, but he was at serious risk of becoming his killer.

The crowd roared as furiously as if the captain of the Scottish guard had injured the king deliberately.

Catherine saw Henry lying in the dust, blood gushing copiously from his face. Although she couldn't tell exactly what had happened, she realized immediately that the king's life was in danger and felt an icy grip clutch at her bowels. Fearing she might faint, she leaned against the balustrade and only managed to get to her feet by summoning all her energies. She wanted to cry, but forced back her tears.

'Hurry!' she cried. 'Call the king's surgeon and take His Majesty to the Palais des Tournelles. We'll await him there.'

She was surprised by her own cool-headedness, but realized that there was nothing else she could do. She looked at Diane, who had turned paler than she had ever been in her life, then turned her gaze to her entourage: the nobles and the ladies stared back at her, their eyes wide, completely at a loss as to what to do. Finally she saw that Michel de Nostredame had risen to his feet: clad in his black kaftan, he was now silhouetted against the fiery sky like some giant crow.

Catherine felt her breath catch in her throat.

Nostradamus nodded, and at that moment the queen knew she was once again on the verge of bursting into tears. She bit her lower lip, so hard that it bled: crying was not a luxury she could afford at that moment. But the prophecy was coming true. What was it Nostradamus had said?

'The young lion will prevail over the old in single combat on the battlefield, and in the cage of gold its eyes will be pierced, two wounds in one, to then die a cruel death,' whispered a voice as black as the pain that rose from her gut.

Catherine once again felt the tremor in her heart which had nearly killed her so many years before. She staggered again.

And then, the voice of Michel de Nostredame: 'You must protect Henry: he is the lion who wins in battle, but he must fear duels in closed spaces. Protect the king, or he will die with his eyes pierced by a blade. Today I saw his end.'

Catherine saw the arena of Rue Saint-Antoine spinning in front of her eyes like some crazed windmill and felt once more that she was about to faint. She would have fallen if someone had not held her up: Raymond de Polignac, who took her in his arms as he might have done a child. And she, for once, let herself collapse against his chest while she felt herself lifted from the ground as if she had taken wing. There were cries of astonishment and exclamations of surprise, a jumble of sounds that sent Catherine spinning into even greater confusion.

'Make way!' shouted a voice. It was strong and hard, and belonged to a man ready to defend her, ready to give all of his blood for her.

Catherine heard it as though from far away, only vaguely audible, like the dull echo of words on a sheet of ice, but she knew that Raymond was there with her and she was reassured. Seeing Henry in the dust had devastated her, and that voice – so firm, so stentorian – at least made her feel that she was not completely lost.

'Get out of the way!' shouted Raymond de Polignac. 'Let us pass!'

He pushed his way through the crowd of foppish nobles clad in foolishly extravagant garments who filled the stand as he searched desperately for the wooden staircase.

'The queen's carriage,' he called. 'Bring it, now!'

When he finally managed to find the stairs, he hurried down them, clutching Catherine in his arms, and ran over to the royal carriage. The guards opened the door and he climbed inside, laying the queen on the soft velvet cushions. Madame Gondi followed him in.

'Smelling salts,' she whispered, handing Polignac a small crystal bottle.

Raymond held them to the queen's nose and waited as she breathed in their perfumed essence. An instant later, Catherine came round.

Polignac jumped out of the carriage. 'To the Palais des Tournelles, quickly!' he shouted to the coachman, the long feather of his wide-brimmed hat swaying in the air. 'I'll follow you on horseback. Hurry, there isn't a moment to lose.'

The coachman nodded, and without another word Raymond de Polignac leapt up into the saddle and spurred his horse towards the Palais des Tournelles, hoping desperately that his fears would not be confirmed. He was afraid that the unfortunate accident would be fatal for the king. He hadn't been able to see Henry clearly, but the size of the splinter and the huge amount of blood the king had lost made him fear the worst.

39

Ambroise Paré

Ambroise Paré stared at his sovereign's face then shook his head. Despite having tried every available remedy, nothing could have saved Henry II.

The king was dead.

For days he had tried to save his life, but without success.

Together with colleagues, he had even dissected four different skulls from as many corpses in a desperate attempt to understand exactly the direction of the lance and therefore the place where the wood splinters might lurk. But it had profited Vesalius and him not at all, and had only procured them remorse, since the skulls belonged to four criminals who had been killed for the express purpose of allowing their investigations.

But nothing. Not even an idea, a hint, or a useful clue.

The muscle tissue of the forehead above the bone was torn along the inner corner of the left eye. Many small splinters of wood had finished up in the eye, but the bone was perfectly intact. There were no fractures.

Not even a scratch.

Paré had not been able to detect and halt the infection, and could find no peace.

When he looked up he saw Catherine.

She was distraught, her face puffy and red. Had she been crying all that time? For the eleven days the king had spent fighting death, the queen had never slept and had never left his side.

'Forgive me, Your Highness,' said the king's surgeon in a faint voice. 'I could do no better. I offer you my life for having failed…'

'It was not your fault, Monsieur Paré,' said Catherine. 'You did everything in your power to avert the death of our good king. It was my fault that I failed to protect Henry, even though I knew the risk to which he was exposing himself. And for that, I will never cease to curse myself.'

Catherine dismissed the surgeons, who – looking like birds of ill omen – left the king's apartments in silence.

The air had grown as stiff and solid as glass, and for a moment she felt unable to breathe. How wonderful it would have been if that had truly been the case, so that she could have died too. But instead she was still alive and, worse, was now truly alone.

In the end, Henry had followed his damned love of fighting – even then when, after so much war, peace had finally arrived. His violent, brooding character had taken him away from her, forever. How many times had she asked him not to take part in the joust? If he didn't want to forgo it for her, he could at least have done so for his children. But it had all been in vain. Not even Diane had managed to talk him out of it.

Catherine was afraid and felt a torment tearing at her, because Henry had been snatched away from her once again. Just when they were becoming closer, just when she seemed to have finally rid herself of the Duchess of Valentinois.

What would become of her, she wondered. And of her children. Of Francis, who was barely able to look after himself? Of Charles, who was always sick and who cried so often? How could she explain what had happened to Margaret? And to Henry? Elisabeth? Claude? She sighed. At least Elisabeth and Claude had their husbands.

Catherine feared for her sons: they were the most fragile, and they were expected to rule France. Above all, she feared for Francis. How would he manage? He was only a boy, and in addition he was physically weakened by a disease that consumed him day after day.

She knelt at the foot of the bed, unable to bring herself to look at her husband's face disfigured by that horrible wound. She wanted to remember him as he had been: handsome, strong, a warrior god.

She trembled at the thought of the hatreds and power struggles which would now be unleashed. For all that time the strange equilibrium between her, Diane and Henry had managed to contain the centrifugal forces of those who fanned the flames of violence and hatred and wanted to destroy the country. There had been wars, of course, but only against the enemies of France, and Henry had succeeded in that difficult task with the help of the obscure pact of blood and shame between her and the Duchess of Valentinois.

But for some time now, after the advent of Mary Stuart, the Guises had been increasing their sphere of influence. Henry's forbidden love for that foolish Scottish damsel had injured Diane, and at first Catherine had enjoyed seeing it happen. The idea that the king's favourite was finally suffering the humiliations she herself had been forced to endure for so many years was almost an unexpected reward.

And then the miracle happened. Henry left Diane of Poitiers and returned to her. He had done it silently, and she had welcomed him with all her heart, because she had always loved him, had never for an instant stopped loving him in all that time. And when she had held him in her arms on that golden spring morning a year earlier, she had scarcely been able to believe her good fortune.

It was the most beautiful memory – a gem she kept in the deepest, most secret part of her heart, and she would continue to cradle there that final gift Henry had given her. If nothing else, it would at least help her temper her regret, which was so profound that it threatened to overwhelm her.

While she knelt there, though, she realized she could not go on like that. She must act.

She would be strong: for Henry, for her children and for herself. She had suffered for so long the harassment and abuses of Diane, and now she had no intention of giving in to the arrogance of a child like Mary Stuart, or to the rapaciousness of the Guises. One way or another, she would manage it. She had Nostradamus, and she had Raymond de Polignac, and that was already much more than she might have hoped.

And furthermore, she was a Medici.

She would rule. Like Lorenzo the Magnificent. Like Cosimo the Elder. She would fight to save her country, which was France, and to honour the memory of her husband and of the great king Francis I.

It was the least she could do.

But there was something she needed to deal with first. For four years, she had been fantasizing about the moment she was about to actually experience, and now she would not hesitate. It would be the beginning of a new period of her life.

As her tears fell copiously, Catherine clenched her jaw until her teeth hurt.

She would fight, she repeated to herself. Until the end.

40

Chenonceau

It was a marvellous day.

From the windows of the castle, Catherine looked out at the river Cher and the splendid, magnificent bridge with its arched foundations that crossed the clear, crystalline waters as they flowed slowly by beneath the summer sun.

Catherine loved this place so much. It made her feel at peace with herself and with her demons, because nature was a better balm for her wounded heart than anything else.

Unlike other queens, she had decided to wear black for her mourning. In France, white was traditional, but she believed that the colour of the night and of darkness – like the darkness that dwelt in her soul and, day by day, devoured her heart – was more suitable.

The sun illuminated the room, and Catherine wondered if Philibert Delorme, the architect who had designed that wonderful castle, had ever seen Venice.

He must have been acquainted with the Most Serene Republic to have so masterfully exploited the effects of transparency and the play of light produced by the reflections on the water in the construction of the staircase which led up to the various floors of the castle. That idea of a central building with a staircase on its side was clearly of Venetian inspiration, and it was for that reason that Catherine loved the castle more than any other – it reminded her of her beloved Italy.

At the door to the gallery, a large French window captured the glimmer on the Cher, and Catherine revelled in the view of the river.

She was standing in the centre of the room when she heard the sound of footsteps on the stairs. That was when she saw Diane.

How old she looked, Catherine thought. The skin of her arms was now greyish and revealed her age without pity. Diane wore a long dress of Neapolitan silk whose bright red tones highlighted her physical decay even more, and her sagging face, painted white with vaguely rouged cheeks, was a parody of vanished beauty: a pathetic memory of a past which was dead and buried.

Catherine felt sorry for her as, still elegant but less splendid, less haughty and less confident than usual, she advanced.

When she was before her, Diane suddenly dropped to her knees and burst into floods of uncontrollable tears then threw herself at Catherine's feet.

'Have pity, *Madame la Reine*,' she said. Who knew how much those words must have cost her – she who had never had to beg, she who had always and only given orders? She, so scornful and brazen, was now asking for mercy.

Catherine didn't help her get up. In her desperation she finally saw the weakness of her old rival, the profound fragility she had been hiding for all that time. She had no need to indulge in some squalid revenge, but nor would it, she thought, be fair to show mercy now to those who had never shown it themselves. She would treat her with indifference, so as not to allow herself to be influenced by those appeals which arrived too late, only after all was lost.

'You must leave,' said the queen in a voice as cold as a knife blade. 'You will give the castle of Chenonceau back to me, as it is the property of the crown. It was reckless of my husband Henry to give it to you, but the gift has no value, certainly not in my eyes. Be grateful to God that I grant you six months to gather your belongings and leave.'

'And where will I go?' asked Diane between sobs, her face resembling that of a capricious and distraught child.

'I am not a woman without pity. Unlike you, who

are so ready to ask today when you have never given so much as a crumb in your whole life. Beauty fades over time, Diane, and eventually vanishes altogether. If you have never been beautiful, as I have never been, you gain an advantage with the passing of the years. Now you and I are identical: equally insignificant in the eyes of men because of an attractiveness we do not possess. But you are the past, and I the future of this state.'

Catherine sighed, as if speaking were a struggle. She realized that there was much truth in what she said, and was surprised she had managed to express her feelings so sincerely. It was as if Diane were, after all, her mirror – the reflection of what she would one day become: a woman dull and desperate, and no longer young.

'You will have Chaumont-sur-Loire instead of Chenonceau, I promise you it. I am firm in my purpose, but not without mercy. I could simply banish you from the kingdom of France and deny you any roof or shelter, but I shall not because I believe that when one triumphs, one must at least triumph gracefully. I have waited, Diane, I have waited for such an infernally long time. I swallowed the poison you administered to me every day of my life. And I hated you.' Catherine let the word ring in the air, illuminated by the blinding reflections of the sun's rays. 'But today, in this magnificent castle, I have realized that life is too short to be wasted upon hatred and resentment.'

Diane looked up, her swollen face devastated by tears

and exhaustion. 'So do I have your pardon, *Madame la Reine*, for all I have done to you?' she asked in a faint voice.

'You will never have my pardon.' Catherine turned away from her as if that request had been a slap to the face. 'The memory of the pain you have caused me is too strong to be silenced with a pardon. Do you remember when you sent Henry to my bed to keep me pregnant so you could keep me out of the way and prevent me from sticking my nose into politics? What was that expression you used? One of my spies reported it to me... "She must become like a baker's oven," you said. You had forgotten, hadn't you? Or when you begged the king to repudiate me because I was nothing more than an Italian merchant's daughter, and as sterile as a desert to boot? Must I go on? I have had more than my fill of pain, Diane, and all because of you! I loved Henry, even though I knew he was completely indifferent to me because he loved you. How can I explain to you how that felt? Have you ever had a wound that never ceases to bleed? Have you ever felt your heart turn to glass and shatter beneath the fist of a cruel woman who glares at you triumphantly as she does it? Is there anything more terrible? If there is, tell me, because I cannot imagine it. And when finally Henry was coming back to me, when he was finally tired of seeking happiness far away, that damn joust took him away from me for ever.'

Catherine stopped, and she too wept.

'If I don't have you killed today,' she concluded, 'it is only because I have finally decided that I want to live. Did you hear me, Diane? Live! Live after having died for twenty years, I want to live after seeing those I loved more than myself die. So don't you dare ask for my forgiveness now because, as God is my witness, you will never have it!'

Catherine watched as Diane staggered to her feet, stunned by those words which had thrown in her face all her evil and all the suffering her acts of power and domination had inflicted.

Overcome by anguish, she leant with both hands on a table then, with difficulty, sat down in an armchair. She tried to speak, but seemed unable to find words to justify herself. Perhaps such words did not exist. Catherine stared at her, the fierceness of her glare seeming almost able to incinerate the Duchess of Valentinois.

'Catherine, I know I have caused you a great deal of pain, and I know too that there is nothing I can say to alleviate that pain, because it is now too late. I wish only to tell you that I am sorry, from the bottom of my heart. And that I am grateful to you for the generosity you show. I don't know if I could have done the same.'

'If nothing else, age seems to have given your words a hint of sincerity. You know very well who you have been, Diane, and there is certainly no need for me to remind you. But I believe that you no longer have any power. Our enemies are pressing in upon us now, and new adversaries seek to do what you yourself sought to do until not so long ago. But I will not allow it. Never again. I have children to protect, children whom I love more than life itself. Do you have any idea what a mother's love is, Diane?'

The Duchess of Valentinois fell silent for a moment, then said, 'I belong to that category of people who are able only to love a single person. Even if I had wanted to, I could not have loved a child because of what I felt for Henry. I know that I should not have, but you, Catherine, must always remember that you came later! After I had put Henry back on his feet, after I had heard his stories of torment upon torment, after I had made him into a man. And all that torment, all that misery, all those nights of weeping when he screamed loud enough to tear his vocal cords, was I supposed to leave him to you? How would you have felt, in my place? Defrauded? Mocked? Do you have any idea of what I have been through? What I have faced for becoming a warrior in a world where a woman can only be a mother, a queen, a wife? And I was none of those!'

'That is why I take pity on you, Diane. But I will never forgive you.' Catherine looked at her one last time. 'Remember – six months from now. Then I want you in Chaumont-sur-Loire.'

And so saying, Catherine left the room.

She went down the stairs, the sunlight blazing in through the windows which overlooked the river.

When she reached the bottom of the staircase she emerged into the courtyard and looked at the clear water, the forest, the old medieval tower of the Marques. The garden on the left bank of the Cher glowed bright green in the July heat.

The sun almost blinded her as she stood there marvelling at the wonders of nature, and she fed upon it, fantasizing about what she had in mind. She would have a long building erected on the bridge: two floors of windows and dormers and a marvellous hall spanning the entire river. Throbbing with life, it would become the heart of the castle, a place for magnificent balls and receptions from which the guests could admire the reflections on the waters of the Cher.

Just as she was admiring them in that moment.

JANUARY 1560

41

Francis II of France

'You see for yourself, Your Majesty, how busy the queen mother is with other matters.'

Francis seemed not to comprehend.

'Speak more clearly, Duke. I do not understand what you are implying.'

'Your Majesty,' observed Francis of Guise with a broad smile, 'what I mean is that, while France becomes a den of reformers, enemies of the crown and of the true faith, your mother goes around with an old soldier, speaking with astrologers and soothsayers, and consigning her soul to the devil.'

'Mind how you speak, *monsieur*. Do not dare make insinuations against my mother...'

'Of course, Your Majesty – it was not my intention to insinuate anything,' replied Guise immediately. 'Indeed,

I am certain that your mother is a woman of untarnished faith. But it is also clear to me that this continuous wandering of hers brings with it no particular benefit for the kingdom. You must take the reins of France and you must do so by punishing the infidels. When all the Protestants have been eliminated, your kingdom will be even greater than it is now.'

Francis sighed. He glanced over at Mary, who returned his gaze, and saw in her eyes firmness and determination – and trust in the Duke of Guise. Francis turned to look out of the window at the Swiss guards in the courtyard of the Louvre.

Once again, he was feeling unwell that day. His illness gave him no respite.

'Majesty,' began Guise, 'aside from the question of your mother, those who worry me most are Antoine of Navarre and his brother Louis, Prince of Condé. They claim to have rights to the crown of France.'

'Of course, but if we had tried to listen to their requests instead of humiliating them... A thousand *écu*! Is not that a miserly amount to pay a prince of the blood to travel to Ghent to sign a peace treaty with an emperor? I warned you that it was a mistake. I know for certain that Condé had to pawn all his possessions to make himself presentable. It is difficult to imagine that he would be on our side now.'

Francis of Guise seemed surprised by the perspicacity of the observation.

'Not to mention,' the king continued, 'that the comment he made in parliament some time ago about the complete inopportuneness of the agreement which would have allowed us to call ourselves sovereigns of France, Scotland and England was far from foolish.'

Upon hearing those words, Mary Stuart seemed to lose patience. 'Francis, what are you saying? As Queen of Scotland I have legitimate rights to the throne of England, especially as Elizabeth is the daughter of a marriage invalidated by Henry VIII himself, since Anne Boleyn was certainly not born a noblewoman!'

'Mary, please…' said the king.

'But neither is that the point, Majesty,' interrupted the Duke of Guise. 'You are right, of course. We made mistakes. But now the Bourbons are crossing the line. Our spies report that they have commissioned a certain La Renaudie, who was declared a forger by the Dijon parliament, to raise an army against Your Majesty in the name of Calvin. What I am trying to tell you is that the Protestant threat must be stopped. They are growing stronger, and there is no limit to what they are capable of doing. It is for this reason that I recommend moving the court to the Château de Blois immediately.'

'Whatever for?' asked the king.

'Because Paris is not safe, Your Highness,' replied Guise, pointing to Mary. 'Not for you and not for the queen. Blois is easier to defend and will allow us protection in the event of attacks by the Bourbons.

What we believed was an empty threat is fast becoming a certainty. The Prince of Condé trusts that Your Highness is in the dark about everything, but this is not the case. And it is for this reason that I suggest moving the court to Blois.'

'But if we do that, they will think we're afraid of them.'

'All the better. We will have the advantage over them.'

The king held up his hands in resignation. 'If you believe that is the only solution...'

'It is certainly the wisest,' concluded Guise.

The Prince of Condé looked at his brother.

'Don't you understand, Antoine? It's now or never! The Guises don't expect to be attacked now, and if we continue to hesitate, all will be lost.'

'Do you think so? You do realize the consequences?'

'Of course I do! But I have no intention of pulling out at the last minute. The Guises want to exterminate all those who follow the Protestant faith, and that cannot be allowed to happen. We must strike, and strike first. The king is a fool – his mother has remained too far from power for too long, and the queen is no more than a girl. What more do you need to move against the Guises? It is they who are the true rulers of France today.'

Antoine frowned at his brother's bellicosity. What

the hell was the matter with the man? Why couldn't he just enjoy the gold his marriage had given him? Why fret so about these plans to conquer the crown? Antoine shook his head. It was as though Louis were trying to involve him in that suicidal rebellion for the sole purpose of ruining his life. Yes, it was true that he was not a particularly committed Catholic, but setting out to take on the Guises at the time was pure madness.

'Do you know that Emperor Philip II supports the Guises proceeding with a complete purge? Do you have any idea what that means? Do you really believe that small groups of peasants, whose only crime is that of following the Calvinist faith, can hold off the armies of France and Spain? If you do, you are completely out of your mind, my brother!'

Antoine wiped the sweat from his brow with the palm of his hand, got to his feet and strode across the hall.

The Prince of Condé, however, had no intention of giving up.

'How can you say such a thing? Coligny is with us as long as we decide to participate in the revolt, legitimizing it as descendants of the Capetians. The presence of a royal family will make the reformist position that much stronger. Aside from anything else, its aim is not to attack the king, but to capture and kill the Guises. Catherine de' Medici is a woman of great intelligence and fairness. I say let us go and take what we deserve! Do you find that so absurd? I certainly do not.'

'Louis,' snapped Antoine. All this talk of war had made his brother lose his head. 'Haven't you heard what happened to Montmorency? The Guises had mercenaries and soldiers invade his lands, and he was forced to take up arms to drive them out of Dammartin! Are we so certain that we want to change the course of history that we are willing to risk our lives for it? Because I don't believe we are for a moment. And in any case, it's not true that Coligny is on our side. You hope that he is, but that is not the case at all: I have heard with my own ears that he is against any military action.' He sighed. All he wanted was to enjoy life, woo the ladies and spend his money – which, luckily for him, he had in abundance. Was that too much to ask? Why the hell should he become a paladin? He had no intention of doing it! But Louis was like a man possessed and spoke of nothing else.

'La Renaudie has organized a meeting with the leaders of the uprising for the first of February in Nantes. They will all be there: Bouchard d'Aubeterre, Captain Mazères, Charles of Castelnau-Chalosse, Captain Lignières, Jean d'Aubigné… We cannot miss it,' he concluded, pulling his velvet doublet tight around himself.

Antoine was not persuaded. 'I think you are wrong. I'm not saying it's not worth trying, but not now and not in this way. The Guises are too powerful, and I would not rule out their already having a counter-plan. We'll end up getting slaughtered, and for what? To become the leaders of a revolt that is doomed to fail? Know that I will support you against my will and only because you are my brother. And as for the rest of it, I remain unconvinced. It is true that I have much more to lose than you do, and this holds me back…'

'You can say that again, since you are King of Navarre!'

'I certainly am! Do you blame me for it?'

'Absolutely not! But I do not believe that fear is the solution. Of course, I can understand that all this' – Louis gestured to the splendid tapestries, the imposing wrought-iron chandeliers and the fine furniture – 'is an excellent reason for being afraid, but I had hoped that for once you might want to obtain something for yourself without having it given to you.'

Antoine stared at his brother in exasperation.

'I don't understand this sudden love of war of yours. I know you've had to tighten your belt and that it hasn't been easy to be Prince of Condé without a penny to your name. If it's a question of money…'

'Money has nothing to do with it, Antoine!' said Louis, slamming his fist down on the table. 'Do you really not understand? The money comes directly from Queen Elizabeth, whose royal rights are contested by that silly Scottish girl. It is not a question of money or securities or land, it is a question of freedom. A question of inalienable principles, like the choice of a religion. There is much more than money in play!'

'Freedom, you say?' murmured Antoine doubtfully. 'Well let's just hope it doesn't end up getting us hanged.'

42

Chaumont-sur-Loire

S he had come to Chaumont.

The great winter had arrived, covering everything with frost and snow, and the dead brown trees that stood out against the leaden sky like ghosts, the dark roofs of the pointed towers and the sharp battlements of the walls made her feel lost. The air was bitterly cold.

She saw the helmets of the guards gleaming in the last rays of the dying sun as the large portcullis rose loudly. Chaumont had a cursed story behind it: just a hundred years earlier, Louis XI had set it on fire and razed it to the ground to punish Pierre d'Amboise for daring to join the League of the Public Weal and rising up against his sovereign together with several other noble rebels.

It was, thought Catherine, the perfect place for Michel de Nostredame, who was currently its lord.

In truth, the arrangement would last only a short time because Diane would soon be taking over the castle, but Catherine already had the perfect solution in mind for her court astrologer.

As her carriage entered the courtyard, she looked at Polignac. Throughout the entire journey, he had never ceased to fiddle with the blade of the dagger he held in his hands. Catherine had not commented upon it because she knew how nervous he was. Nostradamus had that effect on him. It was as if the soldier could sense the astrologer's aura from a distance.

For his part, Polignac was careful to say nothing, firstly because he knew how much faith Catherine put in the prophecies of Michel de Nostredame, and secondly because he knew that the visions and knowledge of that mysterious man were unfathomable to him.

Henry's death had left a tremendous void, and Polignac could not forgive himself for having entrusted the task of protecting him to the man who had killed him. At first he had been tempted to believe that Montgomery had done it on purpose, but it was Henry himself who, as he lay dying, had exonerated the man, reaffirming his innocence in a quiet voice. Not to mention that, during the examination of the corpse, Ambroise Paré had discovered a lump of blood and yellowish matter an inch wide – the beginning of a corruption which would

have been more than enough to determine the death of
the king in any case.

However, Catherine had banished the captain of the
Scottish guard from the kingdom of France. He was
the second Scot to be banished in a short time, following
in the footsteps of Elizabeth MacGregor, but it hadn't
helped. Or at least, it hadn't helped alleviate the guilt of
Raymond de Polignac, who for months now had been
struggling with his failure to prevent the king from
taking the field in that joust.

As Catherine climbed the staircase leading up to
the main hall of the castle, a flock of crows soared
overhead.

She hoped it wasn't a bad omen. Nothing was going
as he wished.

While she was talking to the astrologer, Polignac
would wait in another room, as was his habit. Meeting
Nostredame too often unnerved him.

When Catherine entered the large tapestry-covered
room, the central fireplace was lit, filling the air with
a welcome warmth. The flames burned red and sparks
flew from the crackling logs.

Nostradamus awaited her as usual. For thirty
days and thirty nights he had been preparing for that
meeting.

He gave her one of his evasive looks, his eyes like a
blade flashing with disturbing light. It seemed almost
that his pupils floated in some feverish liquid.

'*Madame la Reine*,' he said in that deep, mesmerizing voice of his, 'please do not be afraid. Approach the fireplace and look in the mirror.'

It was only then that Catherine realized Nostradamus had placed a mirror with blood-red corners directly above the beam of wood which formed the fireplace's mantelpiece.

Looking around her, she noticed that the great astrologer had drawn upon the floor a double concentric circle in white chalk.

'Continue to look into the mirror, *Madame la Reine*,' said Nostradamus.

Blushing like a little girl caught being disobedient, Catherine did as she was told.

Nostradamus began to intone one of his weird litanies, invoking spirits and devils to help him see into the future. The candles all around flickered until suddenly the flames in the fireplace flared up, almost as if the astrologer's words had summoned some arcane force. Catherine felt their heat fill her as though fire were running through her veins, and while she was overcome by that indescribable feeling, she saw something in the mirror.

Her son Francis appeared to her. Catherine raised a hand to her mouth, stifling a cry, but something prevented her from moving away from the vision.

Francis was in a large room which was not one at Chaumont, though Catherine could not have said where it was. Large chandeliers hung from the ceiling, and magnificent tapestries and finely carved wooden furniture certified its opulence. But the scene was slightly blurred, as though flames had partially devoured the details.

Francis walked a circuit of the entire room and then disappeared.

Catherine forced herself to remain silent.

As Nostradamus continued in his invocations, the queen saw another young man appear on the surface of the mirror: it was Charles – her son Charles.

She felt her emotions surge inside her, so powerfully that they were almost overwhelming, and watched while Charles made fifteen circuits of the room before he too disappeared.

Now it was Henry's turn. He was still small, and with his long, sharp face, melancholy eyes and somewhat dreamy expression, he looked younger than he actually was. He too began to walk around the room, completing sixteen circuits before disappearing.

Finally another boy appeared. But he was not one of her sons. After a moment's hesitation, Catherine recognized him. She had seen him playing with her daughter Margaret some time ago.

It was Henry, the son of the Queen of Navarre.

Catherine felt as if she were about to lose her reason.

The boy walked around the room twenty-one times.

The queen cried out and then slumped into a chair.

'*Madame la Reine*, be not afraid,' said Nostradamus. 'What you have seen is only the future.'

Catherine could barely speak. She was afraid that she understood what the vision meant.

'My children...' she said in a low voice.

'They will reign over France,' said Nostradamus, completing her words for her.

'But...'

'Each for as many years as they made circuits of the room in your vision.'

Catherine's face filled with terror. 'Francis...'

'Unfortunately he will soon die, Your Majesty. There is nothing that torments me more than this knowledge.'

Catherine trembled almost as if the armchair might swallow her up, and her nails scratched at the damask. She felt as if she were suffocating. 'Water!' she cried out in a choked voice.

Nostradamus handed her a full goblet.

'Drink, *Madame la Reine*.'

The doors to the salon swung open, the movement of air making the flames in the hearth flicker.

Raymond de Polignac burst in. Despite the years that had passed, he was still tall and imposing.

'You!' he thundered, pointing to the astrologer. 'If you have done anything to the queen, you are a dead man, mark my word! I found you and I will destroy you with my own two hands.'

Nostradamus shook his head then raised a hand to his eyes, seeming to repress a half smile.

Before Catherine had time to speak, Polignac had already drawn his sword.

'You are a true paladin, *monsieur*,' said Nostradamus mockingly. 'But unfortunately I have no power over my visions. Either way, Her Majesty has nothing to fear, neither now nor ever. And certainly not from me.'

'Not another word, or as God is my witness you will find this in your throat,' said Polignac, as the blade glittered in the firelight.

'Put the sword away, Monsieur de Polignac,' said Catherine, recovering her calm. 'It wouldn't help.'

Michel de Nostredame nodded almost imperceptibly. 'Very true, *Madame la Reine*.'

'Tell me,' said Catherine to her court astrologer, 'is there a way to prevent what I saw from happening?'

Nostradamus sighed.

'I confess, Majesty, that if it exists, I am unaware of it.'

'Majesty,' interjected Polignac, 'I will find a way. I will find it for you.'

'Just as you managed to prevent the death of His Majesty?'

Nostradamus had failed to hold back that cruel remark. It was, though, the truth.

'*Mort-Dieu!*' snapped an outraged Polignac. 'Believe

me when I tell you that I will have your heart, you damn charlatan!'

'Monsieur de Polignac!' exclaimed the queen. 'I understand your anguish. You cannot imagine how much I blame myself every day for what happened. Unfortunately, however, though there is nothing that causes me greater pain, reality reminds us of how the events unfolded. I will atone for it by living, and so will you. If you wish to try to prevent the facts prophesied by Monsieur de Nostredame from coming to pass, you have my blessing. It would mean saving my children.' She spoke almost angrily. 'But I will not let you touch this man, whose science is at least able to warn us of what awaits us.' And so saying Catherine leapt to her feet with great agility, shielding Michel de Nostredame with her own body.

Polignac's eyes widened and he shook his head in disbelief.

'Very well, Your Majesty. I shall do as you say.'

And without another word he left the room, his spurs rattling.

'Tell me what to do,' murmured Catherine, turning to face the astrologer with tears in her eyes. But she was not comforted by what she saw.

'Your Majesty...' he murmured. 'Your Majesty...'

'What?'

'*Madame la Reine*... I wish I could help you. But I do not possess the power to bend the lines of destiny to my will. Your children will reign, but in the end the Valois will lose the throne of France to Henry of Navarre.'

Catherine felt the words tear at her. She would almost have preferred to die in that moment.

'It can't be,' she whispered in a low voice. 'It's not true,' she repeated, and she began to beat at Nostradamus's chest with her fists while tears as large as coins streaked down her cheeks.

Nostradamus spread his arms, and his long black kaftan opened as if it were the cloak of the night sky. He let Catherine hit him until she was too exhausted to continue.

'*Madame la Reine*,' he said finally, 'perhaps there is one who can prevent those deaths.'

'Who?' asked Catherine, still sobbing, her tears filling her eyes and reddening her face. 'Who? *Speak*.'

Nostradamus seemed to hesitate for a moment.

'Monsieur Raymond de Polignac.'

The queen felt her tears stop and her sobs subside.

'Really?' she asked.

'I think so. He is a brave man and he is also... in love. And the power of love should never be underestimated.'

Catherine could scarcely believe her ears.

'Do you say so?' she asked, her voice filled with a sudden sweetness.

'Without any doubt.'

'And with whom is he in love?'

'I think you know that very well, Your Majesty.'

Catherine seemed afraid of pronouncing the next words.

'With me?'

'With you, *Madame la Reine*.'

FEBRUARY 1560

43

Blois

'Are you sure of what you say?' asked Catherine.

The Cardinal of Lorraine sighed. He looked at her, and then at Mary Stuart, and finally at the king. He had been preparing what he was about to say for a long time, and he wanted it to be perfect. It must be convincing, so he must leave nothing out.

He let his eyes linger on the flickering flames of the fireplace then raised his hand to his face to simulate deep dismay, and only then did he speak.

'I am sorry to inform Your Majesties only now, but until this morning we had not managed to procure a complete picture of the gravity of the situation. My brother, the Duke of Guise, prudently requested that the king move the court to Blois, and so it was. But the Protestants have not wasted their time over the past month.'

'Come to the point, Monseigneur,' said Catherine.

'Certainly. That Godefroy de Barry, lord of La Renaudie and gentleman of Périgord, was gathering men for a *coup d'état* against Your Majesties, in an attempt to impose the Protestant faith on France, was known. In recent times we have had confirmations in this regard from the Bishop of Arras. But just yesterday I was given this letter.' The Cardinal of Lorraine held out two sheets of parchment paper covered with elegant handwriting which was all flourishes and arabesques.

'Read it, Cardinal,' said Catherine, who had no great affection for Charles of Lorraine, a man deeply enamoured of power and money. And yet she had to recognize his pragmatism and brilliance in successfully making the large spending cuts which had replenished the empty coffers of her state.

It had been no small feat.

'Of course, Your Majesty. So,' and the cardinal read without further delay. '"To His Most Excellent Eminence, Cardinal Charles of Lorraine. Monsignor, my name is Pierre d'Avenelle, a lawyer by profession. I practise in the city of Paris and I am writing to you with a heavy heart because of what I learned today from an acquaintance of mine, Jean Godefroy de Barry, lord of La Renaudie. The latter was in my home for reasons that are of no relevance here, but be that as it may he was boasting of one of his great endeavours which had as its ultimate aim the kidnapping of His Majesty the King of France, as well as the arrest of you and your brother Francis, the Duke of Guise. In this regard, the lord of La Renaudie also mentioned that he had enlisted a large number of armies from Gascony, Brittany and Normandy. Little by little he'd had these troops converge near Tours and had ordered the leaders to that city. He bragged – most foolishly, I must say – that he had given them the name of Huguenots for his having assembled them in an inn near the gate of Hugon."'

'Is that so?' exclaimed the stunned king, who was now red in the face. 'Well we will show those worms!'

The Cardinal of Lorraine, however, had not finished.

'Your Eminence,' said Catherine, realizing immediately that there was more, 'please read the rest of the letter.'

'Thank you, Your Majesty. So, where was I? Ah yes, here it is: "…given them the name of Huguenots for his having assembled them in an inn near the gate of Hugon. Upon hearing this, I thought it might be useful to know more, so I helped loosen La Renaudie's tongue even further by offering him a few glasses of good cognac. This turned out to be an excellent idea, as in short order La Renaudie confessed to me, with the now rheumy eye of the drunk, that behind this monstrous machination there is none other than Antoine of Bourbon, count of

Vendôme and King of Navarre, and his brother Louis of Bourbon, Prince of Condé, and that they found the means to organize this criminal enterprise thanks to the money provided them by the crown of England in the person of Queen Elizabeth."'

'The bastard who sits on the throne without having any right to do so!' spat Mary Stuart venomously.

'Your Highness, please,' said the Cardinal of Lorraine, who did not like being interrupted, much less twice in a row. 'Where was I? Ah yes, here: "... in the person of Queen Elizabeth. When he took his leave, La Renaudie was also vocal about the intention of him and his family to attack Blois and to take Your Highness and the king completely by surprise. I am sure that you will manage to prepare defence measures to avoid disaster. I remain your most faithful servant, please accept my most sincere..." etc. etc.,' concluded the cardinal.

'Well, Your Eminence? What are your recommendations?' asked Catherine. 'Because it is clear that the situation is far more serious than we had imagined, and I think that the aims of this plot far exceed the action we took against the reformers. The edicts signed by the king exacerbated the mood, and hanging Anne du Bourg in Place de Grève was probably a mistake. I think now that it would have been wiser to show some mercy.'

'But what else could we have done?' asked the king,

speaking the words as if they had been fed to him by the cardinal himself. 'We couldn't allow those fools to scoff at the Catholic faith.'

Catherine realized that she had allowed the Guises to take the initiative too much. And yet they were her allies in that moment, not to mention that anyone was better than the Bourbons, who were guilty of having given birth to the one who, in Michel de Nostredame's mirror, eventually supplanted the Valois and placed the crown upon his own head.

'The king is right, Your Majesty,' confirmed the Cardinal of Lorraine. 'Saving Anne du Bourg would have been an unforgivable mistake. We cannot afford to leave ourselves open to these *Huguenots*,' said the cardinal, pronouncing the word as if it were the worst slur in the world, 'or whatever it is they wish to be called.'

Mary Stuart nodded with adoring eyes. Catherine couldn't bear watching the stupid little girl playing at queen and leading Francis by the nose just as Diane had done with Henry. She might be his wife, but the influence she exercised over him was atrocious, and worse still, she hung from the lips of the Guises, who had been responsible for her ascent to the throne of France in order to use her as a pawn against Catherine.

With his elegant face, almost feline eyes and ineffable expression, the Cardinal of Lorraine knew how to turn the arguments in his favour. If nothing else, Catherine was happy to have him on her side instead of among her enemies.

'While we are here, my brother is scouring the woods around Blois. I can tell you that he has already confessed to me...'

The cardinal stopped.

The Duke of Guise entered the hall. He was clad in an elegant doublet and an equally refined jacket with the breastplate of his armour and wore high, mud-stained boots. He took off his feathered hat and made a bow for the benefit of the king and queens.

'Your Majesty,' he said to Francis, adding, as he turned to Mary and Catherine, 'Your Highness, *Madame la Reine*. I do not bring good news.' His words seemed suddenly to shroud the beautiful room with frost. He nodded to his brother, the cardinal. 'The problem, as His Eminence was probably explaining to you, is that the Château de Blois does not lend itself to an easy defence.'

'Is this truly the way things are, then?' asked Catherine incredulously. 'Must we really consider the actual possibility of a siege?'

'We certainly must, Your Highness.'

'And what do you suggest?' asked the king.

'To immediately transfer the court to Amboise.'

'May I ask you why?' Catherine urged him.

'It is soon said. Amboise is in a better position and

is easier to defend. The château overlooks the Loire. On that side, therefore, there is no problem. And it was conceived as a fortress, not a simple residence as Blois is.'

'There are the woods, though...' Mary said, not without hesitation. The news seemed to have terrified her.

The cardinal nodded.

'You are right, Your Highness,' confirmed the Duke of Guise, 'but a forest will not prevent us from maintaining control of the situation. We will patrol it day and night, if necessary. The reformists do not expect to be expected. Isn't that right, Eminence?'

'It certainly is,' confirmed Charles of Lorraine, glancing at his brother. 'I was just informing Their Majesties of the gravity of the situation, but also of the fresh news we received in that providential letter from the worthy Pierre d'Avenelle.'

'Very well,' said the Duke of Guise. 'Then you already have the complete picture.'

'Thank you, Cardinal,' concluded Catherine pragmatically. 'I congratulate you on your work.'

Charles of Lorraine bowed his head with an expression that might almost have been mistaken for humility.

'And I thank you for your insight, Monsieur Duke,' added the queen mother. 'At this point, all we can do is move to Amboise.'

'Without wasting another moment, Your Majesty,' said the cardinal.

And as he said those words, Catherine was certain that she saw a glint of amusement in his eyes.

44

Instructions for a Conspiracy

Louis of Condé could not stop fiddling with the hilt of his sword. Leaning on a chair, he was as bony as a dead tree, with short dark hair, a thin moustache and a hawk-like face: hunchbacked and awkward as he was, in that belligerent pose he might easily have been mistaken for a gargoyle – one of the strange creatures carved upon the facade of Notre-Dame.

Nearby, his brother was drinking a goblet of wine.

With his red hair, unkempt beard and glittering earrings, Antoine of Navarre seemed to be attempting to flaunt the insouciance of better days, but in his heart he was terrified. That conspiracy was a perfect way of committing suicide, he was sure of it. La Renaudie was blinded by ambition, and that idea of his of dividing France into cantons like Calvin's Switzerland was pure madness, yet he kept repeating it as if it were actually a viable proposition. Why on earth had he and his brother allied themselves with him?

The other members of the company undertaking the venture seemed to have supreme confidence in that madman's ideas, but Navarre trembled with a fear that he sought to quell by drowning it in wine.

They were all standing around a table in a shabby inn in Souvigny-de-Touraine, a lousy village that reeked of dung and bad wine. La Renaudie had called a final meeting to decide upon the details and had demanded that he and his brother be there.

The latest news said that Coligny had pulled out of the business. And he had done well, thought Antoine. At least one of them had a head on his shoulders. He instead was there listening to the arrant nonsense La Renaudie was spouting.

'We will defeat the Guises and bring them to justice,' he promised. 'And we will have them convicted of the crime of *lèse-majesté*, usurpation of power and embezzlement of the court treasury.' Such was his expertise at ascribing crimes to the Guises that La Renaudie sounded as if he were drafting a criminal ordinance. 'I want them at my feet, *Mort-Dieu*. They don't expect to be attacked right where they are holing up.'

'I assure you they are well prepared,' observed the Prince of Condé. 'They withdrew to Amboise precisely because they are confident of having better defences there. With the Loire behind and the fortified city in front, it will be no simple thing to take them.'

'True,' said Antoine of Bourbon, without having the faintest idea of what else to add.

'Nonsense,' said Jean d'Aubigné. He was a thin but robust man with blond hair that hung down straight as straw, a thin nose, hooked like an eagle's beak, and two green eyes that darted about restlessly. He pulled anxiously at the pointed goatee which gave him an even more ribald air. 'Not only do we have with us men from Provence, Normandy, Brittany and Gascony, but also Dutch and Lutherans hired in Württemberg. Our ranks are growing – many brothers intend to oppose the excessive power of the Guises.'

'Nobody says otherwise,' replied the hunchback, 'only allow me to recommend caution. The Duke of Guise is the hero of Calais – he who resisted Charles V's imperial troops in Metz and broke his siege. He is not a man to be taken lightly. As for his brother, the Cardinal of Lorraine, it is pointless for me to warn you about his skills as a politician. Not to mention that his network of spies is far vaster than you can imagine.'

La Renaudie shrugged. He looked calm, and his regular face with its strong jaw was the quintessence of confidence. 'We will surprise them in Amboise,' he said. 'However careful and dangerous they might be, the Guises are certainly not expecting an attack. Instead, we will launch a grand offensive and take the city unprepared. I have many men available and ready to fight in the name of Calvin and the principles of the one true faith. We will soon obtain a great victory and put a legitimate king on the throne of France – not a usurper who rules by means of a puppet!'

La Renaudie pontificated as if he were a god, and Jean d'Aubigné was with him. Condé glared at him, but then he glared at almost everyone, even his friends.

Antoine of Navarre avoided meeting the gaze of his fellows and poured himself more wine, which he drank disgustedly.

Admiral Gaspard de Coligny took off his black velvet cap. His doublet too was black, as were his breeches and high boots. His glaucous eyes, though, were pale as fragments of the heavens. Upon seeing the queen mother, he bowed deeply. Catherine had sent for him because she knew the situation was desperate. While his brother François had begun to wall up the entrances to the city and strengthen its defences, Charles, Cardinal of Lorraine, clad in his purple robe, did nothing to hide his fears. He knew that the edict issued by Henry II had exacerbated the mood, and for this reason wanted to know, just like Catherine, what Coligny – who made no secret of his sympathies for the Calvinist faith – had to say.

A little further away, almost in a corner, the young

king also listened attentively, even though he was not at that moment feeling particularly well. He remained curled up in an armchair, ready to take whatever advice Coligny had to give.

Beside him as ever stood the beautiful and seemingly adoring Mary Stuart, ready to soothe his sufferings.

'Admiral,' began Catherine, 'we know all too well how precious you are to France. We know you as a man of great equanimity and diplomatic intelligence. This is the reason I had you sent for: because, as you yourself can see, we risk ending up under siege in our own state. We are being attacked by our brothers. So I ask you: how is all this possible? Do you think there is a way out?'

Coligny considered for a moment. He knew he must choose his words carefully. His beliefs in religious matters were well known and, given the situation, the equilibrium had become particularly fragile and delicate. He weighed every sentence, distilling in his mind what he wanted to say like a true alchemist of politics.

'First of all, I thank Your Majesties for this invitation, which is all the more welcome because it aims to clarify an issue which has long been drenching the fields of our beloved France with blood. So here then is what I think. It is known that our good king Henry, to whom my gratitude is deep and whom I will forever miss, was a man of peremptory choices. He took a stark stance against the reformers with a series of edicts which I will cite for the sole purpose of providing a clear understanding of the problem. In 1551 the Edict of Châteaubriant, which condemned to death the "heretics" caught celebrating the Calvinist belief. Then the attempt to introduce the Inquisition, which failed due to opposition from parliament. Six years later, with the Edict of Compiègne, he strengthened lay power in defence of the Catholic religion, giving the nobles the power to apply the death penalty, which was ruthlessly imposed. Finally, as soon as the peace of Cateau-Cambrésis was signed, with the Edict of Écouen he laid the foundations of current religious policy: the extermination of the Calvinists.'

As he heard those words, the Cardinal of Lorraine started to speak, but Coligny cut him off. 'Please, Eminence, let me finish. I know I have used strong words, but they are necessary in order to take truly effective countermeasures.'

Coligny turned his gaze to Catherine. He knew she was the only person in that room who had enough heart to truly listen to him. She was an independent, courageous woman of great kindness as well as absolute realism who had always had her own opinions, and he trusted her.

'What I believe – and as you have heard, there are specific reasons for what I say – is that the state has been brought to the brink of religious war, so we therefore need some measure, some disposition, that offers hope, and understanding. Your Majesty,' said Coligny, his eyes returning to the young king of France, 'show magnanimity instead of ruthlessness, mercy instead of hatred. A beloved king always wins out over a feared ruler. Do not be guided by grudges and religious fanaticism. I repeat, I had infinite respect for your father and I never questioned his orders. I believe that together with the Duke of Guise he was the greatest warrior I have ever known. But the fact remains that the politics of terror in the field of religion risks tearing France apart from within.'

'So in concrete terms, what are you proposing?' asked the Cardinal of Lorraine, who reluctantly was forced to admit to himself that there was something in what the man was saying, and that the reaction to which they had exposed themselves would be terrible.

'A new edict. Majesty, you must sign and have approved a provision that allows freedom of religious belief. Reformist faiths must not be judged heretical simply because they allow the reading of the Bible in French or German instead of in Latin. The Protestants – the Huguenots, as they call themselves now – are not heretics; they ask only to have a more direct relationship with God, the same God as the Catholic Church. These differences are so minute that they represent nothing more than variants—'

'Do you realize that what you say would be judged as heresy by any religious court?' cried the Cardinal of Lorraine, who was struggling to tolerate Coligny's choice of words.

'You are right, of course, Your Eminence,' said Catherine. 'But my son, the king, who though a young man knows how to look beyond words and rules, has grasped the message underlying what Admiral Coligny has just said. Isn't that right, Francis? It is not a question of equating anything with anything else, after all, only of allowing everyone to be free to choose their own way of loving God. Such a hypothesis does not penalize the Catholic faith, which will remain the strongest and most widespread in the kingdom, but it will avoid the need to exterminate our brothers in the name of these trivial differences of opinion.'

Catherine intervened with diplomacy and authority, her words made even more imposing by the severe appearance she had now chosen for herself. Since Henry's death she had always dressed in mourning. Her black robe was not simply a way to remember her husband – it was a symbol, worn with pride to speak of the pain of a lost love. Rigour and intransigence were an almost tangible way of showing everyone what she had lost. Forever.

Francis understood his mother's words perfectly, and the pleading in his wife Mary's eyes could do nothing about it. In a short time – six months, to be exact – the Scottish queen had seen her star rise thanks to the support of the Guises, but she had suffered with the return of Catherine who, having finally ousted Diane, had no intention of letting the kingdom be snatched from her by a Scottish girl whose sole merit was that of having managed to ensnare her son. Or at least, that was how the queen mother saw it.

In truth, Coligny did appreciate her, since the young queen showed great common sense and intelligence. She was an educated and resourceful woman but, just like Catherine before her, she was a foreigner on French soil, and she too would never be fully accepted. She had a far longer journey ahead of her than that already travelled by the Florentine before she could imagine actually counting for something.

'I will sign that edict, Admiral. I will have it prepared by my jurists on your advice and address. I thank you on behalf of us all for your suggestions, which have proved to be all the more valuable because they are sincere and honest. I will therefore sign a document that puts an end to the persecutions of Protestants, guarantees freedom of conscience pending a council and which repeals the gravest of the sanctions foreseen by the edicts issued by the king, my father.'

Francis had spoken. And despite his youth and his illness, he had spoken well.

'That is a wise decision, Your Majesty,' said Coligny. 'You will see that you won't regret it. Today, I believe, we finally lay the foundations for a reconciliation of the subjects of your kingdom.'

'Let us hope so,' said the Cardinal of Lorraine, 'and let us hope too that the kingdom's privy council will approve such a measure.'

'It certainly will, if it truly cares about the state,' concluded Catherine, and as she spoke, Coligny gave her a look full of gratitude. He knew that if the measure he had proposed saw the light of day, the credit for it would be entirely hers. Did that make her a possible ally in other issues too? Coligny could not say, but Catherine's words had certainly sounded profoundly sibylline.

While she was dismissing him, the queen mother let slip one final utterance, the meaning of which Coligny found himself unable to judge.

'Anything for the good of France,' said Catherine, a strange smile on her face.

It was a smile that reassured Coligny but which, at the same time, frightened him.

MARCH 1560

45

Amboise

Nothing had gone as hoped. Despite the edict, which had been rapidly approved and contained norms granting freedom of belief, the Huguenots had not stopped. Spies and informants confirmed the impending attack, and therefore, despite the agreement with Coligny, the sovereign's disposition would prove ineffective because it had come too late.

Hatreds had been allowed to fester and the conspiracy to move too far forward. Neither now could be blocked by a king's signature.

The admiral himself had abandoned the conspiracy hatched by the Bourbons and La Renaudie, of that the Guises were certain, but it didn't change the situation. It only confirmed the pointlessness of the measure.

And so Polignac stood up on the battlements of the

Château d'Amboise in the cool wind of that gloomy day. It was all wrong, he thought. He could imagine what was going to happen and would have liked to prevent it, but he didn't know how. He only hoped he could avoid a massacre. He was tired, his bad knee hurt and he felt the weight of the years pressing down on him. A thin drizzle had begun to fall, and though the sopping-wet clothes and the sound of raindrops tinkling on armour were familiar inconveniences to an old soldier like him, with the passage of time he found himself less and less able to bear them.

It was Catherine who had asked him to go to the battlements and keep an eye on the esplanade in front of the castle. For the occasion, she had reinstated him in the corps of the king's pikemen, once again with the rank of general commander. The king had been all for it, and even the Guises had not objected.

He must be her eyes, Catherine had told him.

And he had obeyed, without hesitation. He would have done anything for her – that was the most that he could hope for. How could a man of arms, no longer in the prime of life, hope to receive the attentions of the most important woman in France? He could not, as he well knew, so for that reason kept his mind busy with matters of court – matters about which he cared not a dried fig, if truth be told. As far as he was concerned, he would be quite happy if the Guises ended up with their heads in nooses, and the same could be said for the Bourbons who had put together the conspiracy. But palace intrigues and games at least prevented him from thinking about Catherine, who had become his obsession. It had been going on for so long that he'd almost forgotten when the strange infatuation had begun.

He tried not to think about it.

Beyond the walls of the city of Amboise, the grass of the esplanade shifted in the breeze. The sun had broken through the pale clouds and the rain was stopping. A moment later, a magnificent rainbow stretched across the vault of the heavens. Savouring the smell of the falling rain, Polignac stretched his legs and took a deep breath, his chest swelling beneath his armour.

It was then that he saw the first Huguenots advancing from the edge of the forest.

But they weren't soldiers. As black as crows, they wore rough clothes and broken shoes, shabby tunics and moth-eaten cloaks. They were poor men: farmers, shepherds, small merchants, craftsmen. There were women and children too, and they came without weapons. They only hoped to see their right to pray to God in the way they wished recognised.

The king had approved the edict, but Polignac suspected that the Guises would continue do everything they could to stir up hatred. They had accepted the decision in order to avoid problems, but at the same time they intended to take advantage of the possible conspiracy against them to justify a vendetta that would almost certainly result in deaths.

And all in the name of religion.

The crowd was growing. They walked silently, their heads bowed like penitents. With all the humility they were able to muster, they came to talk to the king, preceded by one man.

Polignac saw a soldier take up an arquebus and immediately shot him a glare that froze him in his tracks. 'What the devil are you planning to do? Open fire on defenceless people? Put that arquebus away. Do it immediately or I swear I'll cut off your arm, *Mort-Dieu*!'

The man gave him a resentful look but did as he was told.

'I will report this to your captain later,' said Polignac, growing even angrier. 'What have we become – animals?'

He looked at the men one by one and motioned for them not to open fire for any reason. He was again the commander of the king's pikemen and possessed the authority to be obeyed even by the Marshal of France. And the king had been clear. He wanted to know what his opponents had in mind first.

The Guises had been careful not to show their faces and had advised the sovereign to do the same. But though that prudence was in principle correct, Polignac believed that it made no sense given how things were going. Indeed, by behaving in that way he would risk making things worse. These men came in peace – they were the French people and wanted only to talk to their king. Was there something wrong in that?

No, truly there was not. And yet the king was barricaded in his castle as if he were actually under siege. It had been a mistake.

He waited for them to approach.

Their leader carried a white rag that he waved as if his life depended on it.

'We come in peace,' he shouted.

'I am listening,' said a voice.

It was the voice of the king. Francis II of France stood behind an embrasure upon the castle walls.

'My name is François Grandier, and the good citizens of Amboise have elected me their spokesman.'

'Speak.'

It seemed to Polignac almost that the man was talking to God and that the voice which responded to him came down from heaven. And so it must have appeared to Grandier too.

'Your Majesty, we are your faithful servants who live in these lands. All we ask is that you allow us to celebrate God in his infinite glory.'

'Leave here,' said the king's voice. And then, 'Monsieur de Polignac, make sure that these men receive money to at least give some relief to their pains.'

For a moment Raymond remained in stunned silence.

'Of course, Your Majesty.'

*

At that moment, Catherine was on her knees in the chapel of the Château d'Amboise, praying.

That place was so dear to her: right there the good king Francis I had married her father, Lorenzo de' Medici, to Maddalena de la Tour d'Auvergne, her mother.

Madame Gondi was close by, and not far away Margaret was reciting an Ave Maria. Lately Catherine had noticed that the girl had been growing somewhat intolerant of Madame Gondi. She did not know where that sudden antipathy came from, but she had learned not to investigate too closely.

Everyone knew about the conspiracy. It had been a good idea, she reflected, to give the Prince of Condé the command of the king's personal guards. By so doing, she had forced him to remain inside the castle and prevented him from going out in support of his family. And while she prayed, Catherine was fully aware that Francis of Guise would be going with his men to explore the woods around Amboise in search of enemies.

They knew that La Renaudie would arrive soon, but at least by forcing Condé to stay within the walls she would be able to spare his life. There was no doubt about his involvement in the conspiracy, but she did not want to openly encourage a slaughter.

Not to mention that Condé knew he had been

discovered and that, rather than ending up hanging from one of the castle's windows, he had been happy to take advantage of that opportunity to save his own life and had therefore performed the most incredible of turnarounds. First he had betrayed the king and plotted against him, and then he had accepted Catherine's offer of a position and abandoned the Huguenots when he had realized that the conspiracy had been discovered. Basically, Catherine had offered him a way out that protected him from the wrath of the Guises, and he had made the best of a bad job.

She sighed.

She had asked Raymond de Polignac to be her eyes and ears, and he had obeyed her. Just as he always did.

46

The Attack

Polignac waited until the last minute. The men were ready, the gunpowder tamped down in the barrels, the fuses sparking. He wanted to guarantee his men a clear and deadly shot.

When he judged the enemy was at the right distance, he gave the order.

'Fire!'

The first row of arquebuses thundered almost in unison with a roar that sounded as if it might shatter the very earth.

The enemy's front line was mown down by the spray of lead, bodies hurled to the ground in a grim carousel of death and horror: broken legs, screaming faces, the whistle of projectiles, multiple impacts. The esplanade in front of the city walls was turned instantly into a lake flooded with the blood of the fallen.

The Huguenot soldiers fell, but did not retreat. The second line closed ranks and threw itself at break-neck speed against the walls of Amboise.

Another volley of arquebuses rumbled from above, clouds of blue smoke rising from them as they filled the air with the sinister hiss of flying shot, and the Protestants found themselves under a hail of lead. Men clapped their hands to their chests and fell to their knees, a second shot sometimes took half a man's head off while others floundered in the mud, crawling like worms through the carnage.

Arquebuses were fired in an attempt to catch some of the defenders unprepared, but the favourable position, the defence offered by the walls, and the preparations for the worst that they had been making since the first light of the morning had given the king's men an enormous advantage.

Polignac knew that he must weaken those first offensives and that the cavalry would take care of the rest.

The Duke of Guise waited behind the trees with his men. Hidden by the forest, they awaited the signal to swoop down and overwhelm La Renaudie's troops.

The Protestant commander rode a dappled horse. Less stiff and proud than when the battle had begun, he was still convinced that he could prevail. But Guise had done well to have the court moved there because Amboise was built for war – not to mention that by losing the element of surprise, the Huguenots had lost the only advantage they possessed. La Renaudie was paying dearly for his recklessness.

Their ranks thinned out by the lead shot the king's arquebusiers had blasted down upon them, the enemy seemed to re-evaluate their tactics, and it was at this point that the attack stopped.

The men retreated in small groups, decimated by the firepower of the defenders of Amboise, their leather armour in tatters, their doublets soaked with mud and stained with blood, their swords broken and their pikes snapped.

They had had the worst of it, and none of them now doubted the impossibility of taking Amboise.

Waving a piece of white cloth like a flag and accompanied by his lieutenants, La Renaudie came closer to parlay.

Polignac gestured to his men not to shoot and waited until the leader of the rebellion was at the foot of the walls. Now he saw him for what he was: an unscrupulous adventurer who had believed he could ride the wave of hatred and discontent to his advantage. But he had discovered at his own expense how wrong he had been. Covered in mud, the breastplate of his armour scratched and dented in several places, his dark eyes glowering with bitter disillusionment, he looked upwards. Jean d'Aubigné and Bouchard d'Aubeterre were with him.

'I ask to speak to the king,' he shouted to Polignac.

But the commander general of the pikemen had received precise orders on the matter.

'The king refuses to speak to those who besiege his cities and force him to shutter himself up within the walls of Amboise. The king does not speak to traitors.'

They were harsh words, but they were the only ones possible.

A grin appeared on La Renaudie's face, yet there was nothing amused in his expression: it seemed rather to reveal the mood of one who knows he has already lost and has not the faintest idea of what to do next. He had expected a disorganized, chaotic defence. His spies were to have penetrated the city gates, but they had been walled up by Guise in anticipation of the siege, the guards put on double shifts and the raids in the woods intensified.

And Polignac had at least three more arquebus shots ready, with which he could have annihilated his opponents. Definitively.

'Who are you, *monsieur*?'

'Raymond de Polignac, general commander of the king's pikemen.'

'Curious that your men use the arquebus rather than the pike, *monsieur*. That is not playing by the rules.'

Polignac had to hand it to La Renaudie; he was a

man of spirit – feigning such contempt of danger at a time like that was not something of which most would have been capable.

'Nobody is playing, *monsieur*,' he replied. 'This is war. A war which you desired. It is too easy to ask to parlay after attempting to attack the king. Pike or arquebus, my answer remains the same.'

Polignac loomed over the top of the battlements. His long hair was streaked with silver, his jacket dark blue, his breastplate still worn with swagger, his gaze adamantine. He was an old soldier, and perhaps that made him still more intimidating.

'Then I ask to speak with Louis of Bourbon, the Prince of Condé,' retorted La Renaudie.

Polignac had expected that. After all, had it not been the hunchback who had instigated that madness? But like her great-grandfather Lorenzo the Magnificent, Catherine was possessed of great political intelligence, and in her infinite wisdom she had avoided exacerbating the conflict more than was already the case and removed Condé from the wrath of the Guises.

'Alas, Monsieur de La Renaudie, I must also deny you this. Louis of Bourbon is the new commander of the king's personal guard and cannot therefore appear at my side because, as you will clearly understand, he is engaged elsewhere.'

The news took the Huguenot commander so much by surprise that he was unable to hide his amazement, and Jean d'Aubigné and Bouchard d'Aubeterre looked even more stunned than he, if that were possible.

'Does this news catch you off guard, *monsieur*?' asked Polignac.

'Not at all,' La Renaudie hurriedly replied. 'If the king refuses to parlay with me, why should his personal guard?'

'True,' replied Polignac.

But it was evident to all present just how shocking that news had been for the Huguenots.

'Was there anything else you wished to ask me?'

La Renaudie hesitated, then seemed to summon up his courage.

'In truth, no,' he replied. And without another word he turned his horse around and trotted back to where he had come from, at the far end of the esplanade.

Their shoulders drooping, their heads bowed and their hair soaked with rain and sweat, his captains followed.

47

Without Pity

They attacked them in the flank, slicing through them like an iron wedge cutting into the flesh of a lamb. Francis of Guise led the cavalry charge that would put an end to the Huguenot revolt.

La Renaudie watched as they swooped down like demons, their steel armour streaked with rain, their swords unsheathed, their spears ready to bite. The impact was devastating: the Huguenot infantry was mown down like ripe wheat and the light cavalry was annihilated.

He watched as Bouchard d'Aubeterre was surrounded by the king's knights and torn to pieces: he fell from his steed and was trampled under the hooves of his own horse.

La Renaudie knew he was lost.

His mount leapt to one side, and from out of nowhere two enemy horsemen astride chestnut steeds appeared in front of him. He dodged the sword of one, hearing its blade whistle through the rainy air, then pulled a wheel-lock pistol from his belt – a magnificent model, its stock inlaid with mother-of-pearl. He aimed it at the first rider, who was about to swing at him again – if he hesitated another instant, that man would take his head off.

The flint ignited the gunpowder in a burst of sparks and the pistol fired. The ball tore through the man's neck and he fell to the ground, but his foot caught in the stirrup and his horse galloped away, dragging his corpse through the rain into the forest.

The second horseman was now to his right, and he held a gun in his hand. La Renaudie quickly drew his sword and, before the man could fire, swung it upwards at him. Cutting a perfect oblique arc through the air, the blade struck the soldier at the height of his armpit, the exact point where his leather armour provided him with no protection. Blood sprayed from the wound and the man lost his grip on the gun, which fell to the ground while La Renaudie's return stroke sliced through the man's throat.

In vain, the soldier put his hands to his neck in a desperate attempt to stop the blood flooding from the deep gouge. An agonized gurgle escaped his lips.

Wasting no more time, La Renaudie began looking

for a way to escape into the thick of the woods, his few remaining men behind him. But Guise had been on the lookout, and the cavalry was now racing towards him. The Huguenot infantry had already been dispersed, its horsemen felled one after another by strokes of the sword. Severed heads rolled in the mud.

The flower of French youth had been cut down that day, and La Renaudie was frightened, because he could sense the Duke of Guise's horsemen at his back. Guise would not give up.

Ever.

Guise saw the captain of the reformists ahead of him, on his bay steed. La Renaudie was a skilled soldier and had just killed two riders with admirable coolness. Although he had been betrayed and his assault had proved to be a complete disaster, the duke had to admit that the man had guts.

But guts would not be enough to save him.

Spurring on his horse, Guise herded the fugitives right to where he had hoped they would end up.

He watched as the scene played out before his eyes.

To the left, what had at first appeared to be a wall of green foliage suddenly fell to the ground revealing a line of arquebusiers that had been hidden in the woods awaiting this moment.

He had organized everything. For the last few days

he had been posting patrols among the dense trees so that they could intervene if necessary.

There was a loud crack as the guns opened fire on the last group of fugitives, bringing down a good number of them. For a moment they looked like rag dolls as, riddled with shot, they were flung to the ground, several of their horses falling with them.

As the few survivors surrendered, Guise swooped down on them, but he stopped his soldiers before they could finish them off.

'That will do,' he said, raising his hand. 'Those still alive will be taken prisoner and delivered into the hands of the king, who will decide what he wants with them.'

Then, while his men disarmed their enemies, he went over to La Renaudie who lay on the ground staring up at him.

'You are mine now, you accursed heretic.'

Then, without hesitating, he looked over at one of his arquebusiers and gave him a nod. As soon as La Renaudie got to his feet, the soldier pulled the trigger. There was a flash of sparks and a ball of shot struck him in the chest.

An expression of incredulous disbelief that they would shoot an unarmed man point-blank appeared on La Renaudie's face.

He fell to his knees and then collapsed face-down on the ground.

48

Waking Nightmare

Raymond de Polignac felt as if he were in a waking nightmare. In all those years in the army and at court he could not remember seeing anything like it. He knew war and the hard, bloody, filthy struggle against the enemy, but the shameful massacre that was taking place was something else entirely.

It seemed that nothing could satisfy Guise's thirst for blood, and just because his brother Charles was less blatant in his actions did not mean that he felt pity or mercy for anyone. For him, the Catholic faith justified even the most ignoble action.

Polignac was exhausted. Despairingly, he had attempted to explain to the queen that the appalling violence would backfire upon them. He had lent his martial talents in order to defend the king, not to watch his opponents be slaughtered. They were Frenchmen, they were his brothers. How could the sovereign tolerate this atrocity?

He had gone in search of the Duke of Guise, and had found him in the weapons room of the castle, admiring a newly developed gun. He was turning it over in his hands as if it were an amulet.

'Monsieur de Polignac, what a pleasure to see you! What do you think?' asked the duke, showing him the weapon.

But it was not a real question. Guise had no interest in Polignac's answer – he simply wanted to provoke him so as to delay the moment when Polignac laid into him, because he was well aware the man was at the end of his tether.

'Look: it's a double-barrelled pistol with a flintlock, made of steel, gold and wood. This masterpiece was created by an extraordinary German watchmaker named Peter Peck.'

The furious Polignac interrupted him.

'*Sacrebleu*, if you think I'm interested in talking about a damned gun right now, then it means you don't know me at all. How dare you...'

But, undaunted, Guise continued.

'Every so often the Germans do create something worthwhile. Just think, the mechanism uses an Italian system which vastly reduces loading and firing times. Through a revolutionary firing method, it is possible to prepare the weapon in advance in order to guarantee its immediate use.'

And so saying, Guise stretched out his arm and pointed the gun at Polignac.

'Do you think I'm afraid of that toy?'

'The decorations are by Ambrosius Gemlich, a renowned German painter and artist. And a Catholic,' said Guise, who appeared to be paying no attention at all to his interlocutor. 'Now, as you can see, I am very busy, *monsieur*. Would you be so kind as to leave me in peace? You can do it alive or dead. You decide.'

'Kill me then. I would rather die than remain an impotent witness of what you are about.'

The Duke of Guise smiled but there was nothing amused about his expression.

'Monsieur Raymond de Polignac... where have I heard that name before? Ah yes, you are the protégé of the queen mother. The man who was fired from the king's pikemen following the ignominious defeat at Saint-Quentin, alongside that fool Montmorency, and who was then reinstated at the bidding of the sovereign, which is to say, of the queen.'

'One of the rare times you didn't get your own way, wasn't it, Guise? That must have been a blow to you. What, the hero of Calais not even getting to choose the soldiers? Come on then, pull the trigger. What are you afraid of? Anyone who doesn't share your opinion needs to be got out of the way, right? Exactly as you are now doing.'

'You forget that the men we captured had attacked the castle and the city and had every intention of killing the king.'

'You know perfectly well that is not the case. Those men were exasperated at being persecuted because of their religious beliefs. Do you think I don't know that Coligny himself advised the king to issue a new edict guaranteeing freedom of belief? But it is clear that such a provision will be completely ineffective if you continue to slaughter defenceless men, to say nothing of women and children, in the name of the Catholic religion.'

Guise sighed. The fool was ruining his good mood. Why the devil should he have to endure it? He would kill the man someday – there was no other way to get rid of him, of that he was certain.

In the meantime, Polignac's shouting had attracted the attention of the incredulous guards, who had hurried to the weapons room.

Guise took advantage of the opportunity.

'Get Commander Raymond de Polignac out of here,' he said. 'Despite being given a specific order by his superior, he refused to obey.'

The guards approached Polignac, unsure whether to comply or not. As soon as they put their hands on him, the general commander of the king's pikemen sent one of the two soldiers reeling backwards with a well-placed punch.

'I will go alone,' Polignac exclaimed. 'Keep your hands off me. I don't want to have to hit you again.'

'You'd better get out of this room before I order you put to the sword,' cried Guise.

'It's only a matter of time,' murmured Polignac threateningly. 'Sooner or later you and I will meet again, and on that occasion you will have no one on hand to help you.'

'I look forward to that moment, *monsieur*,' retorted Guise.

The quartered body of La Renaudie was displayed on the Loire bridge. As a warning to the entire population of Amboise and of France, a sign read 'La Renaudie, leader of the rebels'. The river ran red with the blood of those who had been found guilty of rebellion, and even women, old men and children had ended up being drowned in the waters of the Loire, bound together and thrown into the river with rocks tied around their necks.

Catherine could barely hold back her tears. The Cardinal of Lorraine had summoned all the nobles and notables from Nantes to Orléans to attend the executions that took place every day in the square of Amboise, where stages and grandstands had been set up to allow a better view of the horror.

It was not simply gruesome; it was terrible, because the Guises wanted to turn the violence into a spectacle, hoping in this way to slow the momentum of the reformers. They wanted to strike so deeply that they would eradicate the problem, murdering every Huguenot in the kingdom, one at a time, without mercy.

Their intention was to weed out the bad seeds, and by so doing, they sowed the seeds of hatred. New legions of Huguenots took blood vows in the silence of the churches and the countryside, and those who professed to be Catholics were developing a fanaticism that went beyond all human reason.

Whether due to terror or outright madness, not only was the square overflowing but people also crowded the windows of the buildings surrounding it, both men and women like swarms of agitated flies, ready to buzz around the blood of the victims.

That day Catherine was sitting in the grandstand in the square of Amboise. She had been forced into the deathly parade because the Duke of Guise and the cardinal had wished it. Francis, her son, had no strength to oppose them, and now stared in terror at the gallows, his cheeks purple with shame and his mouth sealed shut with fear. The disease was devouring him and Catherine knew that he didn't have long left to live.

Mary Stuart had prayed that at least that day she would be spared the torture of such a vision. She had said she was feeling unwell, but the Cardinal of

Lorraine wouldn't hear of it, so she too was there, as pale as death.

Catherine could not stop the slaughter for she feared that the Guises would retaliate in some way against those she held dearest: her children. She feared for little Charles and Margaret, and for Henry.

Charles was there that day. The lad stared wide-eyed at the blood, seeming almost thrilled by the sight of it. For some reason she could not understand, Catherine felt a terrible presentiment.

Her children were all she had left. She would never endanger them, not for anything in the world, and if their salvation meant the deaths of the subjects of the kingdom, then let a hundred people and a hundred more be killed. She had to protect the kingdom and the Valois above all else. She was a Medici and had consecrated her own person to the state ever since she was born.

The crown, the lilies and the royal lineage were impregnable foundations, and Catherine knew that, however horrible, there was an even deeper reason for punishing those subjects who had rebelled against their sovereign.

She hated the Guises and their complacency in the face of the most aberrant violence, but she hated the Bourbons even more, since it was one of them – a Navarre – who had germinated the poisoned seed that might have extinguished the Valois. Power must be defended, therefore, at any cost. As terrible as it was, this was what Catherine was learning, and those ruthless methods of self-protection and domination were the only ones capable of instilling fear into her enemies' minds. They were, in short, a necessary deterrent to keep the traitors in line.

While she was absorbed in these gloomy thoughts, the guards brought fifty-two of the leaders of the rebellion to the square. They were exhausted men, clad in tattered robes, their faces and bodies scarred by torture and the injuries they had sustained at the time of their capture. Even the foresters had been ordered to wipe out the rebels they found in the forest, and many had fallen under the blades of their axes.

Attempting to feign proud determination, Catherine looked at them. The sky above Amboise was as grey as lead and the crowd in the square rumbled. Drenched with the spit of their countrymen, the prisoners made their way through the parted crowd towards the gallows.

When they reached the platform upon which the Prince of Condé stood, they bowed before him. Everyone held their breath. It seemed to Catherine that the whole world had stopped, plunging into silence that infernal horde of men and women who until a moment before had been shouting the praises of the death sentence.

Condé did not flinch, despite the fact that the Cardinal of Lorraine looked over at him in the hope of seeing him hesitate. In silent tribute to the leader of the revolt, the prisoners did not speak. But then, none of the onlookers could prove his guilt.

When the condemned men got to their feet, the executioner and his aides shoved them towards the gallows, and the crowd began to roar again in expectation, as though wishing to release the tension created by the unbearable silence which reminded them of how deep the hatred that divided France in two ran.

FEBRUARY 1563

49

The Death of the Duke of Guise

Large flakes of snow fell silently to the ground, and the horses snorted out clouds of white steam as their hooves kicked up muddy snow from the filthy road.

Stripped of leaves and needles, the trees seemed dead, their branches black claws stretching out towards a sky that looked like a sheet of polished silver.

The Duke of Guise was tired from the long ride. Now that Orléans had fallen and that damned religious war was about to end, he hoped that he would soon be able to rest.

The years that had passed had taken their toll. As he galloped, he thought back to all the days spent fighting – he, who had always tried to avoid it, but who had finally been forced to respond to the provocations of the Prince of Condé. He had offered him honourable and immediate peace, since everything was conceivable except the throwing open of the doors of the kingdom of France to England, as the Huguenots had done. He had even been willing to acknowledge the free exercise of Calvinism, provided that Condé and Coligny fought alongside him against the hated English dogs.

But, blinded by hatred for their Catholic brothers, they had refused.

Amboise had been a mistake, thought the Duke of Guise. Of course, it was easy to think that in retrospect, but the stubborn desire to drown the rebellion in blood had actually generated even more followers of heresy. He and his brother had been so harsh in their repression of the reforms that they had fomented a fanaticism that was difficult to eradicate.

But now, victory was near. Now, perhaps, it would no longer be impossible to dream of a united kingdom. The conquest of Rouen was a victory of fundamental importance for the Catholic faction, and now Orléans too had fallen. D'Andelot did not have enough troops to keep the city, and Guise had executed a true masterpiece of strategy by attacking it from the quarter of Portereau, which was poorly fortified and undefended, and then moving into the city proper.

It had been a grand idea. Now, though, the duke dreamed of respite. Feeling victorious and secure, he was travelling with a single gentleman by his side, hoping to get to his quarters as soon as possible.

They arrived at a copse, the stumps of the trees poking out like yellowing thumbs from ground encrusted with white snow, bronze-coloured branches sprouting here and there like eruptions of the earth itself.

It was then that they heard the boom of the shots.

Three, in rapid succession, one after another. The projectiles struck the duke in the right shoulder, at the joint of his armour.

Guise gave a cry as his flesh exploded in a cloud of blood, and he clapped his left hand to his wounded shoulder. In the distance, the sound of the hired assassins hurrying away through the snow could be heard even before his lieutenant could take up his arquebus.

But it was of little use.

Francis of Guise felt faint. His vision became blurred and the world faded into a milky fog. He let himself fall forward, embracing the neck of his horse and gripping its mane to prevent himself from falling. And there he remained while his blood flowed copiously like vermilion rain, splashing red onto the white ground.

'They have killed me, Fronsac,' he murmured to the other man.

Then he spoke no more. The silence of the woods and snow cradled his last words.

50

Nostradamus's Farewell

Behind the heavy curtains of the Château de Fontainebleau, Catherine trembled. She loved the magnificent palace so much, and sought shelter there whenever she could, but not even that refuge felt safe in those days. The dispatches announcing the death of the Duke of Guise had arrived, shattering her certainties.

She had wanted power, had coveted it for so long, but since she had managed to obtain it, she had realized that it had begun to consume her, like a fire devouring everything it finds in its path.

She was heartbroken. Her children were dying. Francis had been taken two years earlier – the end had been a liberation for him, and Catherine's awareness that he was no longer suffering was the only weapon she possessed to fight the pain of his passing.

But it was not enough, it would never be enough. Charles was little more than a boy and he already lived like a ghost, tormented by incomprehensible fits, terrified of shadows and seemingly thrilled by the sight of blood.

Mary Stuart had returned to Scotland, and now Guise too was gone.

What would become of her and the Valois? She would protect them, in the name of their noble blood. That noble blood she would never have, despite her marriage to Henry, despite her having always and only ever lived for the crown of France.

It was then that she heard the unsteady steps of her court astrologer on the floor of the ballroom, like the tolling of a mournful bell. She looked up.

He was dressed in black, as always, his large hood on his shoulders, his beard – now whitened by the years – still with its sharp points, one enormous foot, devoured by gout, forced into its slipper almost as if the mass of deformed flesh had been squeezed in there by some crazed butcher. He leaned on his stick as he advanced, as implacable as that pale winter which fed upon fog and human lives.

Catherine had already prepared for Michel de Nostredame the velvet armchair which was his favourite when he visited her. Those visits occurred less and less frequently nowadays, and Catherine had a powerful feeling of foreboding. How distant the times when he had received her in the dilapidated old house in the middle of the forest now seemed.

She waited for him to sit down. Nostradamus could not hold back a groan of pain: that foot tormented him. His prophecies had failed to shield him from the disease, or from suffering.

'How are you, Monsieur de Nostredame?' asked the queen with sincere concern.

'As you can see for yourself, *Madame la Reine*,' he said, his voice still deep but now weak and as fragile as the reflection of a shadow.

'Would you like water? Or perhaps some wine?'

'No, truly, I already have everything I need.'

Catherine waited a moment before asking, 'What news do you bring me, old friend?'

'*Madame la Reine*, I know that what I am about to tell you will not surprise you, so I will do it without delay: I intend to leave the court and retire forever to a place where I can await death. I have come one last time, as you asked me, to tell you what I saw in the stars. No ritual, just a conversation between you and me about what I see on the horizon, always given that you are willing to bear the weight of my words. For, I warn you, the future brings with it dark events. If you did not wish to listen to me... well, I would understand you.'

When she heard his words, Catherine did not hesitate.

'Monsieur de Nostredame, I summoned you here to find out what awaits me. I am saddened by your desire to leave me after we have spent so much time together, but I certainly cannot prevent you from tending to your ills, which as I can see are extremely serious. I would be an ungrateful and heartless woman, and despite what people might say, that is not the case at all.'

Nostradamus had the strength to smile, and then he spoke, his voice like snow falling from the sky or the deep breath of the wind, seemingly inseparably bound to nature.

'France will fall into hatred, *Madame la Reine*. The Huguenots will desecrate churches, burn sacred images, take the sword and the dagger to the masses. As it was in the past, and even worse. It will be the apocalypse visited upon the earth. After this, other wars will follow, wars even bloodier than those already fought. Just as crabgrass infests the fields, this victory in Orléans is the seed from which the conflicts to come will spread. The mercenaries will torch farms and raid barns and you, Your Majesty, will find yourself in the midst of all this. You will lose your daughter Elisabeth, exhausted by her pregnancies. She will die in a lake of blood after giving birth to too many lives. Remember these words of mine.'

Catherine felt the tears streak down her cheeks, but there was nothing she could do. She listened to Nostradamus in silence, her impotence now the incense with which she consecrated the pain she had felt all those years and the pain which was yet to come. She felt as though she had been conceived in torment, her body feeding on it as if it were the only possible food.

She had known nothing else in life, she thought: the humiliations to which her beloved Henry had subjected her, the abominable triangle imposed by Diane, the pregnancies that had transformed her body into a flesh oven, and then the conquest of power with which she had dispensed death and executions. The crown of France was cursed, and the price for wearing it was black as death and red as blood.

'Go on, Monsieur de Nostredame.'

'Are you sure?'

Catherine nodded. In her gaze, there was neither pleasure nor sadness, only resignation. She had surrendered to the curse that had been upon her since she had been promised as a bride to the prince of a kingdom to which she had remained a foreigner despite all the love she had lavished upon it: a love without limit and without qualification which had been rejected as if it were invasive and unwanted. That was something Catherine could not accept. She would never accept it.

'In one night, one single night, you will drown in blood, together with all your children. You will know it when it happens but will be powerless to do anything to halt the evil that will consume you and your offspring.

The house of Navarre will prevail over the house of Valois. Mind your enemies, *Madame la Reine*, for you will receive the greatest torment from he you once looked upon as a friend.'

Nostradamus fell silent and looked out of the window. 'The snow is still falling,' he said, 'and it will fall forever on your heart. You, who have loved so much, cannot open your own soul to the one who loved you more than his own life.'

He shook his head, as if what he had said was now an inescapable truth, a destiny that could not be changed in any way.

'I would have liked to have brought you better news for our last interview, *Madame la Reine*, but it would have been much more cruel to lie to you. In all these years, that is something I have never done.'

'And that is why I have loved you, Michel. In a world of deceit and deception, you and Raymond de Polignac have always been the only ones who have never lied to me. You have a lot in common, you and the commander.'

'He is a good man who could make you truly happy if you only wished to renounce the kingdom.'

'That I could never do. But not because of ambition or personal prestige. In a way that you cannot see, I do love Monsieur de Polignac, and it is for this very reason I remain.'

Perhaps for the first time in his life, Michel de

Nostredame stared at her in amazement, as though he had not expected such a confession.

'Monsieur de Polignac loves France, Michel, more than anything else. Even more than me. He has demonstrated it again and again: he discovered the killer of the dauphin Francis and had him executed, he protected my person and that of my husband so very many times, he allowed himself to be unfairly dismissed from the army, and he accepted with equal fidelity the disposition with which I reinserted him in the role of general commander of pikemen of the king, under the orders of Francis of Guise, whom he hated from the bottom of his heart. He did it for the Queen of France. And so, you see, I cannot give up my crown.'

'Not even if that means you giving up yourself?'

'Not even in that case, if this is the only way for me to keep faith with my kingdom.'

Nostradamus sighed.

'You have great courage, Your Majesty.'

'I do not know if it is courage. I would rather call it love for what I believe in: the kingdom and my children.'

'You realize that you will be damned for it?' said Nostradamus, a hint of resigned fatalism in his voice.

'I know, Michel. The curse began long ago.'

AUGUST 1572

51

The Ambush at Coligny

Catherine hated him from the bottom of her heart.

It was he who had betrayed her in the vilest possible way. After advising her on an edict that would allow freedom of belief, he had had the Duke of Guise murdered, depriving her of one of the most ardent defenders of the crown. Guise had given all of himself to protecting the king, that was beyond doubt. And Coligny had killed him like a dog in Orléans.

He, who had always declared himself faithful to the crown, had plotted in the shadows and become the champion of the Huguenots – the leader of the plague of locusts which was stripping France to the bone.

In that hellish August with its murderous heat, the fields and woods were burning, purified by the Protestant madness, and the whole of France was an expanse of ash. For ten long years she had languished in an apocalypse of hatred and torment and she no longer knew how to save herself.

Now there was a new Guise. Scarred in face and in soul, Francis' son, Henry, had taken up his mantle and, driven on by anger and a desire for revenge, had become even more bloodthirsty than his father. And now he fought for her.

Catherine was closed up in her apartments in the Louvre. At her side was Henry d'Anjou, her favourite son. The youth had grown up immersed in vice, and at sixteen had become head of the French army, triumphing in Jarnac and Moncontour. Lecher, rapist of young boys, a lewd sadist who was dedicated to the most sordid pleasures and the incestuous lover of his own sister, Henry looked at his mother with the purest veneration. With his long dark brown hair falling in perfumed waves like the night tide, his dark eyes, his bejewelled hands bedecked with rings laden with precious stones, puffed sleeves and delicate lace collar, he looked like some fiendish scarecrow.

Catherine loved him above all else.

He had become her confidant, her beloved weaver of conspiracies. She pitied Charles, who was now on the throne. He was weak and ineffectual, a poor little boy who could never make up his mind.

'Henry,' said the queen, 'the Protestant heresy must be eradicated and its seed along with it. Was our man informed? Is he in place? Are we sure he won't disappoint us?' The questions rose to her lips like prayers.

Anjou gave a chilling grin, made even more disturbing by the red-painted lips upon which it appeared. He was like a parody of a man – a fresh incarnation of the devil, who answered her in a soft, sensual voice dripping with lust and deception.

'Of course, mother. Our man is waiting for Coligny to pass within range of the arquebus. He will not miss.'

'Are you certain of it?'

'As certain of it as I am that I worship you like a goddess.'

Catherine smiled, for the first time in a long while. She loved her handsome, tall, strong, impossible son. Henry was her reward for having believed so long in power and in the Valois.

'Very well, then,' she said sweetly. 'Once Coligny has been eliminated, the Huguenots will be like a headless snake. And they will never know who it was who got the better of them, so their suspicions will fall upon the Guises. In this way, we will rid ourselves of the both of them, freeing your brother from their pernicious influences.'

'Soon we will celebrate, mother. The idea of the marriage between Margaret and Henry of Navarre to bring the reformist leaders back to Paris was your masterstroke. And using my sister as bait proved to be a stroke of genius.'

'Come, Henry, be silent. Every word we speak of this matter is a word too many, bear that in mind. We must wait to discover what has happened. Leave me now. I would like to pray that God in his goodness grant me the grace of fulfilling this small wish of mine.'

'As you wish. Your word is law.'

And without another word, Anjou left the queen mother's apartments.

Catherine sent for Raymond de Polignac to escort her in a carriage to Saint-Sauveur. She intended to pray in a church, as she always did when she needed silence and inspiration. She was very fond of the church of Saint-Sauveur, which was not too far from the Louvre palace, so it seemed like a good solution.

Margaret laughed. She was chatting with Sophie de Tourvel, countess of La Motte, the only friend she had in that court crowded with serpents and traitors. In order to survive, she sensed that she must become one of them, but she hardly cared anymore. She knew she had been used by her mother as part of a more complex design. What exactly that design might be she did not know, but she feared it was something grim.

The wedding to Henry of Navarre had been nothing but a stratagem, of that at least she was sure. There had been no lack of splendour at the balls or at the games, but despite all that she felt clearly that an unbearable climate of tension was mounting. By the light of day, peace finally reigned thanks to the pact between the Catholic and Huguenot factions – but in the corridors and rooms of the Louvre it was already rumoured that something terrible was about to happen.

Margaret sensed it beneath her skin, a fear that felt like some insidious damp which gradually crept into one's bones.

Certainly she did not love her husband, an uncouth boor who had emerged from the loins of the Navarre. He was a rough and charmless man, yet serious for all that – and even, perhaps, honest, which meant a great deal in such a place. So neither did she hate him: he too was a victim of the marriage. While deriding him for his ways, she nurtured for him a feeling of pity, and perhaps even of friendship.

But fortunately for her, that hot August afternoon the conversation revolved around matters which were less weighty, at least in her eyes. Like the theft of a ring from the queen's rooms. The guilty party – or rather the guilty *woman* – had been promptly identified and removed from the court.

Forever.

'And so,' Madame de Tourvel told her, 'they finally caught that thief. What a shame for Madame Gondi! Who knows what else she had got up to over the years. It must have been a terrible blow for the queen mother.'

'It was certainly a shock, especially given the trust

she had always accorded her countrywoman. It is a sad story, both for Italy and for the queen herself. She had entrusted Madame Gondi with the most intimate affairs of her life.'

'In fact, I must admit that I was greatly surprised. I mean, isn't it all rather strange? What do you make of it?'

'I confess that I had always suspected her, although, as you can imagine, I had no proof. But Anjou caught her in the act. It was a very poor show, it truly was.'

'Incredible, truly incredible,' said Sophie. 'How magnificent nature is though!' she cried, looking up at the blue sky then taking in the verdant wonders of the Tuileries garden. Around them, lawns and vineyards alternated with splendid flower beds, as well as delicious quincunx, groups of five trees arranged in sequence, which gave a sense of absolute peace and serenity.

'Yes,' murmured Margaret. 'How wonderful it would be if humanity were equally so.'

The barrel of the arquebus burned in his hands. The man was surrounded by too many other people and Charles wasn't sure he would be able to hit him. He was moving slowly forward, yes, but his position was far from ideal. Charles was sweating profusely, and the drops streamed into his eyes. That damned August was driving him insane.

He had prepared everything carefully and gone over

the procedure in his mind to ensure that it had been done properly: the fine gunpowder in the bowl, the coarser gunpowder in the barrel together with the lead ball, which he had tamped down well before closing the bowl at the end of the process.

Just as always.

And it didn't usually fail.

His heart was pounding like a drum and felt as if it might burst forth out of his chest at any moment. He took aim carefully. If he missed, he wouldn't get a second chance: as soon as they heard the bang, the Huguenots would be after him and he would have very little time to make his escape.

Sacrebleu, he was trembling like a leaf! He must remain calm. He waited: he wanted to have the man within range.

In a desperate attempt to maintain his lucidity, he bit his lower lip so hard that it bled and the pain reminded him of what he must do.

He took a deep breath – and finally seemed to have a clear shot.

He reopened the bowl and pulled the trigger. The coil ignited the fuse. He smelled the acrid stench and then the fuse lit the powder, igniting the coarser gunpowder in the breech.

Charles heard the bang and felt the recoil. He hoped that he had hit Coligny, but there was no time to check: he fled at breakneck speed.

*

Accompanied by a troop of about fifteen men, Admiral Gaspard de Coligny was marching towards their lodgings at the Hôtel de Rochefort, just on the corner of Rue de l'Arbre-Sec and Rue de Béthisy. One of his men was submitting for his attention a document. It seemed to be a petition, but before looking at it, he bent down to attend to something annoying in his shoe.

He didn't have time to find out what it was. He heard a bang and saw his right index finger explode in a spray of blood, then felt an indescribable burning in his left elbow like a fire consuming his flesh.

He cried out and fell backwards, and his men closed ranks around him. 'It came from the window of that building!' someone shouted. As he slumped to the ground, Coligny heard the sound of boots running along the pavement. Some of his men were rushing towards the building opposite. He heard another man shout, 'Call Ambroise Paré, Her Majesty's personal surgeon!'

Then he fell to the ground and heard nothing more. He saw only darkness.

52

Polignac's Defence

Raymond de Polignac had taken off his hat. He did not enjoy travelling in carriages, but he'd had no choice.

When he heard the stones hitting the vehicle, he realized that something was wrong. Wondering what was happening, he moved aside the muslin curtains and looked out of the window.

He saw black-clad men shouting angrily. 'They tried to kill Coligny!' he heard. 'Death to the queen!'

Groups of Protestants had gathered and were now running in all directions. There was the sound of gunfire.

The queen turned white.

'Pascot!' shouted Polignac to the coachman. 'Get us out of here! Whip those damned horses!'

But the carriage did not move.

The commander of the king's pikemen wasted no time. He opened the door, and as he climbed out onto the running board, he saw the two mounted guards who had been escorting the carriage lying on the ground in crimson pools.

Polignac climbed up to the box, where he found Pascot, blood gushing like a fountain from the firearm wound in his head.

'*Sacrebleu!*' cried Polignac. 'Majesty, lock yourself inside and lie down on the seat.' And without another word he began to whip the animals, which leapt forward. The carriage started to move and quickly began to pick up speed, but the wretches who crowded the street began chasing after it, hurling stones and insults at them.

There were two gunshots from the right and Polignac gave a cry of pain: a projectile had hit him, opening up a gash in his side. Holding the bridle with his left hand, he pulled a pistol from his belt and fired. There was a flash of light and his shot struck one of the attackers full in the chest. The man threw his hands in the air and went crashing to the ground.

There were more shots and more shouted curses, but the carriage was travelling very fast now, the horses eating up the road. After leaving Saint-Sauveur, Polignac took the carriage down Rue Comte d'Artois, whipping the horses constantly. He hoped to be able to carry on at breakneck speed so as to arrive as soon as possible at Rue d'Orléans.

The pain in his side was hellish. He'd had no time to look at the wound, but to judge from the blood that drenched his jacket it must be serious. He commended his soul to God and prayed that he would reach the gates of the Louvre alive. It had been absolute madness to travel to Saint-Sauveur, but he had not wanted to go against the queen's orders. In all his life he never had, and he'd certainly no intention of starting then.

The carriage careered onward at a mad speed. Catherine was afraid, but she knew that Polignac would protect her even at the cost of his own life. She had committed an imprudence by demanding to go to Saint-Sauveur, that was certain – all the more so in light of the shots she had heard. A couple of stones had hit the doors, but Polignac had been skilled enough to get them out of the ambush extremely rapidly.

As she lay there, hidden like a thief among the velvet cushions, Catherine thought of what she had heard. The rabble along the way had been railing against her, and what else? She remembered those words: 'They tried to kill Coligny!' Had Charles de Louviers failed, then? Just the thought of it made her tremble to her core. If it was so, then she was lost.

Her entire plan revolved around the marriage

between Margaret and Henry, the scion of the Navarre family, champion of the Huguenots. The marriage had been designed for the sole purpose of inducing Coligny to believe that a reconciliation had come, but her intention – as well as that of her son Henry d'Anjou and of the Guises – was to eliminate him so as to sever the rebellion's brain from its body.

In one move Catherine had attempted to take out the protector of Henry of Navarre, the man who threatened the Valois and their crown, to avenge the death of Francis of Guise, and condemn the Guises themselves to be suspected of the possible murder, so as to get rid of them once and for all.

She had hatched the plan over the years and had waited until she had perfected it. She believed it was the best way to bring France back under her control – such a cunning plot would stop the war that was tearing the kingdom apart, and moreover do so in that way that meant there would be few victims, what victims there were being among those who had desired and fomented it. Who was more guilty than they?

They were Frenchmen who hated France, while instead she – a Medici, a woman who had confronted power with all the pragmatism and realism of an Italian – had the solution at hand. She was tired of being used, humiliated and hurt. It had been going on for far too long, and now in one single move she had attempted to turn everything upside down.

She'd thought she had succeeded in her venture, but perhaps all her attempts were doomed to fail.

Every time she thought she had devised a solution, something went wrong.

By the time he arrived in sight of the Louvre, Polignac had long since succeeded in shaking off the rebels who had attacked them. They had tried to pursue the carriage on foot, but as fast as they ran, they had been left behind.

The old soldier was tired, and his side burned as though someone were jabbing at it with a red-hot iron.

When he arrived at the gates of the Louvre, he could no longer resist and only barely managed to halt the horses. The guards ran over to him as soon as they saw him.

Polignac slumped down on the seat, the whip slipping from his hand together with the bridle.

Despite the unbearable heat, he felt as cold as if it were winter. He was feverish. He leaned to the side and felt someone lifting him down.

He heard the voice of Her Majesty the Queen and thought to himself that once again he had managed to do his duty. He deserved a little rest.

He closed his eyes and allowed himself be lulled by that feeling. He wanted to detach himself from everything: from the world, from discipline, from orders, from his sense of honour. He wanted to float in the air and observe others for once, without having to worry about what might happen.

53

The Tears of the Queen

Catherine de' Medici wept.

After climbing unharmed out of the carriage, she had ordered Polignac to be brought to her apartments and had called for the king's surgeon, Ambroise Paré, only to be told that he had gone to the Hôtel de Rochefort to operate on Admiral Gaspard de Coligny, who had been the victim of an ambush.

Catherine had cried out in despair while Madame Antinori immediately sent for another surgeon.

When the surgeon arrived, he found the queen at Polignac's bedside, the white sheets scarlet with his blood, and as soon as he looked at the wound, he shook his head. Polignac was in a desperate condition, and it was a miracle that he was still alive. The man cleaned everything with cold water and applied a bandage.

'There is nothing else I can do, Your Majesty,' he said. 'The only bit of good fortune is that the projectile emerged from the other side, but he has truly lost a vast amount of blood. We are in God's hands now.'

Her teeth clenched with an anger she could barely restrain, Catherine nodded.

Pale and dressed in black, without gold or jewels, she was a portrait of pain. And pain was what she felt: pain for realizing that she was losing the only man who had ever loved her, pain for letting him die after he had been set upon by the people for one of her whims, pain for the failed assassination she had ordered. How could Polignac be saved? She would have given all her blood for a soul as grand and as good as his.

'You must forgive me, Monsieur de Polignac. I have been so ungrateful. I ignored you all this time when I should instead have looked at your handsome face and realized that you were the one who deserved to be loved, and not this accursed crown, stained with the blood of the innocent. *Monsieur...*' stammered Catherine. But emotion strangled her words and prevented her from speaking. Unable to continue, she burst into silent tears.

Raymond stirred – something in those heartfelt words had evidently reached him. He opened his eyes again. A fragile veil clouded the usual brilliance of his gaze. There was no longer the pride, the sense of duty and sacrifice that had always animated him, but he was still there. Polignac clung to life with the determination of the old soldier who does not want to give in to death.

'Your Majesty...' he murmured. His voice was uncertain and hoarse from fatigue and pain. 'Thank you... for these words. Y-you have nothing... for which to blame yourself. But to hear you say all this... is...' He was unable to continue, and spat out a mouthful of blood.

'Raymond,' said the queen, in tears, 'Raymond, stay here with me.' And at these words she raised his head and began to caress his beautiful forehead. She sensed that he was going, and her remorse and regret tore her heart to shreds, because they were both losing everything: what could have been and yet never had.

Raymond de Polignac, the man who had appeared before her like a paladin and who had protected her for all those years at the cost of his own life, was dying. Dying because he had defended her. Again. When everyone else had abandoned her, when she had risked being killed, he had been there: he was there for her, giving everything he still had in his heart to save her.

His many achievements came back to her: the time he had brought Michel de Nostredame to court because she had asked him to, the time he had brought Henry home safe and sound, despite the danger, the time after the death of her husband when he had taken her safely to the Palais des Tournelles, the times he had watched over her while she slept or guarded her while she was absorbed in prayer.

That day too he had been at her side. Protecting her.

She began to weep again, unable to hold back her tears at the thought of such great injustice and such immense love. And she had only realized it in that moment, when it was too late.

For all those years she had denied her feelings and had turned her heart into ice, but he had loved her anyway, with a devotion and a spirit of sacrifice that had been, if possible, even greater than before. And not for France and the crown, as she had believed. It had been her that he had loved – *her*, the woman who had never been loved by anyone.

That thought was devastating, and the pain washed over her like a river. All attempts at resisting it were fruitless, so she allowed herself be carried away by that sea of suffering, gently marooned as she surrendered to the evidence of all that she had not understood and all that she was about to lose.

Forever.

How cruel life had been, and how blind and deaf she had been in her refusal to hear the song of love which had been sung to her. Even though Michel had told her, even though Raymond had done everything possible to make her understand.

Instead all she had cared about had been that damned war. Obsessed with the future of France and her children and the kingdom, she had allowed herself be sucked into that orgy of violence.

She kissed him on his lips. They were cold.

'Raymond,' she whispered in the voice of a little girl. 'Raymond,' she repeated, waiting for him to answer.

But there was no sound.

Raymond de Polignac, commander of the king's pikemen, was dead.

He had left her on her own.

Forever more.

Ambroise Paré had failed to heal the wound as he had hoped. The scissors did not cut properly and he had to try four times before he managed to completely amputate the index finger of the right hand. As for the elbow, there was little he could do: it was completely shattered.

Coligny was resting when King Charles IX and the queen mother had appeared at the Hôtel de Rochefort asking to see him. Paré did not know if it was a good idea, but he certainly could not deny the sovereign access to the room of one of her best soldiers. The gentlemen who were with Coligny, all men who shared his religious beliefs, led His Majesty and the queen mother to the chamber of the Huguenot chief.

'Gaspard, my friend, what has happened to you?'

asked the king, his large, sincere eyes displaying clearly all his dismay.

Coligny's face was grey, his hand wrapped in bandages, his glaucous eyes peering about him in search of the culprit.

'They tried to kill me today, Your Majesty,' he said, his voice tired, but as sharp as a whip. Then turning to the queen, 'Perhaps your mother knows something about it. Am I wrong, by chance?'

Catherine was mortified, but feigned amazement.

'Monsieur de Coligny, I do not understand your allusions. I am instead glad to find you in better health than I had feared.'

'Yes,' he exclaimed with cutting sarcasm. 'I can well imagine. In any case, if by chance you weren't the one who hired the assassin, then surely Guise is behind all this.'

'Coligny, my good Coligny,' said the king indulgently, 'and why should we ever make an attempt on the life of one of our best men? You are raving, my friend, which is understandable, but I would never deprive myself of a soldier like you. Come,' continued the king, 'let yourself be embraced. I promise I will be careful.' And so saying, Charles IX approached his admiral and threw his arms around him in an embrace as clumsy as it was honest and heartfelt, and which left all the bystanders satisfied. Even Coligny himself was convinced of its sincerity.

'I will order an investigation, Gaspard. You can be sure of it.'

The faces of Coligny's fellow believers seemed to relax, at least for a moment.

'You will have nothing to fear, Gaspard,' continued the king. 'I will see to that personally. For the moment, think only of resting and recovering your strength. I want you in shape for our campaigns together. You are not thinking of depriving me of your assistance, I hope? What would I do without you?'

'I thank you for your visit, Your Majesty,' replied Coligny. 'I will do as you say.'

'Very well. And now we will leave you to rest. But we shall see each other again soon'.

'Your Highness. *Madame la Reine...*' he added with an exhausted nod.

'Admiral,' replied Catherine, 'my best wishes for a swift recovery.' And so saying, the queen mother left the room because she could no longer stand the sight of the man and was afraid that she might betray herself more than she probably already had.

'Doctor Paré,' she said, turning to the surgeon, 'Admiral Gaspard de Coligny was lucky to have you as a surgeon. Francis of Guise did not have the same good fortune when he was assassinated and died of an infection.'

Ambroise Paré asked no question and willingly accepted the compliment. 'Thank you, Your Majesty.'

As she headed towards her carriage, Catherine remembered that not even Paré himself had been able to save her husband.

Coligny must die. Otherwise it would be she who did.

54

The Plot

'He suspects, I tell you! There is no doubt of it. Coligny knows and is now plotting to kill us. Not only that: your fool of a brother had the brilliant idea of launching an investigation to find the culprit. We must kill Coligny. We must kill them all!'

Catherine stared at the summer storm which raged outside the windows.

Clad in a blood-red doublet, his earrings gleaming in the chiaroscuro candlelight, Henry d'Anjou's face looked even more sinister than usual. Kneeling before him, his sister Margaret rested her beautiful head on his lap and Anjou caressed her long black hair, which was as shiny as silk.

'Mother, what happened was an accident. Either way, Charles managed to escape without leaving a trace, and he fired the shot from a building owned by the Duke of Guise, so nothing can be traced back to me or to you.'

'He left that damned arquebus there,' thundered Catherine. 'I doubt it will take Coligny long to connect it to your man.'

'Really?' asked Anjou, barely able to believe his ears. His voice grew angry. 'Was he so incautious?'

'He was.'

'Damnation, what an imbecile.'

'We have to kill them, I tell you.'

Fiddling with a small silver comb, Anjou stroked his sister's beautiful hair once again, then suddenly pulled at it.

Margaret shrieked and leapt away from him, drawing a stiletto from her corset.

'How dare you?' she spat, her eyes flashing.

Henry chuckled. He stood up and took her by the wrist then twisted it violently. The stiletto fell to the ground, clanging on the cold marble.

'Let go of me, Henry,' she whispered with tears in her eyes. 'You're hurting me!'

'Enough,' cried Catherine. 'Stop it! Margaret, retire to your rooms. Make sure your husband cannot harm our cause. We must act tonight, but we need the king's support.'

Margaret looked at her in amazement.

'What do you intend to do?'

'I intend to erase the evidence of our guilt.'

'How?' urged Anjou.

'We will convince your brother to give that order.'

'Monster!' cried Margaret. 'You're a monster! First you pair me off with that Huguenot dog and then you want to kill them all. What have you become?'

Catherine got to her feet, walked over to her daughter and slapped her face.

'As it is true that I am Queen of France, you will do as I say. Henry, you will make sure that everything goes as I have ordered.'

Anjou looked at her adoringly, as if her gesture had awakened a wild and bloodthirsty side of him that had remained dormant until that instant.

'Of course, Mother. I will do whatever you want.' He turned to Margaret. 'Did you hear that, little sister?' And he too gave her a slap, and then another, and another.

'That's enough. You understand, don't you, daughter? In my rooms lies the body of a man whose loyalty has been absolute, unshakable. Is it possible that I cannot make myself be obeyed even once? Come, do what we ask of you.'

Margaret wiped away the blood from her beautiful lips, nodded silently, and disappeared.

Henry of Guise looked at Albert de Gondi, Baron

of Retz. Before them, seated on a throne covered in ornamentation as splendid as it was absurd, sat a lost-looking Charles IX.

They were in the Pavillon du Roi of the Louvre.

He took a long, slow breath before speaking then spat out the words as if they were stones. He could no longer keep silent.

'The man was an absolute fool. I should have realized it. I should never have trusted someone chosen by Henry d'Anjou. And now we will be the object of their revenge – there is no doubt of it.'

Retz motioned for Guise to be silent. The king might seem distracted, but that was no reason for speaking too openly in front of him. They often did, though, on those occasions when the situation was particularly tense – and in truth, given the events of recent years, the situation was always tense.

They were still deep in conversation when Catherine tottered in on the high-heeled shoes she had insisted on continuing to wear since her wedding day. Or at least, that was what people said. They resembled small platforms which made her appear far taller than she actually was, rendering her, if not impressive, at least regal. The rest of her clothing, all completely black, gave her an austere tone that made her seem almost untouchable.

'Coligny suspects us,' she hissed. She turned to the king. 'The assassination failed, and now he threatens you, my son, even though you insist on treating him like a friend.'

'That's not true!' cried Charles vehemently. 'It was you who set him against me.'

Catherine looked at Guise and then at Retz. They were her men, but she could not claim to be able to manoeuvre them to her liking. Of the first she feared in particular the blind and bloody fury he had inherited from his father, and of the second, his skill in turning any situation, even the most compromising, to his advantage. But he was as Italian as she, and the veneration he had for the Medici was second only to that for his wife, who had given him at their wedding the marquisate of Belle Île and the barony of Retz.

Guise picked up on the insinuation beneath her words and immediately set about supporting the queen's position.

'That man has already had my father killed, Your Majesty. Like a dog. After he had defended you and your brother Francis' kingdom. He must be stopped. If necessary, in the only way possible.'

'I have no intention of giving in to your murderous whims, Guise,' snapped the king in a desperate voice.

'Am I to believe, then, that Henry is the only one with the courage to make decisions in this kingdom?' Catherine had decided to play the card of fraternal jealousy. She knew that Charles hated his brother because she held him in such high consideration, and hoped that it would serve to inflame the king's soul.

'There, you have said it.' Charles's voice had grown fretful. 'You say his name as if he were your only son. I am tired of you. I am tired of being treated like a frightened child.'

'And I would be glad not to have to treat you as one,' snapped Catherine. 'But that is what I see.'

Retz paled as he saw the awful expression which appeared on the face of the queen as she provoked her son. She did it in such a cold, ferocious way, as though she cared nothing for him, humiliating him with precise determination and exposing his most intimate fears. Catherine was shaking, as if power itself had found its incarnation within her – as if it had been distilled over the years until it had been absorbed into her very blood, saturating the vital fluid that flowed through her veins with resentment and a thirst for revenge.

'But you *do* do it, and in front of my subjects. You have no shame. You are merciless, Mother.' Charles IX stood up and looked with despair at the large windows overlooking the courtyard as though considering taking wing and flying away. He would very much have liked to be able to.

But the queen continued.

'Charles, we aren't asking you for much – just to act for the good of France. Think: if we eliminate them all, there will no longer be any religious wars, any conflict.

By killing a few Huguenots tonight, we will avoid the massacres of tomorrow. Choose the lesser evil, Charles. Do not hesitate.'

'Your mother is right, Majesty,' said Retz.

Looking profoundly shaken by his mother's words, the king tugged at his hair and twisted it angrily around his fingers.

'*Mort-Dieu*, mother, you will drive me out of my mind!' he cried, and clapped his hands to his ears. 'And now even Retz agrees with you.'

Catherine did not lose her patience: on the contrary, she concentrated all her attentions upon attempting to exploit that momentary advantage.

'Come, Charles – the greatness of a sovereign is shown by his ability to make difficult decisions. It is certainly a difficult decision, but not difficult enough to represent an obstacle for you. What matters is having enough willpower to achieve a greater goal, and that result, believe me, is within reach. We need only eliminate those who represent the cancer that plagues our kingdom. A few thousand men, rotten at heart, who over time have chosen to destroy rather than to build, to hate rather than love, and to fight and not to forgive.'

Guise went over to the king. He said nothing, wanting only that Charles felt his presence beside him.

In the candlelight, Charles noticed that the scar that pierced Guise's cheek was even redder than usual.

Without being able to explain why, he was afraid. He stared at it morbidly, unable to remove his gaze. It seemed to him that it was suddenly throbbing with life, its swollen edges seeming ready to split open anew, allowing blood and humours to spill out.

A smile appeared on Guise's face, baring white teeth which resembled those of some predatory creature.

'Come, Your Majesty. Listen to your mother's words. They are full of wisdom. You will not regret it.'

'Just a nod from you, Charles,' she urged him, and so saying she too went over to him. It almost seemed that Catherine, Guise and Retz were trying to physically force the king into a corner.

His eyes staring at the marble floor, Charles fell to his knees. He looked like a desperate child.

'Leave me alone! You are going to make me lose my mind, I tell you! Do you realize what it is you are asking me?'

Catherine looked first at Retz, then at Guise. Charles had his back to them now.

'Very well,' said the queen mother. 'Given your ineptitude, I will go back to Henry and tell him of your pusillanimity and of how once again you lacked the courage to shoulder the burden of your responsibilities. How cowardly you dwell in that weak heart of yours. It is hard to believe that you are the son of Henry II…'

And without another word Catherine turned and

began to walk away. But before she had time to reach the door, Charles spoke.

He had stood up again but was still hunched over, almost as though using his shoulders as a shield to protect himself from the pain they were causing him and from the pain he was about to inflict in turn. When he finally spoke, his voice was a rasping wheeze, like that of a wounded animal ready to fight to the bitter end for its survival. But there was none of the dignity or honour that such a creature might have shown.

The fear that filled his words, making them sound harsh and cowardly, was audible to all.

'Kill them,' said the king. 'Kill them all! None must survive. Or we will have done all this in vain.'

There was a moment of silence. Retz's eyes widened in disbelief and Guise did nothing to conceal the satisfied grin that began to spread across his face.

'Now I know you, Charles,' said Catherine to her son. 'Do not fear. We will carry out your wishes, as always.'

55

Kill Them All

Charles IX was unable to sleep.

Soaked with sweat, his heart pounding, he tossed and turned in his bed. If only he could sleep forever – but he knew that he had just sentenced thousands of people to death. In the darkness of the eve of Saint Bartholomew's day, he heard the threatening tolling of the bell.

He sat up in bed and began taking deep breaths in the hope of chasing away the grim thoughts. The lamps in his room were lit, for he was certain he would not be able to sleep in the dark.

Finally he got up and had the Duke of Guise called. By the time Guise appeared, the king was wide awake.

'Duke,' he said, 'tell the provost of the merchants

and the Marshal of France, Monsieur de Tavannes, to pass on my orders. Close the city gates and kill all the Huguenots in Paris.'

'All of them?' asked Guise.

'Save only Henry of Navarre, who is dear to me as a brother, and Ambroise Paré, since there is no better surgeon than he in all of France.'

'I will do as you wish, Your Majesty.'

Charles IX dismissed him. The Duke of Guise bowed and left his presence, immediately summoning the merchant provost, Fabrice de Santoro, and Costein, colonel of the royal guard.

As soon as the provost arrived, he explained to him the dispositions received by the king.

'Monsieur de Santoro, I have very precise orders to give you. The Huguenots conspire against the king and against the state. If allowed to continue, they will disturb the peace of France's subjects. The king therefore commands that the city gates be closed and that no one be allowed to enter or leave. He also commands that the boats be chained, and that the artillery be assembled in front of the Hôtel de Ville and in the Place de Grève. The militia must be positioned in strategic points in Paris. Go now and pass on the orders to the aldermen so that they may be carried out to the letter.'

Without adding another word, Guise dismissed the provost who, leaving the Louvre and gathering the aldermen, ordered that dispatches containing the king's orders be sent to the militiamen. He also informed Monsieur de Tavannes, Marshal of France.

The dispatches were speedily drawn up and issued, so that the king's commands could be fully implemented by dawn.

The great bell of Saint-Germain-l'Auxerrois tolled twice.

It was the signal the soldiers had been awaiting. Under the command of Duke Henry of Guise, they slipped through the shadows like assassins, coming to the chambers of the noble Huguenots who rested in their beds, flinging open the doors and impaling them upon their swords, snatching them from their dreams and disembowelling them where they lay. They even followed them along the corridors of the Louvre, and blood flooded the salons and sprayed the walls. But Henry had one particular target in mind: Gaspard de Coligny.

As Guise walked with his soldiers through the halls of the Louvre, he saw a figure crawling along the ground. With difficulty the man got to his feet, but then slipped in the blood that covered the floor of the room and fell among the corpses. Guise was on him in an instant, grabbing him by the hair and dragging him to the centre of the salon while the man kicked in terror. Guise threw him on top of another corpse, then held him down with the sole of his boot on the back of the man's neck, crushing him to the ground as he might have done a worm. He asked one of his men to pass him a pike, then raised it and brought it down on the poor wretch's back, skewering him to the body beneath him. The blade sank into the flesh and the man's blood began to flow profusely as Guise pressed down on the shaft of the pike with all his weight.

Around him, his men swung their swords. The blades gleamed in the light of the torches, slashing and slicing at everything that moved while other Huguenots, now lifeless, fell to the floor.

Guise came to the main staircase which led to the Louvre courtyard. At the foot of it stood a group of Swiss guards. Karl von Schulemburg, their commander, had taken steps to carry out Guise's instructions, and the tips of his men's halberds were already red with blood. The orders had spread like leprosy. Men lay in crimson pools, and as he went down the staircase Guise swung his sword, slashing the breasts of a dying woman. Another, who was fleeing across the courtyard, was cut down from behind, a vermilion arc slitting her robe as she sank to the ground.

Blinded by violence and anger, Guise did not even stop to look.

'To the Hôtel de Rochefort,' he muttered.

*

The colonel of the royal guard, Cossein, had received precise orders and now stood at the gate of the Hôtel de Rochefort. As soon as the Saint-Germain-l'Auxerrois bell struck two, he called his arquebusiers.

'Fouquet,' he said to his second in command, 'have the throats of all the guards of the King of Navarre – the ones standing in front of the doors of Coligny's apartment – cut. Quickly.'

Without another word, he entered the courtyard with his party.

At the head of his men, Fouquet entered the palace, walking towards the first of the soldiers who stood at the foot of the staircase and beckoning him over. The man left his post to join him, and Fouquet put his arm around his shoulders.

'My dear Jalabert,' he said, 'I can only imagine how tired you are...'

And as he spoke those words, he slit the man's throat with his dagger. Blood spraying from the wound, Jalabert did not even have time to cry out.

Meanwhile, Cossein was climbing the stairs with his men. He walked over to the guard who stood at the top, rapidly extracting from a sheath in his jacket a stiletto, which glinted in the darkness. Its blade flashed in the light of the lanterns as he stuck it into the soldier's throat, slicing open his jugular. The desperate man clutched at his neck in an unsuccessful attempt to stop the blood, then he fell to his knees, crashing to the ground with a dull thud.

Cossein's men wasted no time in dealing out the same treatment to the other guards.

It was then that Guise's thugs arrived, at their head Besme, a German soldier in the pay of the Duke of Guise, and immediately behind him d'Attin, a knight in the service of Henry of Anjou, and the Swiss guards.

The way cleared thanks to the work of Cossein and his men, they flung open the bedroom door and found themselves facing the leader of the reformists.

Lacking both the strength and the time to arm himself, Gaspard de Coligny was sitting on the bed in his nightgown.

As soon as he saw Besme with his sword drawn, he reached for his own, but d'Attin was quicker and kicked it away.

'Are you Admiral Gaspard de Coligny?' asked Besme.

'I am, *monsieur*,' the old man replied, 'but you should show me a little more respect. If not for the job I hold, at least for my white hair and the wounds that keep me bed-bound.'

Besme smiled.

'Come then,' insisted Coligny, 'is there not one of you man enough to allow me to die with an ounce of honour? Is this rogue all you have left?'

In response, Besme pounced on Gaspard de Coligny and stabbed him with his sword, and an instant later d'Attin did the same, followed by the Swiss guards. When they had finished, they stared at him with crazed eyes: they had finally killed the leader of the rebels – the Huguenots who had wanted to pour down fire and brimstone on Paris. And now they would use his body to issue a warning to all those who dared oppose that night's purge.

They knew that Henry of Guise was below, impatient for evidence of Coligny's demise.

'Let's not keep him waiting,' said Besme, and all present instantly knew to what he was alluding. They opened one of the large windows that overlooked the street.

The voice of the duke came up from Rue de Béthisy. 'Are you done, Besme?'

The German looked out the window. 'We certainly are.'

Guise waited below with his minions, each of them wearing a white scarf tied around his left arm and a cross of the same colour on his hat.

The street was almost dark. Guise ordered the Swiss guards to set torches to light the way. The air was filled with agonized cries and the clanging of swords, and the entire Louvre district was a chaos of skirmishes, gunshots, flashes of red and fallen bodies. The streets nearby echoed with the death rattles of slaughtered Huguenots: Rue des Lavandières, Rue Tirechape and Rue des Bourdonnais were a labyrinth of pain and death.

Amid the flashes of light, Guise smoothed his moustache. He had waited a long time for that moment.

A dark mass suddenly flew through the air and the soldiers watched as the corpse of Admiral Gaspard de Coligny was hurled through the window and came crashing down to the ground.

Grabbing a torch, the Duke of Guise walked over to the body, made black by the red light of the lanterns, then crouched down and stared at the devastated face in front of him. With a white cambric handkerchief he cleaned it of the blood that made it unrecognizable.

'It's him,' he said, 'that Huguenot dog, Coligny.' He turned to his soldiers. 'Courage, men,' he cried. 'We have made a good start, so now let us kill the rest of them. Those are our king's orders.'

56

Dawn of Blood

Margaret could not believe what she was seeing.

She had heard the furious knocking and had climbed out of bed, lit a candle and put on her dressing gown over her nightgown. Then she had rushed to open the door.

Henry of Navarre, her husband, the man she had married only a few days earlier, had stood there begging her to let him in.

Shocked at the state he was in – his face smeared with blood and his clothes torn – Margaret hadn't hesitated, and Henry had taken refuge in her chamber.

When she looked outside, Margaret had seen the blood that covered the floor of the corridor and the bodies lying on the ground in a red lake, some in the last spasms of death.

And when she had seen her brother Henry roaming the halls with a gang of thugs like messengers of death, cutting the throats of everyone they met, Margaret had screamed and locked the door of her room again.

Staring silently into space, Henry was barely able to breathe.

'They're killing us all,' he murmured in a low voice.

'What?' said Margaret.

'The wedding...' he continued, then hesitated for a moment, seemingly to consider whether words were a luxury he could afford in that moment. 'Will you betray me?' he asked. 'Margaret, I know you don't love me. But please don't hand me over to those butchers.'

Margaret was beginning to understand. So they actually had gone through with it, then.

'What are you talking about?' she asked, even though she knew perfectly well.

'Your brother, King Charles IX, has given orders that all Huguenots be exterminated on this accursed night.'

'That isn't possible.'

'I tell you that it is! Don't you see? It's all too obvious. The wedding, the ambush of Coligny... it was all organized from the beginning to eliminate us. Your mother has been very clever, I have to admit it. In one fell swoop, she intends to get rid of the leaders of the two factions causing the religious wars that are tearing France apart. If they had discovered that Coligny's killer was none other than one of Guise's men, they would have chopped off the heads of both the Catholic and Protestant leaders, but something went wrong. The admiral survived and the Huguenots, including me, suspected her of being behind the assassination attempt. It's all too clear what prompted her to embark on this massacre: she wants to erase the evidence of her guilt and free the kingdom of the Protestant threat.'

Margaret could scarcely believe her ears, but at that moment the conversation of the previous night between Henry and her mother came back to her in confirmation of her husband's words.

'They will want my abjuration.'

'Nothing will happen to you, I promise you,' she reassured him. She was no saint and had many faults, not least that she was anything but faithful and loving, but she promised herself that she would honour the sacred bond of marriage as well as she could.

She could hear the rattling of swords and the daggers whistling through the air, the screams of the wounded and those who were dying outside the door.

She felt the cold sweat on her brow.

Catherine was terrified. She had heard the desperate screams of the Protestants being slaughtered in the rooms of the Louvre and seen the glow of the fires in the nearby streets, and the crack of the arquebuses firing had echoed in her ears. The lights burning to indicate the buildings where Huguenots were hiding looked like the hellish eyes of a city craving to devour its own children.

She pressed her face to the glass of the window and stared at the moon, wishing that she could sink into that opaline circle set in the night sky. The fear was like a fever. It seemed to her almost that a voice was whispering her name among the streets where the massacre was taking place and in the corridors of the charnel house which the Louvre had become. She had made a terrible decision and forced her son to go along with it, but in her mind that decision was already melting away in the litany of lies that she repeated to herself to justify her actions: she'd had no other choice, the Huguenots would have killed her if she hadn't killed them first, in a way they had been the cause of their own demise.

And above all, there was the crown.

It had been a bloody solution, but the only one possible for the good of France. She'd had no alternative.

Power demanded its tribute of blood. That same power that she had pursued for a lifetime and which now was subjecting her to all the shades of damnation – because she was certain she would be cursed forever for what she had done.

But she had advised Margaret to save Henry and to protect him. Hadn't that been an act of mercy? And just as it was true that this act would allow the house of

Navarre to survive, it was equally true that without his followers Henry would be harmless.

Charles would ask him to convert: repudiate the Huguenot faith for the Catholic faith.

Henry would convert that very morning. He would have no other choice: that or death. And Condé along with him.

All the other rebel leaders would be killed. Wasn't that, all things considered, a modest price to pay for the salvation of an entire kingdom? Hadn't the Medici exterminated the Pazzi, who were responsible for Giuliano's death during the Easter mass in Santa Maria del Fiore? And had Cosimo the Elder hesitated when the armies of Milan had camped on the plain of Anghiari?

What was she supposed to do in the face of the reformers who threatened to tear the kingdom apart with perpetual war and whose leader was preparing to wrest the crown of France from her children? The Huguenots had tried to kill her son Francis in the conspiracy of Amboise. They had desecrated churches and crosses, spread hatred and false belief, and had refused the peace offered them by the Duke of Guise, killing him like a dog on the road to Orléans. And they had murdered the man who had loved her unconditionally and who now lay in a perfumed wooden coffin.

Polignac. Henry. Francis. She had lost them all, one after another. But even though she did not deserve to be one, she was a survivor, and if in spite of everything she was still there, then there must be a reason. She was a mother, and she had sacrificed her entire life for her children.

They had been used and exploited by unscrupulous, merciless women like Diane, or by ambitious men like the Guises, who had exercised and still exercised a great influence over them, while she instead had only ever loved them: at the beginning, when they were not yet there, and later, when they were born and grown. She had protected and advised them, and in some cases she had imposed choices upon them. She had taught them to become kings and queens.

There was something profoundly tragic about power. Everyone wished to possess it, but the possession of it unleashed only envy and resentment.

Catherine had never really been able to be herself – they had described her as the daughter of a merchant, a heretic, a devil worshipper, a corruptor, a murderess. But none of those definitions, she thought, truly captured what she had always been and what she had never wanted to be: a woman alone.

And that feeling of loneliness was now stronger than ever.

57

The End of an Epoch

Dawn was breaking over the city of Paris. The sky was a dull white and the blazing August heat set small whirls of ash spinning up into the hot summer air.

Dogs lapped at the blood which had been shed during that terrible night.

The city looked like a slaughterhouse. The blood had flowed from the roads into the waters of the Seine and had turned it red – and red it would remain for a long time.

In Place de Grève, the Swiss guards executed groups of desperate people guilty of reading the Bible in French instead of in Latin. The bodies of hanged men dangled from windows, like the rotting fruits of a summer blessed by the devil. Thieves took advantage of the climate of anarchy that reigned in the city, and gangs of brawlers and thugs stoked the mounting fires of hatred. Reassured and urged on by cruel fanaticism, the Catholic militiamen meted out awful punishment not only to those who professed themselves Huguenots, but to all those who were unable to demonstrate their Catholic faith beyond any reasonable doubt.

Even in front of Notre-Dame, the city militia, with white crosses and scarves of the same colour tied around their arms, lined the reformists up in front of the arquebuses, exterminating entire families and pitilessly slaughtering women, children and the old.

It was as though all the city's envy, all its pettiest, lowest feelings, suddenly found justification in that Catholic revenge which, in the name of religion, scattered dignity and mercy to the four winds.

Margaret looked at her husband, Henry of Navarre. He was standing facing the king, her brother.

Catherine, dressed in black, dominated the scene. Her pale face told of a sleepless night, but given what had happened and what was continuing to happen on the streets of Paris, that was the lightest of burdens.

The Prince of Condé stood by Henry's side.

'Renounce your faith, my brother, since I have always considered you such,' said Charles. 'Do it in the name of the true faith and you will save your life. Be converted, Henry, please. As I speak to you, the Duke of Guise is probably quelling the last of the rebels. Do not force me to give an order that I have no desire to give, even if I am forced to do so. Come, Henry!'

The young King of Navarre's deep-set eyes were ringed with black and his sharp cheekbones jutted from his thin face. His dark jacket was spattered with blood and his hair tangled, and he seemed to have aged five years in a single night.

Margaret was silent. Her white dress too was gross with the blood of the innocent.

Henry stared into her eyes. They were large and elusive, mirrors of a perverse reality, but she had saved his life and he had promised her – and in any case, at that moment he could not do otherwise.

'Come, Highness!'

The Cardinal of Lorraine was so cheerful that it was almost embarrassing. But decency and honour were words whose meaning had been lost that night.

'It is the mass or death, Henry,' concluded the king. His eyes were almost crazed, for what had happened had gone far beyond what he had intended, or indeed anything of which his mind could have conceived.

Catherine knew that the night of San Bartolomeo would haunt her forever. Icy chills descended her back and she felt feverish, despite the fact that she was certain she was in perfect health. But the souls of the dead would give her no respite, and she would spend the rest of her days attempting to live with those ghosts.

Catherine, her son Charles and the Cardinal of Lorraine stood there, locked in the king's room, like the instigators of a massacre they were. Margaret, Henry of Navarre and Condé were the victims, and Anjou and Guise the executioners.

'Very well!' said the King of Navarre. 'I will deny the Huguenot faith, if Your Majesty so wishes it.'

'And I will do the same,' echoed Condé.

The king's face finally relaxed. 'My brother, I knew you would not disappoint me.'

And Charles rushed over to Henry and threw his arms around him with such sincere transport that it occurred to the King of Navarre that the ruler must truly be mad. But then, as he saw the queen mother nodding in satisfaction, and the Cardinal of Lorraine so happy that he was actually smiling at him, it occurred to him that they all were.

It was as if the slaughter of the past night and the blood which had flooded Paris had been only a dream, a vague memory, the product of some mental aberration.

But that was not the way it was at all. As they would find out soon enough.

58

The Last Farewell

Catherine had ordered Raymond de Polignac's body to be brought to the church of Saint-Germain-l'Auxerrois in preparation for the funeral.

She observed him with all the tenderness she could still find in her heart: handsome and dressed in military uniform, his eyelids closed to the world, and on his face an expression which was finally serene and at peace. With his death, she thought, she had lost the sweeter part of life. After he was killed, the darkest night of her soul had come.

What was it Nostradamus had said? 'The snow is still falling, and it will fall forever on your heart. You, who have loved so much, cannot open your own soul to the one who loved you more than his own life.'

He had been right.

She wished she could stop being the Queen of France, but she knew that was an impossibility. It would have been cowardly, and meant dishonouring the family to which she belonged. And that must never happen.

She looked again at Raymond de Polignac. Would he have been proud of her? Catherine didn't think so, just as she was anything but certain that he would have understood her actions. How could he have? She felt as though she had plunged into the abyss since he had fallen.

Perhaps Polignac could not have changed the course of her life, but his presence had certainly represented a defence, a bulwark, a guide capable of showing the best possible route.

She put her lips to his forehead. It was cold, just like his hands, and despite the sweltering heat and the thin veil of sweat that covered her face, she felt an icy clutch around her heart.

She knew that nothing would ever return to the way it had been before that night. Words, lies and conspiracies would no longer be enough. She had gone too far.

'Polignac... Raymond... Where are you, my friend? Do you remember how much I mocked you for that romantic way you had of talking to me? I didn't really think it was silly – I liked it very much... Nobody had ever treated me so chivalrously before...'

And once again her voice died in her throat, vanishing into the air above the aisles of the church.

She tried in vain to stifle the tears which ran down her cheeks then, surrendering to her pain, abandoned herself to the ruthless absence. And as she felt the emptiness, the unbridgeable void he had left behind, she shouted his name aloud in the empty cathedral.

One time. Then another, and still another.

But in vain.

Raymond de Polignac would not return.

Ever again.

JANUARY 1589

59

Death of a Queen Mother

Her fever was high. Catherine could barely smell the powerful odour of camphor. Would that be the scent that she would take with her? She could feel her strength abandoning her.

She had confessed and received extreme unction, and the court doctor had already visited her, despite his words of comfort, giving her a sentence without appeal which had remained incomplete because it had been interrupted by tears.

It was a shame to die in Blois instead of in her beloved Chenonceau castle. But soon it would no longer matter.

She was cold from the fever that devoured her body and soul, and the pain was so intense that it prevented her from speaking.

Her eyes went to Margaret and her beloved Henry, who only the day before had confessed to her that he had slaughtered Guise. He had come into her room and with harsh, cold words had unburdened himself of the guilt which must have weighed on his conscience like a boulder.

Catherine knew, though, that if her son had not acted first, Guise would not have hesitated to kill him like a dog.

And yet she was tired. Not even at the moment of death was she allowed to be free of blood and conspiracy.

She turned her gaze to the window and saw the large white flakes of snow falling outside. Her heartbeat quickened and then slowed.

It would soon stop altogether.

She thought of the buildings she had ordered built, the gardens that her will had brought into being, of the castles, poets and artists she had protected. And then of Henry, the great love of her life. And of the first time she had seen Michel de Nostredame. And of Raymond de Polignac, who had presented himself to her at the behest of His Majesty Francis I and from that day on until his death had never abandoned her.

And while her strength drained away, she thought of Florence. She closed her eyes and saw the cathedral of Santa Maria del Fiore looming over the city, seeming almost to challenge the heavens. She saw a little girl trotting towards it. It was her. She saw her aunt watching her worriedly, fearing that she might be frightened by the grandeur of the building. But she was not.

She raised her large eyes to the red dome, as though wishing to measure its height.

'How high is it, Aunt?' she asked, her eyes entranced by its splendour.

Author's Note

I must confess that Catherine de' Medici has been perhaps the most complex historical figure I have faced in this imposing trilogy dedicated to the Medici dynasty. More than Cosimo, more than Lorenzo. I love female characters and was eager to tackle this multifaceted protagonist so rich in contradictions, vices and virtues.

A sort of dark legend hangs over Catherine – a sinister fame that in the past has led to her being called a cursed monarch, a dark queen, a poisoner, and the emblem – in a certain sense – of the evil which lurked within her and which would find its definitive incarnation in the massacre of the Huguenots.

Catherine was a deeply pragmatic and profoundly patient woman, but she had always been queen in a foreign land where no one ever forgave her for being Italian, much less for being a Florentine, and much less still for being a Medici.

And yet it was thanks to her cultural, and perhaps we

should say also genetic, heritage that she managed to survive and reign in one of the darkest and most terrible periods of history.

So this was the point from which I started out in order to tackle the extraordinary story of her personality and her in many ways contradictory, ambiguous and hard-to-define figure.

We see her patiently tolerating Diane, willing to undergo any humiliation, yet ready, where possible, to pay back the evil she receives. Desperately in love with her husband Henry, Catherine paid for her unforgivable crime of not being beautiful, but managed to make up for it with her intelligence, wit, spirit, erudition, culture and taste. It was precisely for this reason that she was a woman and a queen of extraordinary charm.

A skilled politician, as patient as winter, willing to suffer the most atrocious wrongs in silence, aware that with her youth she could, over the years, outwait her opponents, she was an incredible woman: the mother of ten children, she ruled France for about thirty years in a period of history dominated by religious war.

To deal with a character like Catherine, document-ation and study were fundamental to say the least. I immersed myself in her personality through some wonderful biographies, including Honoré de Balzac, *Studi filosofici: Catherine de' Medici*, Milan 1929; Jean Orieux, *Caterina de' Medici: Un'italiana sul trono di Francia*, Milan 1994; Orsola Nemi and Henry Furst,

Caterina de' Medici, Milan 1994; Ivan Cloulas, *Caterina de' Medici*, Florence 1980; Mark Strage, *Women of Power: The Life and Times of Catherine de' Medici*, New York and London 1976; Marcello Vannucci, *Caterina e Maria de' Medici: Regine di Francia*, Rome 1989.

Another very important character for this novel was Michel de Nostredame. I was fascinated by this man, to whom an extraordinary Italian novelist, Valerio Evangelisti, has dedicated a marvellous trilogy entitled *Magus*.

Here I actually made my first deviation from historical fact, since though it is true that Nostradamus was Catherine de' Medici's court astrologer, it is equally undeniable that Cosimo Ruggieri was perhaps the more important figure in this sense. But so fascinated was I with the character of Nostradamus that I succumbed to fiction and made him the only astrologer in my novel.

It is true, though, that the sequences related to the prophecies or to the conversations with Catherine are not wholly inventions, since almost all those 'sessions' actually did take place, even though in a couple of cases I made some modifications for dramatic reasons.

There were some reference texts for the figure of Nostradamus too, including Giuseppe I. Lantos, *Nostradamus: Vita e misteri dell'ultimo profeta*, Milan 2014; David Ovason, *The Secrets of Nostradamus*, Milan 1998; Lee McCann, *Nostradamus*, Milan 1988;

Renuccio Boscolo, *Centurie e presagi di Nostradamus*, Padua 1972.

In terms of narrative, I continued with the method adopted in previous books of telling the story through a series of scenes, so as not to lose continuity. This expedient proved particularly useful for the life of Catherine de' Medici and for her long period of regency on the throne of France. In this case too, the reader can enjoy the novel as a story in itself or, if they prefer, can read it after completing the first two – in this way, I believe, it provides a more effective representation of the Medici dynasty and the Renaissance.

Once again, there were trips. Particular attention was paid to the châteaux of the Loire and, of course, to the city of Paris. For the vast amount of information he provided me on the French capital, I thank my good friend Giambattista Negrin who, over the years, has proved to be a wonderful, passionate guide.

Medici Legacy is perhaps the book of mine which was most influenced by Alexandre Dumas' masterpieces, in particular the Valois Cycle. The serialized novel remains the model for this novel, which drew inspiration from Théophile Gautier and Victor Hugo as well as from German literature: I am thinking here in particular of *Michael Kohlhaas* by Heinrich von Kleist and Friedrich Schiller's *The Robbers*.

To understand the causes and consequences of the religious wars that tore through Europe in the sixteenth century, I carefully read the Corrado Vivanti's *Le guerre di religione nel Cinquecento*, Bari 2007, and Prosper Mérimée's *La notte di San Bartolomeo*, Milan 1975.

The duel and battle sequences owe much to historical fencing manuals, and therefore I must once again cite my essentials: Giacomo di Grassi (*Ragione di adoprar sicuramente l'arme si da offesa, come da difesa, con un trattato dell'inganno, & con un modo di essercitarsi da se stesso, per acquistare forza, giudicio, & prestezza*, Venice 1570) and Francesco di Sandro Altoni (*Monomachia: Trattato dell'arte di scherma*, edited by Alessandro Battistini, Marco Rubboli, Iacopo Venni, San Marino 2007).

Thanks

And so we come to the end. More than eleven hundred pages dedicated to the Medici dynasty.

I would like to thank Newton Compton just for trusting me so much, and my deepest and most sincere thanks go to Vittorio Avanzini, who personally suggested to me some particularly significant episodes. Needless to say, they found a place in this third novel dedicated to Catherine. His profound knowledge of the female figures of the Medici family made the difference. So thank you once again.

I will always thank Raffaello Avanzini for his great courage and the inexhaustible energy lavished on this project, and also for his brilliant flashes of inspiration, always effective and timely. More generally, thank you, my captain, for developing such a fascinating and innovative vision of the publishing world.

Together with the publishers, I would like to thank my agents, Monica Malatesta and Simone Marchi, who as always were able to identify the right solution at the exact moment when it was necessary to do so. This, I believe, is the dream of every professional novelist. I remain speechless with admiration!

My editor Alessandra Penna outdid herself. If I think back to when this all started... it's been an incredible adventure that we've faced together. I couldn't have hoped to have a better professional than her at my side. She's fantastic!

Thanks to Martina Donati for having always been there and for some of the most intelligent and perceptive observations on writing novels that I have ever heard.

Thanks to Antonella Sarandrea for having pushed this trilogy of mine 'furiously', as my friend Simone Piva put it. And for being the kind of chief press officer you don't often see nowadays – a real fighter!

Thanks to Carmen Prestia and Raffaello Avanzini for continuing to increase the number of countries this trilogy will reach.

Thanks to Gabriele Anniballi for his precision and punctuality, virtues which are rare in the modern world and for that reason still more precious.

Thanks also to the Newton Compton Editori team for its extraordinary professionalism.

Thanks to Bryan Adams, for his wonderful songs which help me penetrate the souls of my characters, even when it seemed impossible.

Thanks to Alanis Morrissette for the same reason.

Thanks to Giambattista Negrin, my childhood friend

and the person who more than anyone else taught me to love France and Paris.

Thanks to Patrizia Debicke Van der Noot: she knows why.

I want to thank two great contemporary writers I admire whose work I used as a model during the drafting of this novel: Tim Willocks and Arturo Pérez-Reverte.

Thanks to Nicolai Lilin, because he is an irreplaceable friend and a true enchanter: I could read and listen to his stories for years at a time.

Naturally I want to thank Sugarpulp, who have never stopped cheering me on: Giacomo Brunoro, Valeria Finozzi, Andrea Andreetta, Isa Bagnasco, Massimo Zammataro, Chiara Testa, Matteo Bernardi and Piero Maggioni.

Thanks to Lucia e Giorgio Strukul who taught me to become a man.

Thanks to Leonardo, Chiara, Alice and Greta Strukul: Vienna in the heart!

Thanks to the Gorgis: Anna and Odino, Lorenzo, Marta, Alessandro and Federico.

Thanks to Marisa, Margherita and Andrea 'il Bull' Camporese.

Thanks to Catherine and to Luciano, because they're always an example of how to live.

Thanks to Oddone and Teresa and to Silvia and Angelica.

Thanks to Jacopo Masini & Dusty Eye for all the photos they manage to snap of my rock'n'roll side.

Thanks to Marilù Oliva, Marcello Simoni, Francesca Bertuzzi, Francesco Ferracin, Gian Paolo Serino, Simone Sarasso, Giuliano Pasini, Roberto Genovesi, Alessio Romano, Romano de Marco and Mirko Zilahi de' Gyurgyokai: because your friendship is a privilege and a rare gift in times like these.

To conclude: many, many thanks to Edoardo Rialti, Marisa and Antonio Negrato, Alex Connor, Victor Gischler, Tim Willocks, Sarah Pinborough, Jason Starr, Allan Guthrie, Gabriele Macchietto, Elisabetta Zaramella, Lyda Patitucci, Mary Laino, Andrea Kais Alibardi, Rossella Scarso, Federica Bellon, Gianluca Marinelli, Alessandro Zangrando, Francesca Visentin, Anna Sandri, Leandro Barsotti, Sergio Frigo, Massimo Zilio, Chiara Ermolli, Giulio Nicolazzi, Giuliano Ramazzina, Giampietro Spigolon, Erika Vanuzzo, Thomas Javier Buratti, Marco Accordi Rickards, Daniele Cutali, Stefania Baracco, Piero Ferrante, Tatjana Giorcelli, Giulia Ghirardello, Gabriella Ziraldo, Marco Piva a.k.a. il Gran Balivo, Paolo Donorà, Alessia Padula, Henry Barison, Federica Fanzago, Nausica Scarparo, Luca Finzi Contini, Anna Mantovani, Laura Ester Ruffino, Renato Umberto Ruffino, Livia Frigiotti, Claudia Julia Catalano, Piero Melati, Cecilia Serafini, Tiziana Virgili, Diego Loreggian, Andrea Fabris, Sara Boero, Laura Campion Zagato, Elena Rama, Gianluca

Morozzi, Alessandra Costa, Và Twin, Eleonora Forno, Maria Grazia Padovan, Davide De Felicis, Simone Martinello, Attilio Bruno, Chicca Rosa Casalini, Fabio Migneco, Stefano Zattera, Marianna Bonelli, Andrea Giuseppe Castriotta, Patrizia Seghezzi, Eleonora Aracri, Mauro Falciani, Federica Belleri, Monica Conserotti, Roberta Camerlengo, Agnese Meneghel, Marco Tavanti, Pasquale Ruju, Marisa Negrato, Serena Baccarin, Martina De Rossi, Silvana Battaglioli, Fabio Chiesa, Andrea Tralli, Susy Valpreda Micelli, Tiziana Battaiuoli, Erika Gardin, Valentina Bertuzzi, Walter Ocule, Lucia Garaio, Chiara Calò, Marcello Bernardi, Paola Ranzato, Davide Gianella, Anna Piva, Henry 'Ozzy' Rossi, Cristina Cecchini, Iaia Bruni, Marco 'Killer Mantovano' Piva, Buddy Giovinazzo, Gesine Giovinazzo Todt, Carlo Scarabello, Elena Crescentini, Simone Piva & I Viola Velluto, Anna Cavaliere, AnnCleire Pi, Franci Karou Cat, Paola Rambaldi, Alessandro Berselli, Danilo Villani, Marco Busatta, Irene Lodi, Matteo Bianchi, Patrizia Oliva, Margherita Corradin, Alberto Botton, Alberto Amorelli, Carlo Vanin, Valentina Gambarini, Alexandra Fischer, Thomas Tono, Ilaria de Togni, Massimo Candotti, Martina Sartor, Giorgio Picarone, Cormac Cor, Laura Mura, Giovanni Cagnoni, Gilberto Moretti, Beatrice Biondi, Fabio Niciarelli, Jakub Walczak, Lorenzo Scano, Diane Severati, Marta Ricci, Anna Lorefice, Carla VMar, Davide Avanzo, Sachi Alexandra Osti, Emanuela Maria

Quinto Ferro, Vèramones Cooper, Alberto Vedovato, Diane Albertin, Elisabetta Convento, Mauro Ratti, Mauro Biasi, Nicola Giraldi, Alessia Menin, Michele di Marco, Sara Tagliente, Vy Lydia Andersen, Elena Bigoni, Corrado Artale, Marco Guglielmi and Martina Mezzadri.

I'm bound to have forgotten someone... as I've got into the habit of saying, you'll be in the next book, I promise!

A big hug and my infinite thanks to all the readers, booksellers and promoters who have put and will put their trust in this historical trilogy of mine, so full of love, intrigue, duels and betrayals.

I dedicate this novel and the whole trilogy to my wife Silvia: because every time you look at me you show me the secrets of a wonderful world whose existence I didn't yet know and did not believe possible.

About the author

Matteo Strukul was born in Padua in 1973 and has
a Ph.D. in European law. His novels are published
in twenty countries. He writes for the cultural section
of *Venerdì di Repubblica* and lives with his wife
in Padua, Berlin and Transylvania.